A TIME OF HOPE

*The latest volume in the heartwarming
People of this Parish saga.*

Alexander Martyn is instantly drawn to pretty, but unsuitable, Mary Sprogett – and their rapidly forming attachment incurs his mother's anger. When the couple elope, a Pandora's box is opened and the secret of Alexander's birth threatens to split the family apart.

A TIME OF HOPE

Nicola Thorne

Severn House Large Print
London & New York

This first large print edition published in Great Britain 2001 by
SEVERN HOUSE LARGE PRINT BOOKS LTD of
9-15, High Street, Sutton, Surrey, SM1 1DF.
First world regular print edition published 1999 by
Severn House Publishers, London and New York.
This first large print edition published in the USA 2001 by
SEVERN HOUSE PUBLISERS INC., of
595 Madison Avenue, New York, NY 10022

British Library Cataloguing in Publication Data

Thorne, Nicola
    A time of hope. - Large print ed.
    1. World War, 1939 – 1945 - Fiction
    2. Large type books
    I. Title
    823.9'14 [F]

ISBN 0-7278-7047-5

Printed and bound in Great Britain by
MPG Books Ltd, Bodmin, Cornwall.

CONTENTS

The Story So Far   9

Part One: The Moment of Truth   13

Part Two: A Great Tradition   175

The Woodville Family 1800–1932

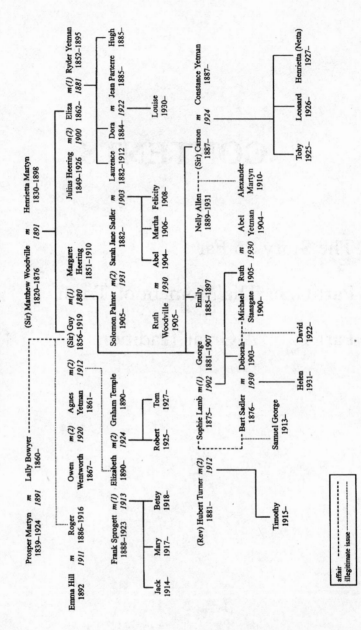

affair ---------
illegitimate issue ·········

The Yetman Family 1800–1932

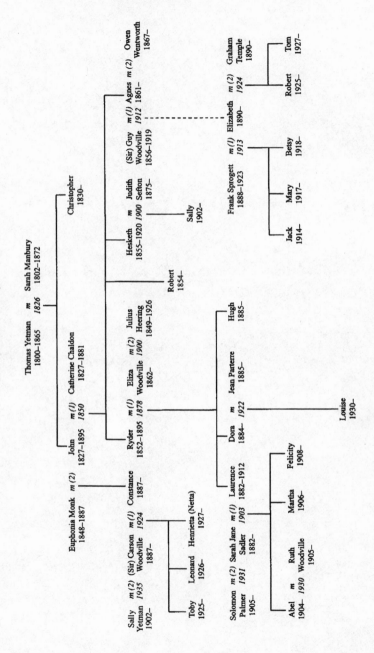

The People of this Parish series

The story so far

In 1880 young Sir Guy Woodville brings his new Dutch bride Margaret to his ancient Dorset family home, Pelham's Oak. With Margaret comes a much-needed dowry to restore the fortunes` of the impoverished but noble Woodville family. Guy has a rebellious high-spirited younger sister, Eliza, who spurns her family's attempts to marry her well. She elopes with Ryder Yetman, the son of a local builder, causing great scandal in the sleepy market town of Wenham over which the Woodvilles have presided for centuries. Margaret and Guy have three children: pious George who elopes with the rector's daughter, Sophie, to Papua New Guinea where he dies of fever; an only daughter Emily, who dies young; and the heir, Carson, a charming rebel with an eye for the ladies who would rather be a farmer than a baronet.

Eliza meanwhile has been happily married to Ryder who becomes a prosperous builder. They too have three children. When Ryder is killed in an accident, Eliza marries the brother of Margaret, her sister-in-law – a cold, mean man who refuses to help his stepson Laurence when he is facing bankruptcy. Laurence commits suicide, leaving an embittered widow, Sarah-Jane, and a young family.

Years later, Sophie Woodville returns as a widow to her birthplace, with two young children. She is welcomed neither by George's parents, who feel she is responsible for his untimely death, nor by her own, who also disapproved of the marriage. Sophie endures many vicissitudes before marrying her father's curate, despite knowing that she is carrying the child of another man.

Carson, after his mother's death, is prevailed upon to propose to a wealthy young girl, Connie, in order to save Pelham's Oak and the Woodvilles from financial ruin. But he does not love her, and when his father remarries, to the supposedly rich Agnes, Connie leaves Wenham to travel the world with her wealthy guardian.

Carson then inherits the title from his dead father, and returns a hero at the end of the First World War, only to find the Woodville estate once more in financial difficulties due largely to the excesses of Agnes, his stepmother.

Soon after Carson's return the rejected Connie, now transformed from a duckling into a swan, once more enters his life. His stepmother, however, contines to plague him, especially after her marriage to a fortune-hunter called Owen Wentworth, who assumes a spurious title and marries Agnes for her money only to find that she has none. He makes off with what jewellery she possesses and she is left destitute, dependent on Carson and Connie.

Meanwhile, Agnes's daughter by Sir Guy, Elizabeth, lives in penury with her war-wounded husband and three children, only to discover that she is a Woodville by birth. She is determined to exact revenge on the family who disowned her, but kind-hearted Carson tries to make amends.

A decade later, Bart Sadler, the former lover of Sophie Turner who left many years before to seek his fortune overseas, returns to Wenham a rich man and makes a conquest of Sophie's discontented daughter Deborah.

Sarah-Jane Yetman, for many years a widow, falls prey to the charms of a much younger man and, to her family's disapproval, runs away with him.

Dora Yetman trapped in a platonic

marriage to Frenchman Jean, renews her relationship with her one-time lover May Williams and goes away with her, but is eventually reunited with her husband.

Meanwhile Sir Carson Woodville after many years of apparently happy marriage to Connie, which have brought him three children, is caught up with the love of his youth, Nelly, the mother of his son Alexander, and risks everything.

Part One

The Moment of Truth

One

Alexander Martyn watched the golden-haired girl playing with the baby on the lawn with fascination.

"She's beautiful," he murmured.

"She's only fifteen." Dora smiled, following the direction of his eyes.

"Never mind. She's beautiful ... and the baby's beautiful too," he added with a guilty start.

"Oh, I know *she's* beautiful."

Louise was eighteen months old and over from her home in France to visit her grandmother, Eliza Heering, who sat nearby listening to the conversation between her daughter and Alexander. There was an air of contentment about Eliza. Normally a woman who lived alone, she liked nothing better than to be surrounded by her family, as she was now, in her family home: Pelham's Oak, where she had been born.

The object of Alexander's admiration was

15

her great-niece, Mary Sprogett, who had been allowed by her mother to act as nanny for the summer holidays to the infant Louise. As well as golden hair Mary had peach-blossom skin, deep blue eyes and a pert, vivacious smile. She was quite tall and expressed her agility in the way she danced about the lawn, clearly entrancing Louise and those about her watching from the comfort of their deckchairs set in the shade of the oak tree higher up the garden.

They could hear the sound of horses' hooves approaching from the rear of the house. Alexander, roused from his reverie, jumped up beckoning to Dora who, like him, was in riding gear.

"Uncle Carson's ready." He pointed towards the beautiful horses, so docile and obedient in the company of their groom who held their reins.

Seated on his black mare, Carson waited for them, his eyes roving over the gathering on the lawn; the seated adults, the playing children. He still thought of Mary, his niece, as a child. Yet in many ways she looked so adult with a slender figure and a small bust. Like her mother, Elizabeth, whom she much resembled, she had grown up before her time.

Carson greeted Dora and Alexander with a curt nod. He had been busy in the stables when they arrived. "Sorry I kept you waiting."

"No trouble," Dora said, as the groom helped her to mount. "We were lazing on the lawn on such a perfect day." For some reason she was anxious to placate her cousin who, these days, was such a solemn, taciturn man. Alexander was already mounted and looked eager to be off. Carson led the way round to the far side of the house, across the paddock and into a field which sloped steeply towards the broad valley which lay between Pelham's Oak and the town of Wenham situated on top of a hill several miles away.

The three set off across country, a soft breeze blowing down from the hills. They were all accomplished riders. When they came to the small whitewashed cottage a mile or so away from the main house, Alexander, who was leading, suddenly slowed down and looked up at the open window.

"Is that woman I saw still living here, Uncle? I thought she was very ill?"

"Alas, she died," Carson said, drawing up beside him. "Oh, over a year ago. But her friend and companion, the good woman who looked after her, lives there now. I said she could stay as long as she liked."

"I said you were good, Uncle." Alexander

17

looked at him fondly. "The day we passed by and she appeared at the window, I told you that you were a good man. Good and kind."

"No I'm not, not at all," Carson said gruffly, and dug his heels into the flank of the horse. "If only you knew me you would not think that."

And he galloped away so fast that a thick cloud of dust from his horse's hooves rose up behind him. Alexander gazed after him in astonishment.

"What was all that about?" he asked Dora, who had reined in beside him.

"I have no idea." Dora, equally bewildered, shook her head.

"Did I say something wrong?"

"You just said he was good and kind, and I agree."

"It's something about that woman. The one who died. She was standing at the window looking at me intently as we passed and I waved to her. I said she was very beautiful and uncle seemed moved by what I said."

"When was this?" Dora still looked puzzled.

"It was about a year and half ago, about when Aunt Connie left. We were riding, just like today. He told me she was tubercular and had not long to live. I never gave it another thought until now."

18

"Mother will know who she was," Dora said. "Mother knows everything. I'll ask her."

And then she gently pressed her heels into her horse's flank and set off after Carson, now a mere speck in the distance.

Breathless at last from her exertions, Mary Sprogett left little Louise to the care of her nursemaid and threw herself on the ground beside Eliza.

"Had enough?" Eliza smiled sympathetically.

"For the time being." Mary tilted back her head and shut her eyes to the sun. "It's such a lovely day." Opening her eyes again she gazed round. "Where's Alexander?"

"He's gone riding. He'll be back for lunch." Eliza looked at her curiously. "Do you ride Mary?"

Mary shook her head. "I'd like to, but Mummy thinks it's too dangerous. Mummy never rode." She looked gravely at her aunt as though to say she knew the reason why. Her mother had been brought up as a servant although she had been the natural daughter of Sir Guy Woodville, Carson's father. It was something that rankled very heavily.

Mary could just about remember the little house in Blandford where her mother had laboured all hours of the day on other people's washing. Her father had been a war invalid and there was never enough to eat, nothing new to wear. Then, one magical day, Uncle Carson had arrived and driven them off in a large car, and from then on their fortunes had changed dramatically.

"Well, Alexander will be here for the rest of the summer," Eliza said. "He can teach you. I'm sure he'd like that, unless your mother won't allow it."

Mary, who in so many ways – maybe due to the rigour of her upbringing – was older than her years, stared at her gravely.

"Maybe you could talk to her, Aunt Eliza. She'll listen to you."

"You have a touching faith in me, my dear." Eliza smiled. "I don't know that I have that much influence over your mother."

And, indeed, her relationship with Elizabeth was a difficult one. Elizabeth had felt slighted for too long by the Woodvilles for them to be able to make full amends, despite the fact that, following the death of her first husband, she had made a good match with a prosperous solicitor and now lived in some style in a large house not far from Wenham.

If anyone she was close to Carson and maybe he could persuade her to let Mary learn to ride, as he was such a good horseman himself.

Eliza could see the three riders, pinpricks in the distance, making their way across the valley and up the steep slope towards the house. Looking across at her son slumbering in his deckchair she gave his foot a nudge.

"Hugh, the riders are returning. Lunch will be at any moment."

A grunt came from Hugh, whose book had slipped from his knee as if he had been half asleep. He tipped back the brim of his hat and peered owlishly at her, his round horn-rimmed spectacles on the edge of his nose.

"What was that, Mother?"

"Lunch darling! Had you better go and have a wash?"

"Do I look dirty?"

Hugh gave her that lazy smile which always so affected her, a strange, shy smile which reminded her that Hugh had always been an enigma, even to her. The baby of the family, he was now a man of forty-seven, an Oxford don who had given his life to scholarship. He had always been self-contained, self-effacing, rather overshadowed as a child by his elder brother, Laurence, and his ebullient and forthright sister, Dora.

His life had not been easy. He had lost a leg in the war and spent many months suffering the consequences, emotionally and physically. The stump had been slow to heal and so had his mind. He had withdrawn into himself even more, seldom took part in family events, and had never shown any inclination to marry. Eliza didn't even know if he had ever had a girlfriend.

"No, you look perfectly all right." Eliza prepared to rise from her chair. "I just thought you might like to freshen up. I'm going to." She looked down at the girl still lying on the grass at her feet. "Mary?"

Mary inspected her grubby hands, smiled and, jumping up, followed her great-aunt into the house.

"Why is Uncle Hugh always so tired Aunt Eliza?"

"He's got an artificial leg. He can't move around like other people. I think he's in a lot of pain most of the time, but he doesn't talk about it."

Mary looked at her with awe.

"How did he get an artificial leg?"

"He lost it in the war. It was amputated above the knee, so the pain comes from the stump that's left."

"Poor Uncle Hugh."

"Poor Uncle Hugh," Eliza echoed, putting her arm around her niece's shoulder. "You must be very nice to him."

"Oh, I will."

When the two returned to the terrace a discussion was going on between the riders and Hugh about where lunch should be eaten. As it was such a lovely day the consensus was on the terrace. In no time David, the butler, together with a small flotilla of maids, had laid a table, provided chairs and, as everyone sat down, a delicious array of cold dishes and several bottles of chilled white wine were somehow magically produced.

Halfway through the meal Alexander put down his knife and fork carefully and looked across at Carson.

"Uncle, you were going to tell me about the woman who lived in the cottage. You said she died. It seemed such a sad story. I remember especially how beautiful she was."

Carson too put down his knife and fork and, joining his hands under his chin, glanced briefly at Eliza before answering.

"It is rather a sad story. She lived in some poverty in the East End of London. I heard about her and brought her here. Alas, not in time to save her. Massie Smith, her friend and companion, now lives in the cottage. That is all there is to tell."

Carson picked up his knife and fork and resumed his meal.

"It's not much of a story," Mary ventured

derisively. "I mean, how did you come to hear about her?"

"Through someone I knew a long time ago." Carson's tone was abrupt as if he wanted to discourage any more questions. His attitude signified that that was the end of the matter.

"How did you know..." Mary began, but Eliza gave her a sharp look and Mary stopped in her tracks.

"You know what curiosity did..." Hugh sat back in his chair and lifted his glass of wine, looking humorously at Mary.

"I don't see why everyone is so secretive." Alexander sounded annoyed. "Uncle said that one day he would tell me the story. I don't see why he shouldn't."

"He has." Dora came to Carson's rescue. "Maybe that's all there is to tell."

"It is." Looking round to see that everyone had finished, Carson tinkled the little bell in front of him. "Perhaps we should have dessert."

Later, when they were at home Dora said to her mother, "Who *was* that women in the cottage Alexander was asking about? I did think Carson was very secretive. It sounded as though there was something he was anxious to hide."

"Oh dear, did it sound as bad as that?"

Eliza's expression was thoughtful. It was nearly ten. They had dined and Hugh had gone to bed early as he habitually did.

"I don't think Alexander was very happy."

"No. I don't quite know what happened."

"But do you know about the woman?"

"A little." Eliza sounded guarded.

"Mother! Now you've gone all mysterious," Dora said protestingly getting up to pour herself a brandy to have with her coffee.

"I do know about the woman, but I don't know that I'm at liberty to say anything."

"It was some old flame of Carson's?" Dora looked speculative.

"Something like that." Eliza remained tight-lipped.

"Was that why Connie left him?"

"I really think you'll have to ask Carson, Dora. I'm sorry. It's entirely his business, not ours."

Dora, who knew her mother and respected her for keeping a secret, nodded. One day she would get the truth out of Carson.

She lit a cigarette and stretched her long limbs before her.

"It is lovely to be here, Mother." She exhaled a stream of smoke towards the ceiling. "I'm so glad we're back in Riversmead."

"So am I." Eliza sighed, and looked round. At last the workmen had gone and peace reigned. The place had been redecorated from top to bottom, and her furniture was in place. It was a large house, but not as large as the one she had left and in which she had lived with her second husband for over thirty years.

But Riversmead was special. It was where she had lived with her first husband Ryder, and where her children had been born.

Eliza leaned forward to poke the fire which they'd lit as the evenings were cold. "It really is lovely to see so much of Hugh. He seems very happy here."

"I think he is happy." Dora had a box of chocolates on the table beside her and began dipping into it. "In his strange way he is happy."

"Why 'strange'?" Her mother looked over at her.

"Well, darling, Hugh never gives much away, does he? I hardly even know what's going on in his mind. Do you?"

Eliza looked thoughtful. "Sometimes I wonder."

"I feel I hardly know Hugh at all," Dora went on. "Being away at school, then the war. You remember how silent he was after the war when he was recuperating? We could hardly get a word out of him."

"I think he's found peace at Oxford. It suits his temperament." Eliza threw fresh

26

logs on top of those reduced to embers. "Dora, tell me, do you think he's ever had a girlfriend?"

Dora shrugged. "Does it matter?"

"No, but..."

"You'd like to know?" A mischievous look came into Dora's eyes. "Maybe he prefers men?"

"Oh!" Eliza hesitated. "Do you think so?"

"Would you mind terribly?"

Eliza knew she was on delicate ground ever since her daughter's one-time attachment to a married woman with whom she'd run away.

"I just think it's a bit of a waste."

"Of what?" Dora's tone was chilly.

"Well, you know, children, the comforts of married life. Hugh seems so alone."

"He's got you. He's got us."

"It's not quite the same." Briefly Eliza looked irritated. "Oh, you know what I mean, Dora."

"I know. Just teasing." Dora could find no other chocolates she fancied and reluctantly put the lid back on the box. "I'll get too fat anyway." She carefully wiped her fingers. "Mum..."

"Yes?"

"What about your birthday?"

"What about my birthday?" Eliza put down her coffee cup.

27

"Seventy coming up."

"Don't remind me."

"Seriously, we should have a celebration. Hugh and I would like to give a party for you here, or at Pelham's Oak if you prefer. Carson's keen. We'll make all the arrangements. You don't have to do a thing, just approve the guest list."

"Well..." Eliza continued to look doubtful.

"Oh, go on. The family will love it. Do you prefer here or Pelham's Oak?"

"It depends on how many people we invite." Eliza began to warm to the idea. "Let me give it some thought." She reached over for her daughter's hand. They had never had any difficulty communicating despite whatever differences they had had in the past. The antithesis of Hugh, Dora was straight, outgoing. "It is sweet of you to think of it, darling. And if it means seeing more of you then, yes. You'll have to come over and arrange it."

Dora laughed and got up. "I knew there'd be a catch." She glanced at the clock. "I'm for bed, Mummy. It has been a long day. Coming?"

"I'll just let the dogs out and then I'll be up." Eliza also rose and walked with Dora to the door, her two black Labradors, Tim and Murgatroyd, who had been snoozing in front of the fire, following her eagerly. She stood in the hall and, after kissing Dora good-night, watched her as she climbed the stairs. Then, the dogs padding after her, she went into the kitchen, unfastened the back door and let them out. For a while she stood in the yard, arms folded, peering into the dark. Then she perched on the side of the garden table, waiting for the dogs to finish their toilets, which would take an age as they invariably went in search of rabbits in the large garden fronting the River Wen.

Eliza felt calm and very peaceful. She loved having her family with her. She was a sociable being and had always liked people about. Julius in many ways had been a solitary man, not much of a companion. But for all the rather tedious years she had spent with him the reward had come at last with his death. He had left her a fortune and she was now a woman of ample means. Her children and grandchildren would never be without the necessities, even the luxuries, of life if they wanted them.

Money, of course, wasn't everything, but it had enabled her to buy back the house she loved and, yes, at last she was happy in a way she hadn't been for years, finally living in her old home. It was home. Full of ghosts from the past, friendly ghosts.

On her marriage to Julius Heering, Eliza

had given the house to her son Laurence and his bride Sarah-Jane. They had also had three children. But their happiness had been cut short by Laurence's suicide in 1912.

Sarah-Jane had continued to live in the house until the previous year when she had fallen in love with a much younger man of whom her children disapproved. When she had decided to go away with him Eliza, temporarily homeless, had bought Riversmead back. And here, finally, she had found peace.

Eliza looked at her watch, saw it was very late and, calling in the dogs, shut the back door and firmly drew the bolts.

Carson put down the telephone with a frown, removed his reading glasses and walked over to the window. He was dressed for riding and had been waiting for Alexander and the carefully chaperoned Mary. Now he had to wait for a call from his solicitor who was trying to arrange for the return of his children from Italy where they lived with their mother.

Carson Woodville, fourteenth baronet, was an unhappy man. Having achieved a degree of contentment in his life he had blown it all away by bringing his former mistress, very ill with tuberculosis, to die at Pelham's Oak. Connie, his wife, had not understood and

30

had left with their three children for Venice, where she had a home.

Nelly had now been dead over a year but Connie had not forgiven him. Nor did he think he needed to be forgiven. There had been no new affair, and to offer succour to a destitute woman seemed to him only fair and compassionate. In failing to understand this Connie had showed a side of herself to Carson which he didn't like. He thought she was selfish and lacked compassion, and had fallen out of love with her.

But he loved his children and wanted them with him. It was possible that a battle would begin in the courts.

The butler knocked at the door and announced that Mrs Temple and her daughter had arrived. Carson went at once into the hall where Elizabeth and Mary were waiting for him, Mary in her riding clothes, Elizabeth dressed for town. As usual she was beautifully groomed and looked very attractive, despite the firm set of her mouth and the steely glint in her eyes.

Carson bent down to kiss Elizabeth on the cheek, noticing the absence of a smile. Then he greeted Mary and told her he would not be long.

"I suppose Alexander is coming too?" Elizabeth demanded.

"He should be here any minute." Carson

consulted his watch. "Are you going to stay, Elizabeth?"

"I am going into Sherborne to do some shopping. I'll pick Mary up on my way back."

"Stay for lunch," Carson suggested, showing her to the door. "You'd be very welcome."

"I'll see," Elizabeth replied curtly and, without glancing at him or Mary, left behind in the hall, made her way down the steps to her car.

Silently Mary joined him and stood by his side.

"Your mother doesn't seem in a very good mood." Carson looked at her. "Something wrong?"

"Father says it is her time of life." Mary shrugged. "I don't know what that means. I wish ... oh, I wish..." she stopped and screwed up her face.

"You wish?" Carson asked gently leading her back to his study.

"I wish I could leave home. I wish I had somewhere to go. Do you think Dora would take me back to France to help her care for the baby? I'd love that. I adore babies."

"My dear." Carson sat her down and with his large handkerchief gently dabbed at the tears which were slowly trickling from her eyes. "Surely it's not as bad as that?"

"It *is* as bad as that."

"Besides you're still at school."

"I want to leave. I'm fifteen, you know, so I can."

"Yes, but your parents want you to have a proper education."

"I *hate* school. I hate my home. Oh, Uncle Carson I wish we still lived with you." Giving herself up to a fresh torrent of weeping, Mary hurled herself into his arms.

Perplexed and not knowing what to do Carson held her close and stroked her hair until the telephone rang and he crossed the room to answer it.

"Carson?"

"Yes." It was Graham Temple, Carson's solicitor and Mary's stepfather. "Have you any news?"

"Not good news I'm afraid."

"Oh!"

"I have had a communication from Connie's solicitors in London that she wants a divorce."

"I see." Carson was aware that a steel band seemed to be encircling his ribs.

"You were not expecting that were you, Carson?"

"I thought it would happen. It is nearly two years since she left and I see no way we can come together again. But I do want the children. They are Woodvilles and this is their home."

"I'm afraid she will not give in over the children. Visitation rights, but that's all."

"Then say I'll oppose a divorce. I have done nothing wrong. She left me. The blame is entirely on her side. I can stay married as long as I like. Tell her I will not give her a divorce and I want my children. If necessary I'll fight her in the courts for them."

"Don't forget she is a very wealthy woman."

"I am not without funds myself," Carson replied loftily. "I have made several good investments lately."

"All right. I'll telephone her solicitor and ring you back as soon as I can. Don't go out."

When he put down the phone Carson saw that Mary's tears had dried and she was looking at him gravely.

"You're unhappy too, Uncle Carson?"

"Yes." Carson sat by her side and tucked her hand in his. "My wife wants to keep my children and I love them very much."

"I wish I could live with you."

"I wish you could too, but you can't." Carson looked up as the door opened and Alexander put his head round the door.

"Sorry I'm late. Ready?"

"Well," Carson glanced at the phone. "I

have to wait for a call from my solicitor. I think you'd better go without me. I'll be waiting for you when you get back and we can have lunch. Now be careful won't you? Mary's very good, but she's still learning. No galloping."

"I'll look after her, Uncle, never fear." Alexander held out his hand towards Mary who flew over to him, her eyes shining.

Mary and Alexander had been riding together for over a month, always accompanied by Carson or a groom. This was the first time they had been alone together and Alexander experienced an unusual sense of awkwardness, a curious feeling of unease. Normally not at a loss for words, he felt tongue-tied, but Mary seemed quite happy trotting by his side. She was indeed an adept learner, already quite an accomplished horsewoman, at ease in the saddle.

They descended the hill towards the white cottage. Alexander noticed that, on this occasion too, the top window was open and also the front door. As they got nearer he slowed his pace until he had stopped completely. He gazed across at Mary. She also slowed until they were side by side.

"Do you know, I'd like to go in?"

"Well, go," Mary said with a smile. "Do you know the person there?"

"You remember that day at lunch, when Aunt Dora was here with Louise and I asked Uncle Carson what had happened to the lady who used to live here and he said she'd died?"

Mary shook her head. That day she had been too excited to take much in; too excited at the proximity of all the grown-ups and, in particular, of Alexander. It had seemed impossible then that she would see him again, never mind so soon and so often, and now, for the first time, she was alone in his company.

"Why does she matter to you?" Mary looked puzzled.

"She doesn't matter to me, but I'm curious about her, and Uncle Carson's answer was so strange. I smell a mystery and mysteries fascinate me."

"If she's dead she can't be here now," Mary said prosaically.

"No, but her companion is here, the woman who looked after her. Let's go and see her."

"All right." Mary looked guiltily back at Pelham's Oak, as if aware they were doing something they shouldn't. "If that's what you want."

They trotted to the gate of the house and Alexander dismounted, tethered his horse to the railings and then helped Mary, taking her hand firmly in his as she leapt down. For a moment he clung onto her hand and, their faces very close together, they stared at each other. He stifled a wild impulse to kiss her and drew away, flinging open the garden gate as a comfortable body of about Mary's mother's age with plain, well-scrubbed features, came to the door. When she saw Alexander her mouth fell open in amazement and she nervously wiped her hands on her blue pinafore.

"Massie?" he asked.

The woman nodded. "Why..." she exclaimed and stopped, hand to mouth.

Alexander, surprised at her reaction, gave her a reassuring smile.

"Do you know who I am?"

"Mr Alexander," she gasped.

"Oh! I didn't know you knew my name."

"Well, I see you riding with your ... Sir Carson," she stumbled.

"And this young lady here?" Massie gave Mary a hesitant smile.

"This is Miss Sprogett."

"D'je do, miss." Massie gave a half-bob as if to the quality and pointed the way inside.

"Would you like to come in? I'm afraid I'm not used to receiving visitors. But you are most welcome."

"That would be nice." Alexander looked encouragingly at Mary, who hesitated. "We shan't be long. We just wanted to know how you were. How you're keeping."

Alexander looked appreciatively round the modest but pleasant and comfortable sitting room with chintz-covered chairs, rugs on the stone floor and a large bowl of fresh flowers on a scrubbed deal table in the middle of the room. To one side was an inglenook with the remains of a log fire.

"Can I get you something to drink, sir?"

"Thank you." Alexander smiled. "But please don't call me sir. I'm Alexander."

"Alexander," Massie echoed obediently, and scuttled out of the room. Almost immediately they could hear her clattering about in the kitchen beyond. Alexander winked at Mary and leaned towards her. "This is fun," he said.

"I think you've made her nervous," Mary hissed, and then giggled at the sound of a pan dropping, as though this confirmed her remarks.

"It's just because of my association with Uncle Carson. She knows we come from the big house." He jerked his head in the direction of Pelham's Oak.

In a few moments Massie was back bearing a large tray on which there were cups, a teapot, milk jug and a plate of biscuits, which she set on the table.

"I'm not used to company," she said

again, "but you're very welcome I'm sure." Then she began to pour and shyly handed them each a cup of tea.

"I was very sorry to hear about..." Alexander paused "...your friend." As Massie looked at him blankly, he hurried on, "The one who died."

"Nelly," Massie echoed woodenly.

"Oh, her name was Nelly." Alexander nodded. "I think you might remember some time ago I was riding with my uncle and we saw her at the window. I told him I thought she was very beautiful."

"Yes, she was." Massie had a sob in her voice.

"I wondered who she was exactly. How she came to be here."

"Oh!" Massie pursed her lips in a thin, stubborn line. "Did he not tell you?"

"No." Alexander looked more and more mystified.

"Then I can't tell you. I'm sorry but I can't."

"But what *is* this secret?" Alexander demanded, his expression stern. "What is so mysterious about Nelly that no one wants to talk about her?"

"You will have to ask Sir Carson," Massie said firmly. "I'm afraid that's all I can say." Then, leaning urgently forward so that she perched on the very edge of her chair she looked at him pleadingly. "And, please, don't say you spoke to me. Sir Carson has been very good to me and I should hate to lose this cottage and the little allowance he gives me. I *beg* you not to say you wus here."

Two

The Martyn-Heering business empire had its imposing headquarters in the City of London, overlooking London Bridge. From the window of the chairman's office on the top floor Alexander was able to see up river and down. Boats of all sizes busily plied up and down, past the warehouses in Lower Thames Street which were the depositories of the teas and spices, the jutes and silks, the rice and tobacco, carried by the company's boats from the Far East.

The company had been run for many years by Alexander's adoptive father. Prosper Martyn had been joint chairman with Julius Heering, Aunt Eliza's second huband. Both men had died within a couple of years of each other but, before that, the chairmanship had passed to a nephew of Julius, Pieter Heering, who was now in his late fifties and not in the best of health. His son Joachim was not interested in the business and there were no Martyns left so, consequently, the

41

future of the company was a question mark, though control still remained in the hands of the family.

The door opened and Alexander turned as Pieter Heering entered accompanied by two men who he introduced as the general manager, Jeremy Sydling, and Philip Preston, the financial controller. The men shook hands and chatted about this and that, while Pieter consulted with his secretary, who had entered unobtrusively by a side door.

"Now," he said, a hand on Alexander's arm, "I want to talk to this young man and in a while we'll join you in the dining room for lunch. Shall we say," he glanced at his watch, "in about half an hour?"

The two men nodded, withdrew from the room, and Pieter indicated a chair in front of his desk. As Alexander sat down, he held out a silver cigarette case. Alexander shook his head. Pieter looked surprised.

"Don't you?"

"I do, but I don't want one now thank you, sir."

Pieter smiled, snapped the case shut and sat down behind his large imposing desk which faced the river. He joined his hands under his chin and regarded the handsome young man sitting in front of him.

"So, Alexander."

"So!" Alexander placed his hands across his knees and smiled at a man he liked, but didn't know very well. Like Prosper Martyn, Heering was childless, although he had been married for many years to a large, friendly Dutch lady called Beatrix, who preferred to live in Amsterdam and rarely accompanied her husband to London.

Occasionally Pieter would come for dinner at the Martyn's house in Montagu Square which, since Prosper's death and until recently, had been shut up.

"I hope one day you will sit at this desk in this chair, Alexander, as chairman of the company. Should you reach this position, you will be a man of great fortune and influence." Alexander looked round while Pieter watched him closely. "Tell me, do you feel drawn to business, Alexander, or is there something else you would rather do? It is no use coming into this if it is not for you. I believe at different times both Sir Guy and then his son, Sir Carson Woodville, worked for this firm with unhappy results."

"I am not related to the Woodvilles," Alexander replied smoothly. "In fact I am not related to anyone. I think that you know I was adopted in infancy, my parents unknown. I come to you, then, with a very clear slate, and I am most interested in all aspects of the business."

Pieter looked pleased. "You are very honest."

"You see there is nothing in the blood, as it were. I do not know who I am."

Pieter's face puckered with sympathy but Alexander appeared unconcerned. "There is no need to feel concern on my behalf. I feel nothing but gratitude to my adoptive parents. I was never very close to my father, but my mother has given me all the love and affection a man could possibly want."

"She adores you," Pieter agreed. "I am glad that you feel so relaxed about your origins. With reason. You have had a wonderful home, much better than the one you might otherwise have been brought up in, and you will lack for nothing as your mother's heir. You are already, I understand, a very wealthy young man, yet anxious not to fritter your life away."

"I am interested in making a good career and doing something useful," Alexander assured him. "I would like to start work as soon as I can. I've had a very good summer: I travelled abroad; I helped a young friend to learn to ride; and I spent a lot of time in the country."

"In your beautiful Dorset home?"

"Exactly. The Woodvilles and their relations are my mother's friends and my friends. I regard them as a kind of family. We are close. But I do not take after them."

Alexander stood up and walked again to the window. Then he turned to gaze steadily at the chairman. "What happened to Sir Guy and Sir Carson, whom, incidentally, I revere, has no bearing on what will happen to me. I am eager to learn the business from the humblest beginnings."

Alexander walked home in the late-afternoon sunshine reflecting on his meeting with the Chairman of the Board, a position he might conceivably occupy himself one day. Although at twenty-two it seemed a very long time away, perhaps another twenty years.

He was not ambitious to be chairman but to fulfil himself, to justify himself, particularly to Lally, the woman who had adopted him and given him unstintingly of her love. Although he had had everything a boy, then an adolescent, then a young man, could have wished, he had not been spoilt. He had been brought up with kindness but a certain firmness. Lally never tired of telling him of her own humble origins, and thus reminding him of his. In other words they both had much to be grateful for.

Pieter Heering was quite right. If he'd been abandoned as an infant his parents must have been poor, possibly destitute. His mother might have been a woman of the streets, perhaps plying her trade in the environs of nearby Hyde Park, knowing that only wealthy folk lived in the surrounding squares. The Martyns' home might have been chosen at random as a place to dump him.

It was an issue that from time to time absorbed him. Nevertheless, he enjoyed his leisurely walk along Fleet Street, through Trafalgar Square bustling with traffic and pedestrians making their way home, through St James's, London's smart clubland where, in due course, he would probably be a member of a number of distinguished gentlemen's clubs, as Prosper Martyn had been. He walked along Piccadilly and through Shepherd's Market where he noticed more acutely than usual the number of women strolling casually along the streets, loitering on the corners, or hanging out of windows ogling him. Maybe his mother had once been among them? He shuddered and hurried on through Mayfair, across Oxford Street and into leafy Montagu Square, which had been his home ever since he could remember.

It was with a sense of relief that he put his key in the door and let himself in.

"Is that you, darling?"

"Mother!" he cried with genuine pleasure

as Lally came along the hall to greet him, the enticing fragrance of her perfume enveloping him as he stooped to kiss her. "You look divine," he breathed.

And indeed she did. He thought of her as his mother and called her by that name. Sometimes he felt not only that he loved her, but that he was a little 'in love' with her, as though their relationship, although not in any way sordid or reprehensible, had another dimension that would have been called into question if they had been blood relations. They doted on each other, loved each other's company, could while away many happy hours alone together, hated to be separated for too long, were almost like lovers in their joy when they saw each other again.

Lally was a petite woman with a slim, beautiful figure, her cornflower-blue eyes still vivid and serene, her skin flawless. Her blonde hair was carefully tinted and worn as it had been since anyone could remember in a mass of tight little curls on the top of her head with dozens of tiny ringlets behind. It was almost impossible to think that this woman, who looked no more than forty or forty-five, had been born in 1860. But to Lally appearance had always been of utmost importance. She had lived for the admiration of men and now she lived for the love, the worship, of Alexander.

"How was the day, darling?" she asked him in caressing tones. "How was Pieter?" She led him into the drawing room which gave onto the square. In the twilight the gas lamps were being lit, their soft glow casting shadows, the trees taking on mysterious shapes. It was a long gracious room with a high ceiling, but at present it was in a state of chaos. With the prospect of Alexander joining the business, Lally was in the process of refurbishing the house and was up to her elbows in samples, swatches of material and catalogues of all kinds, that, when not in use lay on the carpet, the sofas and the chairs. However, the untidiness was controlled and, as Alexander sank into one of the chairs covered with a white sheet, Lally solicitously poured him a drink and handed it to him.

"I thought we'd have champagne," she said fetching her own glass. "It's such a lovely way to start the evening."

"It is," Alexander agreed and, raising his glass, toasted her.

"Tell me about Pieter."

"Well, it was pretty much what you expected. He wants me in the firm. I was given lunch with the board who were all very charming and," he put his glass on the table beside him, "I can start when I like."

"That is wonderful, and one day you'll be chairman?" Lally looked at him anxiously. "Pieter promised me that."

"Well, not immediately." Alexander laughed. "Not for many years."

"It was Prosper's wish, and Julius's," Lally said stubbornly.

"I can't understand what happened to all the Heerings and the Martyns." Alexander scratched his head in bewilderment. "I mean Julius had brothers, so did Prosper. Why does it come down to me when I am not even a relation?"

"But you are a relation..."

"By adoption, not by blood."

He had that familiar feeling of sadness, of alienation, almost of rejection, of a person who had no roots. Sometimes the sadness threatened to overwhelm him.

Lally came quietly over to him, the folds of her tea-gown making a slight swishing noise as she walked. She changed several times a day even when she was by herself. This afternoon she wore a dress, the hem about ten inches from the ground, made of a clinging voile with a pattern of large navy-blue flowers on a white background and a large blue bow at the scooped neckline. She always smelt delicious never varying her perfume, that of the subtle Arpège by Lanvin. Perching on the arm of Alexander's

49

chair she let her fingers run delicately up the back of his neck in a caress that was almost lover-like.

Her love for Alexander was unsurprising. Apart from his sweet disposition and his place in her heart as her adopted son, in looks he was a lady killer: tall, athletic, yet languid when it suited him, with the air of an aesthete and the manners of a dandy. At Oxford he had cut a swathe among the ladies with his charm, his elegance, his undoubted beauty. He had thick straight black hair, high cheekbones and deeply recessed, dark, unfathomable eyes that seemed all-seeing and all-knowing.

"What is it, darling? You're broody, out of sorts. I don't like my boy like this. Do you *really* want to work for Martyn-Heering? Is there something else you'd like to do? Would you like to farm, go into the army or simply be a man of leisure and travel round the world?" She sat up, an expression of sudden excitement on her face. "We could do that together, Alexander. Take a trip through Europe, the Middle East and Asia. Oh, I'd *love* that..."

"Mother, Mother." Alexander chuckled, taking her hand. "Don't get carried away. You know that I would despise myself if I did nothing. No, I do want to work and the sooner the better. I told Pieter Heering that but, at the same time, I would like to know who I am. Don't you understand?" As he looked at her gravely she lowered her eyes.

"I am so afraid, Alexander."

"But afraid of *what*?"

"That if you knew the truth you might..." she hesitated.

"Might *what*?" He clasped her hand tightly, sensing something. Lally wrenched her hand away and walked rapidly across the room.

"You know ... maybe not like me as much, love somebody else. I couldn't bear that."

"That's impossible." Alexander rose and, crossing the room, put his arm around her tiny waist and nestled his cheek against hers. "Nothing that I could ever learn would interfere with my love for you, Mother." He raised his head and looked at her closely. "Is it remotely possible that, even after all this time, I can find out how I came to be left here, find any clue as to who my parents were?"

Lally shook her head, hands clenched in front of her, fighting desperately the feeling of panic that invaded her heart.

Connie Woodville tossed the letter across the table to her companion at breakfast.

"I have been invited to Eliza's seventieth birthday. Shall I go?"

Paolo Colomb-Paravicini picked up the letter and quickly assimilated its contents. Then he handed it back to her and smiled.

"It is entirely up to you, my love."

"I think not."

Connie rose and, going over to one of the long windows, gazed across the Venetian lagoon. Its shimmering water, on a fine September morning, was a wonderful sight with the gondolas gliding by and the little *vaporetti* skimming swiftly over the surface. For a while she remained there, arms folded, lost in thought.

Paolo had arrived for breakfast after the boys had been taken to school by their nursemaid, Mafalda, who also took Netta, the youngest, along for company. They would stroll back, stopping to gossip with the many friends Mafalda would encounter on the way, dallying by one of the street markets that proliferated in the city, and possibly not come home before lunch.

It was almost two years since Carson had brought his ex-mistress home without a word of explanation to his wife. For many weeks, she had endured a situation which she found intolerable. It was true that the woman had been very sick. Perhaps she should have tried to be more sympathetic, but Carson had taken too much for granted and in the end Connie had had enough. He probably hadn't even noticed she had left.

But, there, waiting for her in Venice like a patient old dog, had been Paolo ready to comfort and commiserate despite the fact that years before she had thrown him over for Carson. Left him, as it were, on the heap. It was a wonder he had forgiven her.

Count Colomb-Paravicini had one of the oldest names in the Venetian aristocracy. His forebears had been statesmen, soldiers, princes of the church. He was gentle, scholarly, tender and warm. She knew instinctively that he would never have brought an ex-mistress to his home, however sick, and expect her to be treated like royalty.

Paolo, trying to divine her thoughts, watched her with love in his eyes. He had lost her once and he didn't want to lose her again. But he had to be patient and wise and, above all, not too possessive. She was seventeen years his junior and, though not a girl, one had to respect her desire for space. Although she had been disappointed in her marriage, perhaps she was still in love with her husband, and could not be hurried.

Connie turned and strolled slowly back to the table, sat down opposite Paolo and stared at him.

"I have asked Carson for a divorce. I can hardly go back to Pelham's Oak for a party."

Despite the joyful leap of his heart, Paolo's

53

well-bred features remained remarkably composed, scarcely a muscle in his face flickered.

"When did you decide that?"

"About a month ago."

"And what does he say?"

"No." Connie smiled briefly. "But I think it is only a bargaining point to get the children.

"But you wouldn't let him have the children?"

"Of course not. I mean he can see them, as he does now."

"And he wants to have them living with him?"

"Yes."

"Meanwhile he won't give you a divorce and you've got the children. It seems like stalemate."

Connie shifted restlessly in her chair and poured herself another cup of coffee.

"I thought I might agree that the boys should be educated in England. I mean Toby is his heir. Through his own fault, Carson didn't have much of an education but he wants his sons to have a good one, and I agree. I'm going to suggest that that happens, in exchange for a divorce."

"And then will you marry me?"

Paolo looked hopefully at her. Connie gave him a brief, tantalising smile.

"Perhaps. If you're good."

"I'll be *very* good," he said and, leaning across the table, took her hand and kissed it.

Deborah Sadler threw the letter on her husband's desk her cheeks scarlet with excitement.

"*We* are invited to a party!" she cried with an emphasis on the pronoun. "What do you think of that? To Pelham's Oak for Aunt Eliza's seventieth birthday."

"My, my." Bart Sadler took up the letter and read it. "Signed by Dora," he said looking up. "Do you think this means peace has broken out at last?"

Deborah stared at her husband with an air of exasperation.

"Don't you want to go?" she demanded.

"What do you want?" He leaned across the desk towards her and she thought yet again what an unreasonable man he was. He only thought of himself, never considering her wishes or those of others. Once, when she had been lonely and depressed he had seemed very attractive: a strong, forceful man much older than her, of experience and wealth, who had swept her off her feet, turning Cinderella into a princess. Alas, that seemed rather a long time ago.

"I know you don't like Aunt Eliza," she said petulantly.

"No," he corrected her gently, "she doesn't like me."

"My mother won't go if we go," Deborah said.

"That's your mama's loss."

Deborah sighed and turned away from Bart who got on with the accounts that he was working on, as if she didn't exist. She stood for a while, arms akimbo, gazing broodingly out of the window. Of course he didn't understand. Ever since their marriage Bart and Deborah had been ostracised by those people in Wenham and beyond who were connected to the Woodville family either by blood or friendship. Bart, a man of fifty-two at the time, had eloped with the daughter of a woman who had once been his mistress, Sophie Turner, now the wife of the much respected rector of Wenham. This was, understandably, a matter of considerable regret, mortification and shame to Sophie and she eschewed all contact with her daughter, her son-in-law, or her grandchild, their infant daughter Helen.

Bart really didn't care, but Deborah longed for reconciliation and friendship. She missed her mother and her stepfather, her younger half-brother, Timothy-James, but not the elder one, Sam. She saw her younger sister, Ruth, and her Uncle Carson, but Bart had offended Aunt Eliza by tricking her, with his customary ruthlessness, into selling him her house.

It was thus rather a lonely world that Deborah inhabited. She had too much time to herself in which to brood and think how much better off she might have been married to a man more her own age.

Bart was indifferent to the opinion of the townspeople of Wenham. After many years abroad he, once a ne'er-do-well, had returned to Wenham a rich man and all he cared about was becoming even richer. He had thrown himself into creating new business enterprises and had begun to neglect his capricious, wilful, and also rather selfish, wife who had caused a good deal of hurt and embarrassment to her family when she was a teenager by eloping with a workman and bearing his child. Thus Deborah was twice ostracised: for her past as well as for her present.

Deborah turned to Bart whose head was still bent over his figures.

"As you don't want to talk about it—" she began.

"Deborah, it is not worth talking about. These people don't matter at all to me."

"They do to me." Deborah's cheeks had started to flame.

"That's your affair. Look," he raised his head and gazed at her wearily as though she had begun to irritate him, "do whatever you like. I'll fall in with your wishes."

"In that case we'll go. I've decided!" Deborah said and flounced out of the room. Her husband flinched as the door banged behind her and, for a few minutes, he sat gazing thoughtfully at it.

The age gap of twenty-seven years was really a very large one. Too large when you coupled it with a young woman who thought only of herself, when he would have preferred a docile obedient woman who thought only about him.

Three

October 1932

Bart Sadler halted awkwardly on the threshold of the cream and gold drawing room which was, once again, the scene of a splendid reception at Pelham's Oak. He did, in the end, feel very nervous, although he had assured himself he would not. After all why should he? He was man of substance, a power in the community, a town councillor, maybe a future Mayor of Blandford. He had married a beautiful young wife and fathered her child. Reminding himself of his importance he squared his shoulders, thrust out his chin, made sure his black tie was properly centred and tucked his wife's hand firmly under his arm. He gave their name to the functionary at the door who called in loud clear tones, "Mr and Mrs Bartholomew Sadler."

Simultaneously, it seemed, everyone in the room stopped talking. All eyes swivelled towards them as they walked towards the receiving line stationed just beyond the door.

It was a moment of truth.

Carson, first in line, reached forward to shake Bart warmly by the hand and kiss Deborah on the cheek. Eliza, a little more formally, took Bart's hand avoiding eye contact. He bowed, looking at his feet.

"Happy birthday, Mrs Heering."

"Thank you."

"Happy birthday, Aunt Eliza." Eliza looked up and took Debbie in her arms. For a few moments, the women clung together. "I so missed you," Eliza whispered in her ear.

"Me too," Debbie whispered back. Then, after a short pause she asked. "Is Mummy here?"

Eliza released her niece from her embrace, stepped back and shook her head. "I thought she'd come, she said she would, but at the last minute she sent a note to say she had a headache. Your stepfather is here." Eliza pointed to where, a few feet away, Hubert Turner hovered, an anxious expression on his face.

Deborah hesitated only a moment and flew towards him.

"Oh, *Father*!" she cried. "It is so *good* to see you.

"And you, my dear." The emotional rector

wiped a tear from his eye. A collective sigh seemed to rise from those in the room still entranced by the drama being enacted by the door.

"Your mama had a headache," the Reverend Turner said. "I think she wanted to come but..." he glanced behind Deborah to Bart, who was watching the proceedings. Debbie nodded as if she understood.

"But I do wish you would come and see us, my dear. Your dear mother pines for you, and the sight of her grandchild."

Debbie glanced at Bart, who stood with a black scowl on his face. "One day, perhaps."

Hubert nodded, and reached out to shake Bart's hand.

Bart and Debbie then completed the handshakes – Dora and her husband Jean, and Hugh – before joining Hubert once more and then losing themselves in the crowds where, slowly, almost reluctantly, conversation had resumed again. Few backs were turned on them. Everyone wanted to see what happened, or if anything would happen. On a night that promised to be full of surprises no one wanted to miss a thing. Bart Sadler and his wife at the Woodville home was an event.

There were many at Eliza's seventieth birthday who were well acquainted with Bart Sadler. His family were prominent in the locality: they had farmed hundreds of acres for years; his sister had married a Yetman. Many of the more prominent citizens did business with him, or sat with him on the town council to which he had been speedily elected. A man of so many parts, such wealth; the town needed him. They knew him well, and gradually they drifted towards him shaking him by the hand and introducing their wives who were anxious to gawp at the couple who had been a source of such delicious scandal. In a way it was a pity that it was all over and tiresome respectability had intervened.

Slowly quite a crowd gathered round the hitherto ostracised couple and, watching from the far side of the room, now that the stream of new arrivals had reduced to a trickle, Eliza could not help but be intrigued by the attention given to Bart and his wife. She had had to steel herself to shake his hand, but it had been done. It was a problem no more. She would invite them to Riversmead and they undoubtedly they would one day ask her to her former home. She would see her great-great niece. Imagine being a great-great aunt at the early age of seventy! In a way it was something of an achievement. Observing them absorbed by a curious crowd she thought that, in a way, Bart and Deborah deserved each other, though perhaps 'deserved' was not the word. Deborah had hurt many people and shown little gratitude for many kindnesses that had been done to her. Dora and Jean had once scoured the country for her when she went missing. Carson had taken her into his home when she fell out with her mother. In the end she had run off with a man no one liked. Maybe it was simply that she and Bart suited each other, locked together in mutual selfishness and self-esteem, with little care for the feelings of others.

It was an evening of contrasts, of pleasure and pain. Pleasure to see so many friends, pain to know that family discords continued. Elizabeth was studiously ignoring her mother, Agnes, who sat on a chair in one of the corners, a glass of champagne in her hand, looking dignified, but a little frail and perhaps rather lonely. In a minute she would go up to Agnes and invite her to sit at her table for supper, but then what would she do about Elizabeth who was entertaining a coterie all of her own, as far away from her mother as she could get? Or Sarah-Jane who had arrived with her husband, Solomon Palmer, whose extreme good looks enhanced the age difference between them. Sarah-Jane, it had to be admitted, was looking a little worn.

Enjoying a moment alone as the receiving

line broke up and its members dispersed among the guests, Eliza helped herself to a glass of champagne from a passing waiter. She contemplated not only the people who filled the room, but the beautiful room itself with its ornate plasterwork and cornices, the magnificent crystal chandelier, and the oval painting of *Diana the Huntress*, attributed to Sir Thomas Thornhill, the eighteenth-century painter, who had also owned a house in Dorset not far from Pelham's Oak.

Off the drawing room was a larger reception room, only used for big occasions when there was to be dancing. It was being prepared for supper with small tables lit with glittering silver candles.

Eliza had seen so many occasions in these rooms over the years. The one which most vividly came to mind was the wedding reception for her brother, Guy, and his new wife, Margaret, in 1880, which was when the modern history of the Woodville family began. It was the first time Eliza had become conscious of her heritage. She had been just eighteen, a rebel on the threshold of life, caring little for family icons and convention.

The last time this room had been used had been for the baptism of Carson's only daughter, Netta, now with her mother in Venice.

Eliza gave a deep sigh and looked up to

find Alexander gazing down at her, his face creased with concern.

"Are you all right, Aunt? You look so sad on your birthday."

"No, I'm not sad." She took his hand. "I was just thinking over many eventful years. Let's go and say 'hello' to Agnes. She does look a little lost."

"No one seems to talk to her." Alexander obediently set out with Eliza across the floor.

"Well, a lot of people don't know her now. She's become rather a recluse since Owen Wentworth ran off. Oh, I suppose you're too young to remember that."

"Tell me about it." Alexander looked intrigued but, above the noise of the crowd, could hardly hear Eliza's reply.

"I'll tell you another time, this is not the place."

Although she was alone Agnes seemed quite content, sipping her champagne and observing the crowd. However, as Eliza and Alexander approached her face broke into smiles and she half rose as Eliza stooped to kiss her.

"You look so lovely," she said. "I can't believe you're—"

"Shh," Eliza smiled, finger to her lips. "I can't believe it myself. And I can't believe it of you Agnes." She stepped back to admire the woman in front of her. "Your outfit is ravishing."

Agnes gave a tight little smile of pleasure. "Thank you. I think so too."

Agnes had always been fashion conscious, even at home alone she maintained high standards. Her evening gown of grey silk had a high neck and long sleeves tapering to the wrists and seemed, as well as the acme of fashion, to cling to a body which had defied the years. Agnes was not slender, too many years of good living had inclined her to plumpness, but her flesh was firm and supple and kept in control by good corsetry and dignity of bearing. In her younger days her breasts had been celebrated for their beauty and admired by many men even though few got any closer than a glance from a distance.

Agnes had had all her jewels stolen by Owen Wentworth, the man who had married her and so grossly deceived her. As they had not been insured they had not been replaced, so she did not glitter and gleam like half the overdressed women in the room, whom she far outshone in elegance. She wore a pair of rather good diamond earrings that Connie had given her, and her hairstyle was simple, if unfashionable. Rather like Lally, almost her exact contemporary, she clung to the old style which suited her: tight curls and waves, a little like Queen Mary, only hers were blonde, but not too blonde so that the onlooker was left wondering if it could possibly be natural.

Agnes accepted Eliza's compliment and Alexander's admiring look with equanimity and patted the seats on either side of her.

"You must keep me entertained, though just looking around does that. I never saw so many people in my life, most of them strangers, most of the women plain. When do you think *my* dear family are going to come and see me? Apart from Dora and Carson, a word or two with Hubert Turner, I have spoken to no one. Am I some kind of pariah? Have people forgotten I was once mistress of this house? Don't I deserve some kind of memory, some respect? I think I should have been in the receiving line, Eliza. I'm surprised I wasn't asked."

Eliza blushed. "I imagine Carson thought there were enough people there, Agnes. I mean, so many hands to shake..."

"Don't make excuses," Agnes snapped. "You can't take me in. You feared a scene with my daughter. Elizabeth might have snubbed me."

"Would have snubbed you, Agnes," Eliza interjected. "It would not have been pleasant."

"The truth at last." Agnes glared at her malevolently. "I hear my niece Sally Yetman is here. Her father, my brother Hesketh, I believe did very well. Died of a heart attack, poor man, some time ago. I don't suppose she even knows who I am."

"Oh, but she does," Eliza glanced around. "She wants to talk to you. Very much."

"Is she pretty?"

Eliza looked thoughtful.

"I would say not so much pretty as nice. She seems an awfully nice girl and I'm glad Carson asked her. He invited all that branch of the Yetman family, but Sally is the only one who came. See, she's with Dora now." Eliza pointed to a group of people in the middle of the room, mostly young or youngish. Among them was a tall, fair woman of about thirty who bore a remarkable resemblance to her cousin.

"You see," Agnes said plaintively, "they have no time for me, those young people. Ah well, it's all I can expect I suppose now that I have no money and am dependent upon charity. They know they won't inherit anything from me."

"Oh, Agnes," Eliza protested, "that is a silly thing to say. The situation is not as bad as that."

"It is as bad as that," Agnes insisted, stamping her neatly shod foot. "And what about my granddaughters, are they going to talk to me?" She spoke rapidly as if she was afraid her audience would go away, and her tone grew increasingly querulous.

Eliza attempted to stop the torrent by patting her hand.

"My dear the evening is young. I am sure all that will happen in good time."

"I will fetch Mary if you like," Alexander said eagerly. "I know she is dying to talk to you."

"Then why does she not come?" Agnes looked at him reproachfully. "Is it because her mother won't allow it? I was in half a mind whether to come or not, but Carson was persuasive and even sent a car for me, which was rather nice of him considering we haven't always seen eye to eye."

Those eager, piercing eyes of hers – slightly menacing like those of a bird looking for its prey – darted about again. They were violet and rather small, close together, calculating, missing nothing. They followed Alexander as he made his way through the throng, stopping every now and again to greet someone he knew.

"He's so handsome," Agnes murmured. "He has a look of his father..."

Eliza glanced at her sharply.

"How on earth do you know?"

"Oh I know." Agnes pursed her mouth

knowingly and smiled mysteriously, the squiggly curls bobbing up and down as she nodded her head several times.

"But how ... ?"

"A little bird told me. Does he not know yet?" She looked slyly at Eliza, who shook her head. "Well, he should. It's not right that he doesn't know who his parents were."

"I know," Eliza said. "Believe me, it troubles me, but it is up to Lally to tell him – I think it is her duty – and yet she can't bring herself to."

"Why ever not?"

"Well..." Eliza glanced at her sideways. "In a way you can understand it. He might have divided loyalties. He might feel very angry. You can't predict how he will react. They have such a rapport that she cannot bring herself to, for the moment, though I daresay she will in time."

"I don't think it's fair to the boy," Agnes began, but stopped when she saw Alexander approaching with Mary Sprogett close by his side.

The girl looked radiant, her fair hair and blue eyes offset by a dress of turquoise taffeta, the bodice ruched over her tiny bust, the narrow shoulder straps accentuating her slim white shoulders. The fashionable mid-calf length of the skirt showed her white silk stockings and dainty pointed shoes which appeared to be made of the same material as her dress. Agnes, always deeply conscious of fashion, looked at her with approval as she held up her powdery cheek to be kissed.

"Well, my dear, I haven't seen you for quite a while."

"No, Grandma." Mary sounded nervous.

"Mother doesn't allow it, I don't suppose."

"No, Grandma." Mary's voice quivered, as though she was afraid of this remote and august relation.

"Well, what will you do if she sees you now?"

"She's gone into supper. In the other room."

"Will you tell her that you saw me?"

"I have wanted to see you," Mary burst out, her voice ringing with sincerity. "But..."

"I know, my dear, I know." Agnes held up a hand on which there was a solitary platinum wedding band, the only thing Owen Wentworth had left her with (and that only because she was wearing it at the time of his theft). "There is no need to explain, but if you can come and see me, I would like it. I would like it very much. And," she looked up at Alexander, "bring this young man with you. I like him too. Now run off to Mama and tell your sister and brother they must come and visit me too ... when they can."

"Yes, Grandma." Mary flung herself at Agnes who, for a moment, clung to her with a very real emotion. As the girl pulled herself away, Eliza saw there were tears in Agnes's eyes.

"I *will* come, Grandma. I will come soon." Alexander held out his hand, Mary clasped it and sped away with him across the room anxious not to offend her mother.

Agnes dabbed her eyes. "That was all very emotional. Not the thing for a party. Not the thing at all." She looked over at Eliza and smiled. "I don't think you've any idea how much a gesture like that means to me. Mary is a very sweet girl. I hardly know my grandchildren. Elizabeth has been very cruel to me. And," she cocked her head towards the door, "I like that young Alexander very much. Don't you?" She looked across at Eliza, who nodded but, to her dismay, found that for some reason her heart was full of foreboding.

Even in Agnes's lonely old age Eliza felt that, somehow, she was still capable of much mischief.

Carson wandered among the supper tables talking to his guests, sometimes sitting, sometimes standing, leaning over, an arm round one, a hand on the shoulder of the other, thoroughly enjoying himself. He was

72

surprised how wholeheartedly he had thrown himself into the party. Perhaps it was because it helped to take his mind off his marriage difficulties: his wife's intransigence and lack of cooperation.

It was at a time like this that the family was particularly important, and he had gone out of his way to track down people with whom they had long ago lost touch. It was Dora who had been keen to trace the branch of the Yetman family of which she knew almost nothing. She had only been eleven years old when her father died. It was the first time Dora had seen her cousin, Sally Yetman, since she was very small, and Carson had never met her.

Sally sat at the table with Dora and Jean, her aunts Eliza and Agnes and Lally and Alexander. Alexander kept on glancing at the table where Mary sat with her parents. Not far from them were Sarah-Jane, her husband Solomon and her children Abel, the eldest, with his wife Ruth, and her daughters Martha and Felicity. Also at the same table was Hubert Turner, Deborah and an unusually silent Bart Sadler.

Carson looked round, drew out a chair and sat down next to Sally.

"You and Dora could be sisters," he said.

"I know." Sally smiled, a frank, refreshing smile, which Carson immediately found attractive. She had fair hair, stylishly cut in a page-boy bob with a fringe and a long, rather slinky evening dress that showed off her figure. She had blue eyes, a broad nose and a firm, decisive-looking mouth. When she laughed she showed a set of beautifully even teeth. She was not conventionally pretty but, like Dora, was a good-looking woman, along with many others in his family. She seemed a cheerful, jolly sort and he liked her. She was also a bit like Connie.

"It's so wonderful to find this family," Sally said. "And Aunt Agnes, who I don't think I've ever met."

"Never," Agnes shook her head. "I was off abroad before you were even born. Hesketh was a very poor correspondent. I didn't even know he was dead." She didn't look very sorry.

"And your mother?" Carson asked. "Is she well?"

"She's well. Leads an active social life in Bournemouth."

"Can I get you something to eat, sir?" A black-coated waiter hovered by Carson's side and pointed to the serving table still groaning with food despite the fact that the plates of the hundred or so guests were full.

"I'll help myself." Carson smiled, looking up. "I'm not hungry yet. Maybe when the dancing begins."

"Oh, there's dancing. Good." Sally turned her attention again to the food on her plate. "This is a lovely party. I'm so glad you asked me." She smiled at Carson, who smiled back.

"I'm glad too," he said. "Maybe we'll see more of you."

Sarah-Jane had repeatedly told her husband she didn't want to go to Carson's party. She hadn't been back since she'd left Wenham and, as far as she was concerned, that was that. She and Solomon had started a new life, where no one knew them, in Brighton.

But the new life hadn't been quite the success Sarah-Jane had hoped. She knew nobody in Brighton and making new friends was difficult. She'd had a large family in and around Wenham, besides her own children, and even if she didn't see much of them, she knew they were there.

Her family had thought she was foolish to run off with a man twenty-three years her junior, younger than her own son and only a little older than her daughters. They were all solid middle-aged farming folk and they couldn't understand what had got into their sister to make such a spectacle of herself. No one had attended the quiet register office wedding and, as if they had known she was coming, none of them were here tonight except her brother, Bart, and he was something of a black sheep himself. Two of a kind.

But Solomon had insisted on coming. He found life in Brighton dull and there was little work to be had as an architect. The economy was in a depression, millions were out of work, a lot of people had lost money and were not building houses.

Sarah-Jane had not been a wealthy woman and all the money she had came from the sale of her house, Riversmead. Her husband only had what money he earned, so they were not well off. Discontent was beginning to set into a marriage only just a year old. Solomon hoped that maybe his stepson, Abel, who had formerly been his partner, might find something for him to do, or Bart Sadler, whose house Solomon had worked on after Bart had bought it from Eliza.

There was little merriment at their table. Sarah-Jane's children sat glowering at her, as though she was somehow tainted. They too had not come to her wedding, and seemed rather to wish they were not here now. Hubert Turner manfully tried to keep the party going with trivial tales about the parish, which were of little interest to anyone, and Deborah chatted away to her sister Ruth who she saw most days anyway. Bart looked unsmilingly about him, obviously not in a happy mood, until the tables were pushed back and the dancing started. The small ensemble which had been entertaining the crowd with airs from Mendelssohn and Schubert showed its versatility by a change of mood and broke into a foxtrot. Couples who had been waiting for this moment pushed back their chairs, and Bart jumped up and immediately led Deborah to the dance floor.

"Do you want to dance?" Solomon looked at his wife who shook her head, raising her full champagne glass unsteadily to her lips. "Don't you think you've had enough to drink, dear?" he enquired anxiously.

With the vigour of the inebriate Sarah-Jane shook her head.

"No I do not."

"Come on let's dance." He tugged urgently at her hand but she shook him off.

"No, I don't want to."

"Do you want to make a spectacle?"

"But we're not a spectacle."

"Everyone will look at us."

"So?"

"I don't like it."

"Why? Because everyone will say 'Look at Solomon Palmer and that awful old hag of a wife. She's years older than he is. God knows what he saw in her.'"

During this exchange Abel hurriedly got

up and led his wife onto the dance floor. Hubert, realising his labours had not been appreciated, had his attention diverted by some parishioners and eagerly crossed the room to talk to them. Besides, he was not much of a man for dancing. Sarah-Jane's daughters Felicity and Martha remained at the table stonily observing their stepfather's unsuccessful attempts to entice their mother onto the dance floor. Finally, with a sigh of exasperation, Martha rose, held her hand out to Solomon, and said almost in a tone of command.

"Come on, let's dance."

"But..."

Solomon looked at her, but Martha seized his hand and propelled him into the crowd packed tightly together in the small space that had been cleared between tables.

"Sorry about that," Solomon mumbled.

"Can't you see she's drunk?" Martha demanded wrathfully. "I can't bear Mummy making a spectacle of herself."

"She doesn't usually. We shouldn't have come."

"I'm surprised you did."

"It's a very isolated life we lead in Brighton."

"You should have thought of that before."

"There's no work, nothing to do," Solomon went on as though he hadn't heard

78

her. "Sometimes I think…"

The music stopped in time, unfortunately, to coincide with a commotion at one of the tables on the edge of the dance floor. Sarah-Jane appeared to have collapsed and was lying face downwards, her head in the bowl of fruit in the centre of the table. Felicity was making an attempt to revive her with a napkin, but everyone else just remained where they were, staring. Martha and Solomon hurried across to her, just as Sarah-Jane began making a feeble attempt to lift her head.

Carson, suddenly stirred into action in the middle of dancing with Sally, stood anxiously next to Martha trying to help.

"Shall I call a doctor? Doctor Hardy might be here somewhere." Carson looked about him, but the family doctor, who had been invited as a guest, was nowhere to be seen.

"I can manage," Felicity, who was a nurse, muttered, "if someone can help me get her out."

"What's the matter with her? Is it her heart?" Carson appeared seriously alarmed.

"Mummy's *drunk*!" Felicity announced in scathing tones. "Hadn't you noticed?"

Martha shot her a warning glance but Felicity was defiant. The few people within earshot exchanged glances.

Solomon helped Felicity get Sarah-Jane

into an upright position, but her head lolled like a rag doll's.

"We've got to keep her upright to stop her from choking," Felicity said, and with Solomon's help they began to half lift, half drag her out of the room.

Meanwhile, at a signal from Carson, the valiant little band – consisting of two violins, a flute and a piano played by three perspiring men and a red-faced woman – broke into a brisk foxtrot and everyone started to dance energetically again.

Alexander was very conscious of Mary's nubile, pliant body so close to his. He had waited all evening for another chance to be with her again after he had returned her to her family following their meeting with Agnes.

He put his mouth very close to her ear.

"What did your mother say?"

"She didn't notice. There were so many people."

"I rather like your grandmother."

"So do I. I feel very sorry for her."

"Maybe we could go and see her together? You know, without telling anyone."

Mary looked doubtful. "When?"

"We'd find some time. I'm working in London during the week."

"Oh, you've got a job?"

"With the family firm. I'm starting at the bottom. We could go one weekend."

"We must be very careful. My mother will be furious."

"Why does she hate your grandmother so much?"

"Because she rejected her when she was a baby."

"I can imagine that..." Alexander began, but the band played harder, the music got louder and it proved too difficult to continue the conversation. Instead, Alexander took advantage of the crowd to press Mary even closer to him. He could feel the beat of her heart next to his.

Lally tried to keep her eyes on the couple on the dance floor but it was very difficult. The lights had been lowered and some couples were openly smooching. A far cry from the decorous dances when she was a young woman, not that there had been much that was decorous about her youth. She was not at all happy about Alexander's obvious interest in Mary Sprogett, a girl with an awful name, whose father had been a carter, without any education or breeding.

Eliza was tapping her foot. Next to her Lally turned and studied her profile for a moment, reflecting that Eliza had weathered well. She wore an elegant black sequinned, close-fitting evening gown. The streaks of white in her dark hair, which she had had cut fashionably short, a variation on the Eton crop, gave her a decided air of distinction. She wore little jewellery, unlike Lally, who sparkled like a Christmas tree with gems on her fingers and her wrist, and a pearl necklace of great antiquity around her throat.

"I do wish Alexander would leave that Sprogett girl alone," Lally whispered to Eliza. "He'll be giving her ideas."

Eliza looked at her friend in surprise.

"But she's rather sweet."

"She's only fifteen for goodness' sake."

"Well I'm sure there's no romance. She's scarcely more than a child."

"There'd better not be,"

"Would you really mind?"

"I would mind terribly. For one thing I would hate an alliance with Elizabeth."

Eliza patted her hand comfortingly.

"I'm sure you can put it out of your head. He will meet a number of very glamorous young women in London. He'll be spoilt for choice."

They both looked up as Carson appeared and sat down at their table.

"Aren't you dancing?

"No one to dance with."

"You must dance with me."

"That would be lovely."

"Enjoying the party?" He looked across at Lally.

"Wonderful. The food was superb. You must tell me where you got your caterers from."

"Have some more champagne." Carson beckoned to a passing waiter but Lally put a hand over her glass. "I really think I've had enough."

Carson stood up and extended his hand to Eliza and together they glided on to the floor.

"I can't quite get the hang of these dances," she said. "They're all so vigorous. So much jumping about."

Carson laughed and pressed her close.

"You're doing splendidly."

"And you're doing splendidly." Eliza looked at him with approval. "It's a lovely party and you're a very good host."

The music stopped. Suddenly, all the lights went out and the band began to play 'Happy Birthday'. Through one of the doors a waiter emerged carefully pushing a trolley on which there was a large birthday cake with its candles already alight. Eliza put her hands up to her face in surprise. Carson led her forward and as all the dancers stepped back, and everyone joined in the chorus, he invited her to blow out the candles, which she did, but not all at one go. There were cheers, laughter and a massive chorus of 'for she's a jolly good fellow', after which Carson held up his hand for silence.

"I would like to say how pleased my family and I are to see you all here tonight," he said, "to celebrate the birthday of my dear Aunt Eliza."

There followed more cheers and applause as the lights went on again.

Carson continued, "She has been a wonderful wife, mother, grandmother and aunt and I, for one, owe more to her wisdom and good advice over the years than I can say. I ask you to raise your glasses and drink the health of Aunt Eliza, born in this house seventy years ago today."

When the noise had subsided Eliza stepped forward and, as silence fell, she joined her hands in front of her.

"Thank you all so much," she said simply, turning to Carson. "Especially Carson for giving me this lovely party, my daughter Dora for helping to organise it," she looked towards Dora, who waved back and blew her a kiss, "and all of you, friends and relations, who have come here to celebrate this special day. For it *is* special. It seems that more than seventy years have elapsed since the year 1862 when I was born. Queen Victoria had another forty years on the throne. It is, indeed, like a bygone age, and we have seen so many changes, so *many many* changes: the arrival of the motor car, the aeroplane, electric light. When I was a child, Pelham's Oak was lit by candles and gas and oil lamps. The only means of transport was by horse or horse-drawn vehicle. Now there is wireless, telephone – you can hear and speak to people many hundreds of miles away. There are moving pictures in the cinema. It is all miraculous. Quite miraculous.

"We, as a family, like most of you, have suffered many tragedies as well as had many joys. We have seen a terrible war that has changed the world and decimated so many lives. Even now our country is going through trying times, with thousands out of work and many more living in poverty. Some people still have their lives ruined by ill-health from the effects of the war.

Nevertheless, I believe that this is a time of hope, and I pray that we keep faith with the future, with unborn generations entrusted to us, and that we never see another war."

Eliza, who had never made such a long speech in her life, was almost choking with emotion. She raised both her hands to her lips and blew kisses to her audience who, with one accord, rose to their feet to salute her.

Four

March 1933

The Becketts and the Martyns had been friends for many years. Frank Beckett was a successful City banker. His beloved only daughter, Minnie, was twenty and had been carefully reared and nurtured: she had gone to one of the best schools in the country, had been finished in Switzerland and had all the accomplishments necessary to make her a fine wife to some fortunate man. But, above all, she was quite beautiful with thick, luxurious black hair, limpid brown eyes, high cheekbones and a secretive rather alluring smile, full of hidden promise.

Alexander knew the Becketts. He had met Minnie several times, he had played cricket with her brother Ronald, and had lunched in the boardroom with her father, who was a close friend and colleague of Pieter Heering and was one of the company's bankers.

Lally's house in Montagu Square had, in

the last six months, undergone a complete refurbishment. There were new carpets, curtains, wall coverings and in many rooms new furniture, though most of it was in fact not new but old: antiques that Lally had bought in her restless trawl through the salerooms, many of them in Dorset. Lally had an eye for fine furniture and exquisite taste, and she now felt she had a house fit for Alexander to live in during the week when he was in London, and maybe to settle in if he got married.

She herself preferred to live in the country, though she enjoyed her trips to town. Shopping was her weakness. She loved to entertain: to plan the food and wine with the cook and butler; to order the flowers and arrange them tastefully in large bowls in the hall and reception rooms was a task she always enjoyed. She would play hostess for Alexander, giving a dinner party two or three times a month with a view to introducing him not only to people of interest and importance, but to a variety of suitable young women in the hope that, eventually, he might choose one for a bride.

The talk at the dinner table was grave. The war had been over for fifteen years, but the consequences continued. The economic situation was still serious, though the National Government, under the leadership of Ramsay MacDonald, was beginning to succeed in re-establishing British credit. On the whole, businessmen were satisfied with the government. However, there were still five million people unemployed and the Labour leader, George Lansbury, had up-braided the government for its indifference to the sufferings of those without work.

In Germany, Adolf Hitler had become Chancellor, but many considered him a renegade who couldn't possibly last long.

This was not the view of Frank Beckett.

"His party has just polled almost fifty per cent in the German elections. I don't think you can write him off. I think he might actually be quite good for Germany."

"Are *you* worried about Herr Hitler?" Minnie, her fine intelligent eyes sparkling with amusement, turned to Alexander, who was sitting next to her.

"I know very little about him," Alexander replied with a deprecating smile. "But what I know I don't like, though some people say he will be good for Germany."

"I agree with Frank. Germany is in an appalling mess. People who have met him say he is quite charismatic." Sir David Lankaster leaned across the table towards Frank Beckett, but next to him Reuben Schwartz shook his head. He was a distinguished art dealer and critic who often advised Lally on her purchase of paintings.

Sir David, founder of the Lankaster Engineering business, sat on the board of the Martyn Heering bank. Unmarried, he was a very old friend of Lally's who she often invited to make up numbers if there was an excess of women.

"Hitler is a rabid anti-Semite," Schwartz said. "I have been back to Germany and I have seen what he is doing to the Jews."

His wife Alma nodded vigorously in agreement.

"In fact," Schwartz went on, "I intend in time to sell my Berlin apartment and withdraw altogether from Germany; take all my money out and settle permanently in London."

There was an awkward pause. As they had finished dessert, Lally, with her usual tact and intuition realising that the talk might become controversial and therefore an embarrassment to her guests, rose from her chair and invited the ladies to accompany her out of the room. This practice had ceased in many houses after the war, but it was a tradition Lally adhered to. With a backward glance she asked the men not to be too long.

The four men then closed up round the table and, as the port was circulated, lit cigars and resumed their discussion.

"I think that was a very successful evening," Lally said, turning indoors with Alexander as the Schwartzes, the last guests to leave, drove off. "Thank heaven we avoided any arguments, though I know David Lankaster is an admirer of the new German Chancellor and, of course, the Schwartzes hate him."

They went into the hall where Roberts, the Martyns' elderly butler, stood waiting to receive final orders.

Now in his seventies, Roberts should probably have long ago retired, but he had nowhere to go, no relations or even close friends and, as he was youthful in outlook and enjoyed his work, Lally would not dispense with him. He was one of the family and when she did let him go, it would probably be to a comfortable retirement in a cottage on her Dorset estate.

Lally told Roberts to lock up and go to bed. She and Alexander went into the lounge for a nightcap, to dissect the evening as they usually did after a party. Alexander dropped into an easy chair and ran his hands over his face.

"Tired, darling?" Lally enquired solicitously, placing a small glass of fine cognac into his hands.

"Thank you, Mother." Alexander looked

up with a grateful smile. "A little tired. It seemed a long day."

"You mustn't work too hard, my precious." Lally perched on the arm of his chair and began to stroke his brow tenderly. Alexander caught hold of her hand and kissed it.

"I wondered if we should invite the Becketts to Forest House for a few days, darling? Would that please you?" She leaned forward so that she could see his reaction.

"Not particularly." Alexander played with her fingers and then gently let her hand fall.

Lally looked disappointed. "Don't you *like* the Becketts?"

"I think he's a bit of a stuffed shirt and so is Lankaster. It says everything if they approve of the Nazis. It was all I could do to stop myself – well, let it pass."

Lally appeared taken aback. "But I didn't *dream* that you felt so strongly."

"I don't *feel* strongly. I just don't like the look of the Nazis, all that militarism."

"I don't think they actually *like* them," Lally ventured. "I just think they're trying to see their point of view and that of the German people who felt so terribly humiliated by Versailles."

"Serve them right. They started the war. Damn it all, Mother," Alexander turned on her savagely, "look at how many people were

91

killed or wounded. Hugh Yetman lost a leg, and he was one of the lucky ones."

"I just thought..." Lally hesitated, surprised by her darling's outburst. "*She* was rather nice – Minnie."

"She's all right."

"I think she is very pretty and intelligent. Often the two don't go together. I believe her father has already settled twenty thousand a year on her."

"Mother, you're matchmaking." Alexander jumped out of his chair so suddenly that Lally nearly fell off the arm and righted herself just in time.

"I am not matchmaking, dear. But I think Minnie is a catch. I'm surprised she's not engaged already. I understand a lot of young men have been after her since she came out."

"Well, she will be spoiled for choice, then. Frankly I'm not interested." Alexander looked at the clock on the mantelpiece. "Time for bed, Mother." But Lally remained on her precarious perch anxiously gnawing at her fingernail. Finally she looked up.

"Every time I see you with that little Sprogett girl you seem *very* interested."

"I like her very much." Alexander gave her a chilly smile. "She's very unaffected."

"Unaffected!" Lally burst out, getting to

her feet. "Well, she hasn't much to be affected about, has she? I mean she's a nobody with a very common mother who pushes her forward at any opportunity. As for her father ... he was a useless individual."

"A war invalid I heard." Alexander's tone was still icy.

"Well that's what was said. He was a coward, if you ask me. He was sent home as unfit."

"That's a grave misjudgment. He was honourably invalided out of the army and never able to do another day's work in his life. It wasn't as if he didn't *want* to."

"You sound very knowledgeable," Lally's tone was sarcastic. "I suppose you got that from the daughter."

"As a matter of fact, I did. She loved her father. Besides, Mother, as for being a 'nobody' Mary's mother, Elizabeth, is Sir Guy's natural daughter. In fact, she's a Woodville."

"But brought up as a servant, nevertheless."

"No fault of hers. If she is the daughter of a baronet she can hardly be called common. Whereas we don't know who my parents were, do we? It occurred to me my mother might have been a prostitute. My father may have been one of her clients. I wonder what

93

the Beckett family would think about *that*! Really, Mother, you're the most awful snob and considering where *you* came from I wonder you've got the nerve."

And without the customary solicitous and tender good-night kiss Alexander stormed out of the room and slammed the door behind him, in a rare display of temper.

It was the first row they had ever had, the first harsh word between them.

Lally didn't sleep at all that night, her mind in turmoil. At around eight she heard the front door close and knew that Alexander had gone to work without putting his head round her door, as was his custom, to say goodbye.

One day she would have to tell him who his parents were, and what would he say to her then? If he was angry with her now, how would he ever find it in his heart to forgive her when he knew the truth?

She would put off that evil day for as long as she could. She feared losing Alexander for ever.

April 1933

Bart Sadler glanced up with surprise as his visitor entered the room, having been announced a few minutes before by his butler.

"Solomon, what a pleasure!" he cried rising and crossing the room to shake the young man's hands. "Is Sarah-Jane with you?"

"No, not this time." Solomon, clearly nervous, avoided Bart's eyes.

"Do sit down, do sit down," Bart said expansively, pointing to a chair near the fire. "It's so terribly cold."

"It is." Solomon rubbed his hands together, but remained standing, looking at Bart.

"Cigarette?" Bart proffered a case. "Or do you prefer a cigar?"

"This will be fine." Solomon accepted a cigarette and as he held it to his mouth Bart saw that his fingers were trembling. The cigarette lit, Solomon sat down. Bart abandoned the shelter of his desk and sat opposite him, curious about the purpose of the visit.

"Is all well? Is there anything I can do?"

Solomon drew on his cigarette, gazing as he did so into the fire. Finally he raised his head.

"The fact is, Bart, I am in very much need of work. I haven't worked since I left Wenham."

"You amaze me." Bart settled back in his chair, cigarette between his fingers. "You are so very talented."

"It is nothing to do with talent. There is no work to be had. Believe me I've tried. I've even been up to London stumping the streets. I have been everywhere. There is no work about and we are living on my wife's money, which will soon run out and then we shall be penniless."

"I am very distressed to hear this," Bart said getting to his feet. "Very distressed indeed. If I can let you have..."

"I am not begging, Bart. I am not looking for charity. I would like work and I wondered if you knew of any opportunity here?"

"Well, of course, I have a lot of contacts. I'm sure I can find you something. Would you be prepared to move back to Wenham?"

"If necessary I would go anywhere."

"Have you talked to Abel? I believe he is still doing well, despite the bad economic times."

"I can't talk to Abel. He has not forgiven me for going off with his mother."

"I find that an absurd situation." Bart lit a fresh cigarette. "However, I can talk to Abel. After all he is my nephew and he is such a nice man. I'm sure he will do what he can."

"I would rather you didn't talk to Abel. I wouldn't want him to know my circumstances. I feel I should have been able to provide for my wife. After all, I persuaded her to come away with me and I'm ashamed

96

that I have to ask for help. I would much rather that if you are able to effect some introductions for me they should be without Abel's knowledge."

"But he will have to know some time. Especially if you return to Wenham."

"I would rather wait until that happens," Solomon said, "and then I can decide what to do."

Bart Sadler was a man of his word. It was nice to help people, not only for the sake of doing someone a good turn but because it helped to show how powerful you were. You could unlock doors that were shut to other people, open avenues that had been closed.

Bart was an influential man in the community and people were anxious to do him favours in the hope of being able to ask for favours in return. However, he found that the services of architects were not much in demand: builders were managing to do without them and drew up their own plans. Very few people were wealthy enough to build houses on the scale of Bart's house, Upper Park, which had been built in the heyday of the eighteenth century.

The house, situated seven miles from the town of Blandford, was a fine example of Georgian architecture. Standing on an incline facing north-south, it was built of

Dorset brick and faced with Chilmark stone. On all sides were magnificent views of the countryside. Surrounding the house were extensive formal landscaped gardens with an orangery. The stables and out-buildings had been refurbished and extended by Solomon Palmer when, in better days, he had worked on the house with Abel Yetman after its purchase by Bart.

Solomon was a first-class architect, with a fine imagination, and in a happier, more affluent age he would undoubtedly have flourished.

Now neither he nor Bart could find any work for him. Despite Bart's range of contacts that went from the north to the south of the county and beyond, no one was able to offer a young architect, however talented, any work of any kind. Everywhere Bart drew a blank, offered with the greatest possible number of apologies and expressions of regret.

Bart was driving home one day about six weeks after Solomon's visit brooding, among other things, on his lack of success on behalf of the young man, reluctant to admit defeat, when he was struck by an idea. The depression wasn't going to last for ever, even now there was money to be made and people were making it. He knew that munitions were being shipped to Germany

98

which was trying to pull itself up from the effects of the war under the able leadership of Adolf Hitler, whom Bart could not help but admire. He felt that he and Hitler had much in common: they were both men who had made something of themselves from humble beginnings, men of determination and stature. Bart, had left England penniless and had returned years later with a fortune, made by his own wits. Whatever people said, and critics abounded, you needed strong leadership in a country that had suffered total defeat as Germany had. Its currency had been devalued so as to be practically worthless, and it had millions unemployed. Bart knew of a number of small-arms companies which were exporting to Germany. He was interested in the business himself. In fact, he already had feelers out.

But the idea that came to him as he was driven home on a beautiful spring day through the Dorset countryside was that if he speculated and built a few fine houses, well designed to the highest specifications, and offered only to people of wealth and discrimination, he might well be on to rather a good business venture. And who better to act as architect for him for the high quality houses he had in mind than Solomon Palmer?

And, for that matter, who better to build

99

them than Abel, his very own nephew?

As soon as he got home Bart telephoned Solomon and asked him to come and see him. For the moment he decided not to confide his plans to his wife.

Solomon could hardly believe his ears when Bart told him of his scheme over dinner at The Crown in Blandford where Solomon was staying.

"I have plenty of money, you see," Bart said expansively, "and my fingers in a number of pies. I have many investments and I also have funds overseas which I can call on when need be without having to pay tax in this country. In fact I pay hardly any tax at all.

"I thought if we planned, say, four or five houses to start with, built on the grand scale with every modern convenience, rather like Forest House – though even better – we would sell them without any difficulty."

"Are you *sure*?" Solomon, beside himself with excitement, looked incredulous.

"Eventually we will sell them. It might take a year or two but I have no doubt that the economy will improve. It has to, and when it does there will be a lot of very rich people around anxious to show off. I will form a company. Indeed, I have already taken steps to do it, and I am offering you the post of architect at a starting salary shall we say of six hundred pounds a year?"

"Six *hundred?*" Solomon gasped.

"Plus bonuses, of course, on satisfactory work completed. I don't want to throw my money about but I want you to be properly rewarded. However," he looked candidly across the table at him, "you will have to return to this part of the country. What will Sarah-Jane say to that?"

"Sarah-Jane will have to do as she's told," Solomon said firmly, "for once."

"Until you have everything arranged you are very welcome to stay with us," Bart said.

"But would Deborah mind? After all her sister Ruth is married to Abel. I don't know how Debbie feels about the situation."

"Like your wife, mine will have to do as she's told," Bart said with a smile. "We can't have women wearing the trousers can we?" He raised his glass, brim full of fine claret. "Cheers," he said. "Here's to our partnership."

"To our partnership," Solomon said, fervently raising his glass in reply.

Bart looked round Abel's house with approval. It was large and built of Ham stone to a conventional design, double-fronted, with an imposing portico to fit in with the big house that was its neighbour.

101

The grounds were not yet landscaped but inside it was beautifully proportioned and finished, with gleaming paintwork and shining parquet floors. Bowls of spring flowers were scattered about on highly polished tables and the whole place exuded an atmosphere of wealth, taste and refinement.

The house was built on land given to the couple by Carson as a wedding present. It had been designed and supervised by Solomon Palmer and executed by Abel. It had been an ideal partnership, in Bart's opinion, before Palmer seduced Abel's mother and thus found himself out of a job.

A blushing maidservant showed him into the drawing room, which was large enough to entertain a considerable party of guests. It stretched the width of the house. The front looked out onto the Blackmore Vale and Pelham's Oak, a couple of miles distant, the back faced the town of Wenham, also a similar distance away. In between were acres of Dorset countryside: copses, thickets, streams and lush pastureland grazed on by fat contented cattle.

Bart was fond of his nephew Abel. He was a grave, rather solemn young man who had assumed the burden of the man of the family at a tender age after his father's death. He had grown up very quickly and, following in his father's footsteps, had eventually qualified as a master builder and started his own business. He had married his pretty cousin Ruth in the spring three years ago. As yet there was no sign of a family, rather, one imagined, to their regret.

The young Yetmans seldom received a visit from their uncle and Abel came hurrying into the room followed by Ruth, who greeted him with a kiss.

"Do excuse this impromptu call," Bart said, sinking into a deep, well-upholstered armchair. "But I had an idea and wanted to communicate with you as soon as I could."

"You're always welcome, Uncle," Ruth said. "We don't see enough of you. You're so busy. Would you like coffee?"

"Coffee would be very nice."

"Debbie not with you?" Ruth looked hopefully out of the window.

"Deborah has gone into Blandford on a shopping expedition, I believe. Anyway this is a business call."

"Oh well, in that case I'll leave you to it." Ruth prepared to leave the room, but Bart held up his hand.

"No, I'd like you to stay Ruth. This concerns you too."

"Sounds interesting." Abel sat down opposite his uncle, prepared to listen, while Ruth briefly left the room to order coffee.

"You really have a lovely place here." Bart lit a cigarette and looked around. "You must feel very pleased with it."

"We are, and grateful to Uncle Carson for his generous gift of land."

"It's a beautiful position," Bart agreed, "and a fine house, beautifully designed." Neither Abel nor Ruth, who had returned, replied, and Bart felt as though a chill had entered the room. He also began to feel a little less sanguine about the success of his mission. "I might as well come to the point," he said at last. "Solomon Palmer has been to see me."

"We don't mention his name in this house, Uncle," Abel said quietly.

"But he hasn't done anything wrong," Bart protested.

"Still, if you don't mind, we'd rather not discuss him."

"Heavens above," Bart said heatedly, "Sarah-Jane is my sister. I can't abandon her."

"Is something wrong?" Ruth asked, quickly taking the tray from the maid who had entered with the coffee. She put it on a table and started to pour.

"They are practically destitute from what Palmer told me. He has not worked since he left here."

"I'm surprised." Abel accepted a cup from

104

his wife. "He is a very capable architect."

"He says it's almost impossible to find work. He has been everywhere, including London."

Abel's face was impassive as he regarded his uncle.

"Are you asking us for financial help to support Mother? In that case—"

"Of course I'm not asking for financial help. He has not asked me, and he would not take it. He wants work, and that I am prepared to offer him."

"Where? Here?" Abel looked at him with surprise.

"I am optimistic about the future. I thought that I would like to enter the building business myself, extend my field of operations, as it were, and construct several fine houses on a speculative basis." He paused and looked from husband to wife. "With you as the builder, naturally, and Solomon as the architect. I am prepared to finance the whole operation, which will be of undoubted financial benefit to you both. In fact I hope to us all."

Abel finished his coffee and stood up.

"I'm afraid this proposal is not of the least interest to me, Uncle. I will not work with Solomon Palmer again. I couldn't." He looked at his wife, who nodded her agreement.

"We felt their behaviour was disgusting and demeaning." Ruth walked over to her husband's side. "And they were very deceitful and indiscreet. Why, even the servants knew what they were up to. They caused great scandal in the neighbourhood, and the whole town condemned them. I don't think it would welcome them back."

"Well, I think this town has no business to condemn them. Your mother had a right to her own life. She was widowed for many years. She was lonely."

"Be that as it may, I don't want to work with Palmer, and that is that," Abel said. "It was bad enough having to sit with them at Aunt Eliza's birthday party. And then Mother had to make an exhibition of herself, which shamed us all. We were horrified. No, thank you. Work with Solomon Palmer if you will, Uncle Bart, but please don't expect me to join you."

"Then I shall get other builders to do the work."

"That's entirely up to you. I'm afraid I can't compromise. If I do, then I shall look a fool and people will think the worse of me."

"You realise this will cause another rift in the family?" Bart said, looking closely at his nephew, "that we could well do without."

"I agree, but the rift is of your making not ours."

Bart had a feeling of desperation. "But I've already made Palmer an offer. I can't go back on my word."

"You only have yourself to blame, Uncle," Abel said with an air of indifference. "You should have spoken to us first. You should have found out which way the wind blew."

Five

It was one of those rare things in a normal English summer: a brilliant day, the sky cloudless, the air balmy. The colours of the flowers and shrubs in the garden were of a peculiar intensity as though an artist had been round during the night and daubed them all with a fresh coat of paint. Agnes sat in the shadow of a tree in her pretty garden attempting to read a book but, in reality, seeing very little of what was on the page.

Agnes Wentworth was not by nature a restful woman. She felt life had dealt her a blow – a series of blows really – by condemning her to a life of solitude in Wenham, the small town where she had been born and which she detested.

Not that she blamed herself for the various misfortunes with which life had beset her. Agnes was inclined to blame other people and had very few friends because no one could really trust her not to say cruel things behind their backs.

However, those who were close to her, who knew her best, had a grudging respect and admiration for her, and they came nearest to loving her. They included her former sister-in-law Eliza; Sophie Turner, who had just missed being her daughter-in-law, and Lally Martyn who, as a former adventuress herself, perhaps appreciated best all the vicissitudes Agnes had suffered and her skill in overcoming them. But, unlike Agnes, Lally had for many years had a stable marriage, a beautiful home, and had wanted for nothing.

Agnes's home was not her own. She regarded her allowance as paltry, and there were many things she wanted that she couldn't have. She pined, above all, for that deep, unquestioning love that comes from family. This was denied her by her daughter Elizabeth, who refused to have anything to do with Agnes or allow her children to see her, except a stiff, formal visit once a year. It was very, very cruel, in one's old age, to be deprived of the love of a family and Agnes, whenever she thought of it, which was quite often, gave herself up to waves of self-pity. She never thought to blame herself for rejecting her own daughter in the first place.

Agnes had lunched sparingly, as she

usually did. She was still figure and fashion conscious. She began to doze, her book fallen onto her lap. She was conscious of the pleasant warmth of the sun, though protected from its rays by the leafy branches of the chestnut tree under which she sat. Although only half awake she became aware of a presence and, expecting to see Grace hovering by, opened her eyes and looked sharply to one side.

The pert, pretty little face of Mary Sprogett was looking gravely down at her. For a moment Agnes scarcely recognised her.

"Hello, Grandma," Mary said, laying a small parcel on Agnes's lap. "Did I surprise you?"

"You certainly did," Agnes said, "but it is a nice surprise." She began to undo the gift lying in her lap. "I hardly recognised you, Mary." Finally she removed the paper and exclaimed with delight, "Chocolates! My favourites! How thoughtful!" She put up her cheek for a kiss. "My, how you've changed since I last saw you. You're quite a young woman."

Mary smiled and slumped on the grass by the side of Agnes's chair.

"Go and get yourself a seat child." Agnes flapped her hand towards a pile of folded chairs beside the summer-house, but Mary shook her head and wrapped her arms around her knees.

"I prefer it here, Grandma."

Agnes's stony features relaxed into a smile. She had once been a beauty, but years of disappointment and frustration had left her with an almost permanently sour expression. She put out a hand and touched Mary's head.

"It's so sweet of you to come and see me, dear, but why did it have to take you so long?"

Mary shook her head, eyes downcast.

"I suppose your mother..."

Mary suddenly raised her head and looked urgently, almost desperately, into her grandmother's eyes. Agnes was surprised and a little alarmed, to see such an expression of timidity, almost of fear, in them.

"Grandma, I've run away!"

"You've run away?" Agnes repeated.

"From home. I didn't know where to go and then I thought ... no one would think of looking here."

"But Mary you can't stay here if you've run away." Agnes's expression was aghast.

"Only for a while."

"And what will you do then? You'll have to go home some time and I will get into terrible trouble."

Mary shook her head vehemently. "I'm

never going to go home. I hate home. I hate my mother."

"Oh, but you mustn't say that."

"Mummy always picks on me. I think she hates me too."

"I'm sure she doesn't."

Agnes didn't know exactly why she was defending her daughter. She supposed it was the sort of thing one did instinctively, however alienated one was.

"She hates me, Grandma." Mary paused before thrusting in the barb. "And she hates you."

"Oh, I know that." Agnes put back her head and gave a melancholy laugh. "But why does she hate you?"

"She has always preferred Betsy and my brothers, especially the new ones," Mary said on a note of contempt. "She says I am most like my father and she despised *him*. She said I was a snivelling brat when I was young. Now she wants to send me away."

"But where to?"

"Switzerland."

"Switzerland," Agnes echoed. "But Switzerland is very nice."

"I don't want to go. It's to a finishing school. My mother thinks I need to be made into a lady and I want to remain as I am. I don't want to be a *lady*." Mary derisively emphasised the word 'lady'.

Agnes smiled and placed her hand on the child's head again.

"I see. Your mother wants you finished off." Agnes giggled at her own joke.

"I want to leave school, but I don't want to go to another, especially not one abroad."

"But what will you do, dear? It is a very sensible thing to have a good education." She paused and sighed deeply. "Had I been better educated I would not have become so dependent on men. Men keep us in subordinate positions because they know we are superior to them, and they are afraid we'll catch them up, overtake them. You should never close your eyes to the advantages of a good education. Never. Now," Agnes sat upright in her chair, "we shall have a cup of tea and then I shall call a taxicab and Grace will take you back to your mother who need never know you've run away."

"I left her a note," Mary said defiantly. "I have taken all my things."

"But where are they?" Agnes looked around in dismay.

"I left them in the hall."

"Then you must take them back. You must tell your mother you're sorry and—"

"No, no, no." Mary burst into hysterical tears and clutched at Agnes's skirt. "I will kill myself if I have to go back, and you will be responsible for my early death."

Elizabeth Temple stood at the drawing-room window looking out for her expected visitor, her hands playing agitatedly with the necklace at her throat. She recalled the awful moment when she had found the note and realised Mary had gone. Cleared out. Of course she had not slept the night before, not a wink. Graham had snored away beside her, but Graham was not Mary's father. He was concerned, but he was an optimist, a man of equable temperament with no imagination. He was convinced that no harm had or would come to his step-daughter. She was playing a prank.

Mother and daughter had had a great row the previous day and Mary had run away while her mother was out on an errand in Blandford. Telephone calls to her various school friends had failed to find her.

The last thing Graham Temple wanted was a fuss: a hue and cry. It was bad for business and he was a prominent and respected solicitor. Once it got out that his stepdaughter had run away from home it would do his position in the community no good at all. People would suspect some sort of ill treatment. He begged Elizabeth to wait another twenty-four hours before raising the alarm. If Mary had not left a note but just disappeared, it would have been different.

Just then Elizabeth saw a car coming up the long drive to the house. She ran to the front door as Eliza got out and looked anxiously at Elizabeth, who was running down the steps.

"Any news?" Eliza asked. Elizabeth put a finger to her lips and shook her head.

"The servants don't know. I told them that Mary was staying with friends."

"Perhaps she is."

"Well, she's somewhere, the little wretch, and when I get her home I'll..."

Elizabeth took Eliza's arm and hurried her up the stairs and into the drawing room.

"How hot it is!" Eliza said fanning herself with her hand.

"A glass of cool lemonade, Aunt Eliza?"

"That would be lovely." Eliza sank into a chair while Elizabeth rang the bell to summon the maid. She waited until she had left the room before speaking.

"We had a big row yesterday morning. Graham and I want her to go to a finishing school in Switzerland. Mary's no scholar, she has no manners and her deportment is poor. Frankly, I think she's a very lucky but ungrateful child."

"What does she want to do?"

"God knows." Elizabeth shook her head and helped herself to a cigarette from a box on the table. She lit it with trembling hands and threw the match into an ashtray. "She refuses to return to school to complete her education. She is sixteen and I suppose she could get a job, if she could find one. She seems to have no interest in anything and I am at my wits' end. Now this—" She turned to Eliza but, as the maid came in with a jug of lemonade and two glasses, conversation was suspended until she left. "I felt I had to ask your advice, Aunt Eliza. I know we have not always got on, but I think more of you than other members of my family, except Carson, of course, and he is away."

"Gone to Venice to collect his children. Have you contacted the police?" Eliza asked as she put her glass to her lips.

"Certainly not! There is no need to cause such a commotion, not for the moment anyway. She left a note saying that she was running away. We are sure she has come to no harm but, to put it bluntly, is just plain *naughty*. It is many years since I smacked Mary but she will get the hiding of her life when she returns. I don't care how old she is."

"In that case she will run away again."

Eliza looked at her niece for a long, long time aware of conflicting emotions: guilt, exasperation, even a kind of affection that still persisted. After all Elizabeth was part of Guy and she had adored her brother. But

Elizabeth was vain, proud and domineering. She was in a way as damaged as her poor daughter obviously was if she hated her home enough to run away. Elizabeth was, in fact, very like her mother, Agnes.

This gave Eliza an idea.

"I'll see what I can do," she said. "As long as if, and when, Mary comes back there is no punishment, but an attempt at understanding. I want you to try and build bridges with your daughter. Will you do that?"

Elizabeth nodded but her expression remained defiant. She didn't say she would and she didn't say she wouldn't.

Silently she saw Eliza to her car and silently Eliza drove away.

Eliza said "I don't suppose you've seen Mary?"

Agnes shook her head.

"She's run away."

"Fancy," Agnes said, pointing to a chair close by under the chestnut tree. The good weather had continued and she spent a lot of time in her garden.

"You don't seem surprised." Eliza watched her closely. Devious woman that she was, it was almost impossible to fathom whether she was telling the truth or not.

"I know that Mary and her mother don't

get on. That's why I'm not surprised."

"I think she's here, Agnes," Eliza said looking round, aware of a sense of something unusual about the house. She was one of the few people who could talk bluntly to her sister-in-law. They had crossed swords many times in the past and she felt no fear of her.

"I don't know why you should."

Eliza was more convinced than ever by Agnes's off-hand tone that she knew something.

"If you are close to any of your grand-children it's Mary."

"Fat chance I have to be close to *any* of them." Agnes sniffed.

Then, as if knowing the quality, the tenacity of her opponent, her expression slowly relaxed and a secretive half-smile played on her lips.

"All right she's here. I made her a promise I wouldn't tell, but I know you. You're determined to ferret out the truth. I think you sensed it."

"Somehow I think I did," Eliza acknowledged. "However I think you should have let her parents know. It wasn't kind."

"Why should I?"

"Because they were worried."

"Huh!" Agnes scoffed. "I think they would be glad to be rid of the poor child. They want to send her to Switzerland."

"Only for her own good."

"To get *rid* of her," Agnes repeated. "I intend to keep Mary here for as long as she wants to stay." Her expression grew soft. "I love having her. She is a dear child, a sweet girl and she loves her old granny. Elizabeth has deprived me of the company of my grandchildren and has not proved a good mother herself. I will fight to keep Mary here for as long as she wishes."

At that moment Agnes looked beyond Eliza's shoulder and made a beckoning gesture with her hand. Eliza turned to see Mary advancing slowly across the lawn as if rather afraid of the presence of her great-aunt. Eliza rose and, with a welcoming smile, embraced her.

"Hello, Mary."

"Hello, Aunt Eliza." Mary gave her a dutiful smile.

"Your parents are very worried about you. You should have told them where you were going."

"I was afraid Grandma might get into trouble." Mary draped her arm round Agnes's neck and Agnes, relishing the gesture, put her own arm tightly round the young girl's waist. Eliza felt an instinctive pity for the pair of them, as though they were orphans sheltering from a storm, both outcasts in their respective ways, both sharing the same stubborn, aggressive streak.

She saw a striking resemblance between the granddaughter, now that she was nearly grown up, and her grandmother. Agnes in her day had been a beauty: not very tall but with blonde hair and lustrous blue eyes flecked with grey. Her granddaughter mirrored her exactly. As yet, though, Mary's eyes had the open honesty of innocence not yet lost, while Agnes's had the quality of steel, the grey over the years seeming to dominate the blue.

Eliza stood up. "Mary I am going to see your mother to put her out of her misery. She will be very annoyed with you, also very sad. It's understandable. After all, they only want to send you to finishing school. I would have thought you'd have liked that. If you are unhappy with your parents for whatever reason you would get away from them."

"I don't like school," Mary insisted stamping her small foot. "I am finished with school."

"Then what will you do?"

"She can stay with me," Agnes said with an imperturbable smile, "and be my companion. I'm sure we can rely on your tact to arrange that, dear Eliza."

Eliza, as anticipated, placated Mary's parents, at least for the time being. That summer was a very precious time for Agnes, one of the happiest she had had for many years. She had a fearsome reputation, but only because she was so lonely and felt so rejected by her family who in the past she had treated quite badly. She relished the company of her granddaughter and they whiled the summer weeks away chatting on the lawn or taking trips in Carson's motor car, visiting Sherborne or Bournemouth to shop and indulging their appetite for sweet cakes and hot chocolate, the latter taken in some of the fancy hotels in that fashionable seaside resort. Agnes had little money of her own, but what she had she lavished on Mary, doting more and more on her with each day that passed.

But, best of all, Agnes enjoyed the visits of the handsome, personable young Alexander Martyn, which started soon after Mary took up residence with her and continued through the summer. At weekends they would go riding together at Pelham's Oak, accompanied by Carson and observed from the terrace by a fond Agnes. Frequently, however, Mary went off alone with Alexander in his motor car.

Agnes, a lifetime schemer and manipulator, enjoyed the intrigue, the deception. A frustrated romantic, she delighted in the spectacle of mutual awareness as, slowly, Mary and Alexander fell in love.

Carson, who had had business in Yeovil, sat on the terrace smoking a cigarette and watching the young riders in the far distance. He noted how Mary's seat had improved, with what skill she managed jumping the hedges and crossing the streams, her exhilaration as she sped off leaving Alexander to follow on behind, as though tempting him to chase her, which he did, gladly. Mary had grown into a beauty. She was almost womanly in her manner, older, much older than her years, with a kind of unwitting sophistication.

Finally, Alexander and Mary reached the top of the hill. They slowed their mounts as they passed through the gate onto the lawn, still laughing, where Carson awaited them.

"I wish I didn't have to go back." Alexander jumped down from his horse while the groom, who had run over from the stables, helped Mary down from hers.

"Why must you go back?" Mary shook herself. She ran her hands through her thick hair and patted her horse that, together with Alexander's, was led away by the groom, and flopped into the chair next to Carson.

"Because I have to work."

"You don't need to," she said teasingly. "Grandma says you're a very rich man."

"That's why he needs to work," Carson said laconically. "so that he doesn't spend his time in idleness."

"Besides, I like work," Alexander glanced at Mary. Then, as if an idea had suddenly struck him, "Look, do you suppose your grandmother would let you come up to London? Just for a visit?"

"Oh, I'd love that." Mary clasped her hands together in rapture. "I would *adore* to go to London. Do you think I could go, Uncle Carson?"

"I think your grandmother would miss you."

"Only for a while," Alexander said excitedly, "and Mother would be there." He looked across at Carson. "I mean Mary would be properly chaperoned." Carson noticed a slight blush on the young man's cheek and suddenly he wondered if things weren't going at too fast a pace.

Alexander jumped up.

"Come on, let's go and ask your grandmother." He held out a hand. Mary clasped it eagerly, her eyes shining with excitement.

"Take care," Carson said, looking at them as they got into Alexander's car. "Don't rush things. You have your lives before you, you know."

But his words, which once upon a time could have applied to himself, were drowned in the sound of the car's engine as it vanished down the drive.

There was something different about her grandmother at luncheon that day, Mary thought, her happiness suddenly evaporating, something that made her look warningly at Alexander, shaking her head as though this was not the time to suggest a London visit. Agnes sat there, very stiff and upright, preoccupied, scarcely smiling, and did not even ask them if they'd had a nice morning. She had reprimanded them for being late and hurried them into the dining room where a light luncheon was served by Grace.

It was not until Grace had left the room that Mary said, "Is there something wrong Grandma? You're very quiet. Are you quite well?"

"I am quite well thank you, Mary," Agnes said glancing at the door, "but I am afraid I'm the bearer of bad news. Your stepfather was here this morning and he insists on you returning to your home in preparation for going to Switzerland. He thinks this period of grace has lasted long enough. They are to take you to Geneva next week. It's all fixed, I'm afraid. I can't keep you here without their permission. Your stepfather even murmured something about a court order if I opposed them, as you are still a minor. I also think that news has got to them of the amount of time you're spending with Alexander. You're seen gadding all over the place together, apparently."

"What's wrong with that?" Alexander demanded.

"Nothing, as far as I'm concerned. I know the relationship between you is one of friendship, and properly conducted. I reassured Graham Temple on that score. However, I'm afraid, my dear, you will have to pack your bags. Your stepfather is coming for you tomorrow. Meanwhile, you two had better make the best you can of the short time you have together."

After lunch Agnes pleaded a headache and went up to her room. Alexander and Mary wandered into the garden and sat in the low chairs under the chestnut tree. It was very peaceful. Alexander put his head back and, closing his eyes, held out his hand, seeking Mary's.

As her cool palm slid into his he brought it to his lips and he felt a tremor run through her.

"I love you," he said. He opened his eyes, leaned over towards her and kissed her. For a long time they clung to each other oblivious of the possibility of observers from the house.

"I didn't think it would come to this so soon," Alexander murmured when, finally, they broke apart.

"Come to what?"

"We have to decide what to do."

"I am *not* going to Switzerland," Mary said. "I am going to run away."

"Don't be silly. You can't." He looked at her aghast.

"I can. And I'm going to do it tonight."

"Where are you going to go to?"

She looked at him. "Could I go to London with you?"

"They will know where you are."

"Then you can lend me some money and I'll catch a train somewhere. I'll write and tell you where I am."

"Don't be ridiculous." Alexander let go of her hand and leant back in the chair and closed his eyes again, deep in thought.

"You can go to Switzerland and I can come and see you there. We can write. Or..." he opened his beautiful brown eyes and a suggestion that took her breath away seemed to lurk somewhere in the depths.

"Or?" Mary felt her heart suddenly start to race.

"We can run away together. I can't let you

126

go by yourself."

"Where to?" Her heart went on pounding with excitement.

He raised a hand expansively, flourishing it about.

"Rome, Paris, Vienna ... all the places Aunt Agnes has described to us. We can get married and then you will never have to do what your mother tells you, ever again."

Later that night Agnes watched as the Alexander's car sped away, away from Wenham, away from Dorset and England, on the lovers' big adventure. In her heart she would follow them, all the way, hour by hour. She had no qualms about what she had done. She didn't want a granddaughter she adored making the mistakes that had so ruined her own life and deprived her of happiness in the past.

She wished them godspeed.

Six

November 1933

With the lowering sky, the skeletal trees heavy with frost and the ground hard underfoot it was difficult to imagine what the landscape might one day look like if Bart's ambitious plans came to fruition.

Wearing heavy coats and thick mufflers the men tramped over the uneven ground. With his tape measure Solomon paced the boundaries of the house, which would be the first to be built on this newly acquired piece of land on the outskirts of Wenham. Finely positioned overlooking the River Stour it would be a large, elegant dwelling with all modern conveniences as well as outbuildings, stables and a garage for three motor cars. Solomon had lost no time in drawing up plans even before the purchase of the land was completed.

Also competing to buy this desirable tract of real estate had been Abel Yetman, who had lost out to Bart, who had offered more money. The negotiations had been conducted through solicitors and the two men had not met. In fact, they had not met since Bart had suggested that he and Abel should go into business together employing Solomon Palmer as the architect.

Deborah and Ruth still saw each other, but family gatherings had come to an end. As Abel had predicted bad blood had been stirred up and Bart's attempts to reintegrate himself with his family had been set back by years, perhaps for ever.

But once he had his nose into a piece of business nothing stopped Bart. Sentiment, family connections – nothing was allowed to stand in his way. He had not made a fortune in South America and got a reputation as a hard man to do business with for nothing.

Solomon carried a set of plans as well as his tape measure and, from time to time, the two men stopped, looked at the plans and examined the lie of the land.

"It's an ideal site," Solomon said, cheeks pink with cold but also excitement. "Exactly in the right position facing north-south, and a beautiful view of the river." He waved his hand towards the meandering Stour which, flanked by trees and fields, snaked off into the distance to dawdle past Blandford and Wimborne, finally finding its exit in the broad waters of Christchurch Bay.

"Well, now that we have completed the purchase," Bart turned to his young companion who was so full of enthusiasm, "we can begin as soon as the weather improves. I have no shortage of workmen ready, able to start as soon as we give the word."

"No hope of Abel..." Solomon began as they started towards Bart's car.

Bart shook his head. "I wouldn't ask him again even if he *is* my wife's brother-in-law. I did a lot for that young man and in my opinion he did a very foolish thing in turning down my overtures. I've no intention of being snubbed again."

"Still, it is a pity," Solomon said, as Bart got behind the wheel of his custom-built Lagonda. "He was a very good builder. If you employ casual labour you don't have the same kind of control."

"Oh, I'll have control all right," Bart put the car into gear, "and you're mistaken if you think I'm employing casual labour. I have engaged a very good manager who also happens to be a relative. He's my nephew, Charlie Hardcastle, the son of my youngest sister Maureen, whose husband was also a builder. Oh, Charlie knows the ropes. He's very keen. You'll like him. We also have a plasterer, a roofer, a plumber, an electrician and several bricklayers and general workmen."

"You've been very busy." Solomon was impressed.

"I'm going to build new premises, but I'm also thinking of adapting ones that exist already. I'd like you to look them over."

"No intention of retiring, Bart?"

"None at all." Bart laughed. "I mean to work harder than ever. In fact I intend to expand. You see, once you have the capital you can hardly help making money. You just put it to work for you and, without lifting a finger, the sum increases." He frowned. "Or it should if it is invested properly. Now young man," he looked keenly at his brother-in-law, "when are you and my sister going to move to Wenham? We need you here, now."

"Well," Solomon scratched his forehead, "Sarah-Jane is not keen to come back. She feels they're very stuffy here in Wenham."

"She can't stay in Brighton for ever!" Bart expostulated.

"That's what I tell her."

"You needn't live in Wenham if she doesn't like it."

"It's not so much that. It's her family. They haven't been very nice to her."

"*I've* been nice to her," Bart protested.

"I mean the children: Martha, Abel, Felicity."

"But only Abel is here."

"Sarah-Jane is self-conscious; I can't explain it."

"It's the age difference." Bart gave him a knowing look. "It matters in a woman but not a man. I'm much older than my wife. Nobody gives a fig."

"Exactly. I tell her it's not important."

"And is it?"

"Not as far as I'm concerned," Solomon said, but Bart thought his tone lacked conviction.

"Well you'd better stay with us until you get fixed up," Bart said, as they turned into the drive of Upper Park. "You're very welcome and so is Sarah-Jane. But you can't live here indefinitely and once we get busy, as I think we soon shall, you can't be traipsing off to Brighton every weekend, whatever your wife says. Incidentally," he looked at Solomon as he stopped the car, "I shall be going abroad to Germany on business for a few days, but by all means stay on here as long as you like. Why don't you invite Sarah-Jane over? She'll be company for Deborah while I'm gone."

To have Solomon Palmer as a house guest was, for Deborah, a welcome diversion. The whiff of scandal about him made him interesting. She thought he was extremely good-looking and, not for the first time, wondered what on earth he had seen in Sarah-Jane.

The first impression was of his height. He was very tall and lean, with an awkwardness of gait and a hesitant manner which betrayed his shyness. He looked much younger than his twenty-nine years and his youthfulness, his smooth skin with little show of beard, coupled with his casualness of dress, gave him the appearance of a scholar, maybe still a student. His tousled, curly brown hair and warm brown eyes, which lit up engagingly when he smiled, only added to his appeal. In short, despite his apparent diffidence, Solomon was most attractive to women who wanted either to mother him or take him to their beds, sometimes – perhaps, in the case of Sarah-Jane – both.

The first night Bart was away Deborah and Solomon went into the dining room as usual. Normally, Bart sat at the head of the table, but tonight Deborah sat there with Solomon on her right. Harold, the butler, was in his customary place and the servants stood by the huge walnut sideboard waiting to remove dishes and replace them with fresh ones. From time to time Harold refilled their tall crystal glasses with wine. Between courses there was a pause while Deborah and Solomon smoked cigarettes.

"How are you finding the new site?" Deborah asked as soup plates were removed and Harold came forward to light her cigarette.

"Oh, it's excellent. I can't wait to get started." Solomon drew on his cigarette as the butler moved back to issue fresh orders.

"Bart says you're looking for a property to buy."

"Well not yet. I mean—"

"But surely you'll move back to Wenham? I hope so."

"It's not decided." Solomon's tone was abrupt.

"Sarah-Jane must be anxious to see her family again."

Solomon pointedly didn't reply and they both fell silent as the next course was served. Because of the proximity of the servants the conversation for the rest of the meal consisted of generalities.

After dinner they stood awkwardly for a moment in the hall. Solomon was not sure what was expected of him or how to behave in the absence of the host. He didn't know Deborah very well, nor did he know what she thought of him. In truth she made him slightly nervous with her direct glances and rather flirtatious manner. It surprised him too.

"Well," he said shuffling his feet and

looking towards the stairs, "I think I'll have a look at my plans and then have an early night.

"Oh, come and have coffee." Deborah playfully tugged at his arm and led the way towards the drawing room. "I thought we might play a record. Do you like jazz? Coffee please, in the drawing room, Harold," she called out to the butler who stood stiffly by the dining-room door.

He bowed and withdrew into the dining room.

"It's such fun without Bart," Deborah said gaily, as she threw open the doors of the drawing room and ran over to the gramophone in the corner. She turned and looked mischievously at Solomon. "I feel like a naughty little girl let out of school." She indicated a silver cigarette box on the side table. "Help yourself to a cigarette and light one for me."

She started going through a pile of records, some she put on one side and some on another. Soon the room was filled with the sound of Jelly Roll Morton's trumpet. Deborah, hands wiggling by her side, shimmied over to Solomon, took the cigarette from his mouth and put it into hers. Then she held up her hands and, as he stood looking at her rather bewilderedly, clearly not knowing what was expected of him, she seized him by the arms and together they began to gyrate round the room.

Solomon realised that she was a little drunk. He didn't know how much wine she was used to but they'd consumed a bottle between them, with a couple of gin and Italians each beforehand.

The music came to an end and Deborah returned to the gramophone. This time, instead of jazz, a soft smoochy air filled the room. To the sounds of 'What is this thing called love?' Deborah sashayed over to Solomon, her arms extended invitingly. He hesitated only for a fraction of a second before encircling her waist and slowly bringing her left hand up to his breast, tucking it in his. Deborah rested her cheek against his and together they danced slowly in time to the music until it stopped. The record went round and round on the turntable.

"Better change the record," Solomon muttered trying to break away, but Deborah held on to him.

"Don't you want to?" she asked looking up at him.

"Want to what?"

"You know."

"Of course."

"Well then..."

Solomon succeeded in disengaging himself as gently as he could and went rapidly across the floor to stop the gramophone. Then he lit a cigarette before rejoining Deborah, who stood by the fire, her hand resting on the marble mantelpiece.

As he stood by her she sought his free hand with hers.

"I don't think we should," he said.

"Why not?"

"Well..."

"Are you afraid of Bart?"

"Of course. He'd kill me if he found out. He might kill you too."

"He would never find out."

"What about the servants? They're all over the place."

"They have their own quarters. Nowhere near us. Harold has already gone to bed and he's always the last."

Solomon threw his cigarette stub into the fire. "Let's do it then."

"You could sound more enthusiastic." She put her arms around his neck and looked into his eyes. Then, drawing his mouth towards hers, she kissed him.

Later that night they woke to the sound of the toddler crying. Solomon sat upright in bed but Deborah remained where she was.

"The baby's crying," he said, turning to her.

"I know. One of the nurses will see to her. That's what they're there for." Debbie reached up and drew Solomon down beside her. "Don't worry about the baby. What's the matter with you? Is it Sarah-Jane? Did it make you feel guilty?"

Solomon gave a sarcastic laugh. He turned on the bedside lamp and groped for his cigarettes.

"Sarah-Jane is a drunkard. She's no wife to me." He lit his cigarette and put out the lighter. "Sorry," he said turning to her.

"No, I'll have a puff of yours." She took the cigarette from his mouth and drew hard on it. "Are you sorry you married her?"

Solomon leaned back against the pillow. "Now I am. At the time I thought it was the right thing to do."

"What do you mean 'at the time'?"

"Well, I thought I was in love with her. I mean I suppose I was in love with her. And then when the children found out and were so annoyed I felt I had to do the right thing. I couldn't just abandon her."

"When did you know that she drank?"

"Not really until we moved away. I think the problem began then. I used to come home worn out from looking for work and sometimes find that she'd passed out. You remember she made a spectacle of herself at Eliza's birthday? It wasn't the first time. But

I can't just leave her. I don't know what would happen to her."

"Is that why she doesn't want to come back to Wenham?"

"Partly. But it's very complicated. It's to do with her family and me and her age. When she's in her cups she says she's ruined my life, but it's my fault as much as hers."

"You're a very sweet man," Deborah said gripping his hand. "I mean genuinely nice. Not like Bart."

"Bart's not nice to you?"

"Well, he doesn't beat me. I suppose you must think something is wrong if I can do this with you."

"I'm afraid I wasn't very good."

"You were better than Bart."

"Really?" Solomon looked surprised. "I'm astonished."

"Why, did you think he was a good lover?"

"I thought – well—" Solomon shrugged. "I don't know."

"You think he's good at everything. You admire him."

"Well, yes, I do. He certainly gets things done."

"He certainly gets his own way, you mean."

"That too." He looked at her sideways. "Don't you love him any more?"

"I'm not sure. He no longer makes me feel

very special. I don't think it's other women. I think he's so wrapped up in his work. The honeymoon was wonderful. It was very exciting to be wined and dined and treated like a great lady. But when we came back things weren't quite the same. It was as though that part of Bart's life, the romantic part, was over and he immersed himself in his business affairs. I don't think he really knows what I do half the time, or cares."

"I have to be honest and say that I felt he cared about you very much."

"You can't always tell by appearances," Deborah said. As if making an effort to dispel her gloom, she threw herself on her stomach and ran the palm of her hand titillatingly across his chest.

Solomon felt himself aroused.

This time it would be better.

December 1933

Dearest Mother,

I have never been happier and know I have found my true love. Mary and I have been together now for several weeks and we are certain about this.

I didn't want to hurt you, dearest Mother, but I knew you would never consent to our going away, and Mary's parents would have done all they could to separate us.

140

I know I have placed you in a terrible situation and, believe me, I regret it with my whole heart. I don't want you to think that because I love Mary I love you less.

I want to marry Mary. She is to have our child, and I want to have the blessing of the Church. I ask you to do all you can, with the help, perhaps, of Aunt Eliza, to bring Mary's parents round, particularly her mother.

Nothing now can be undone. The doctor confirmed yesterday that the baby will be born in the summer.

Anyway, I want to return to England and to my work and show that I am capable of the trust Pieter Heering put in me.

We would prefer to be married in England, but if that is not possible we shall somehow contrive to be married here. Could you please send me my birth certificate?

With all my love, dearest Mother,
Your
Alexander

Eliza put down the letter and looked across at her friend whose face was still tear-stained.

"You see he will have to know now," Lally exclaimed.

"You should have told him before," Eliza said. "It was bound to happen. But that is

141

not the only problem, Lally. What are we going to do about Elizabeth?"

"The deed is done. Carson will have to talk to her. If the child is pregnant the sooner they get married the better."

Lally picked up the letter again and perused its contents for about the tenth time since it had arrived that morning. It was not the first communication from Alexander since he had gone away with Mary, but it was the first letter. Shortly after they had eloped he had cabled to say they were well. He had also written to Pieter Heering to say he was taking a few months' leave and he hoped this was not inconveniencing anybody. As he was a major shareholder in the company and possible future chairman this was a forgone conclusion. Besides, Pieter had a fondness for the young man and admired his spirit.

"I don't know how I shall survive this." Lally, who had aged visibly over the past few weeks, put down the letter and gazed into the fire, her handkerchief screwed up in a ball in her hand. "I will have to tell Alexander the truth about his birth and I will have a pregnant daughter-in-law of sixteen years of age. Well," she looked across at Eliza and gave her a wintry smile, "thank heaven for Carson. He will know what to do."

Mary knew that Alexander was becoming restless. He spent a lot of time on the telephone to his office in London, sent and received cables and watched the post anxiously for a letter from his mother.

She sat on the balcony of the villa they had rented on Lake Como gazing out on the beautiful still waters of the lake towards the town of Como itself. They'd passed the villa one day on a trip out of Milan to the mountains that towered over the lake. There had been a small sign saying it was for rent, which they'd almost missed because Alexander liked to tear along in his high-powered Bugatti. Mary had said 'what a lovely place' and at the same time they had seen the notice and stopped. They had instantly fallen in love with it and decided that their wandering days were over for the time being. It was just at that point Mary had discovered she was pregnant, a fact she hesitated to tell Alexander, except that he'd guessed. Her urgent run to the bathroom in the morning had given the game away.

Mary often wondered if he'd planned the pregnancy. She was just an ignorant girl, a virgin when they'd first slept together, but Alexander had more experience. He knew about these things and she knew nothing, not even, really, how babies came. All that scared her a good deal. She had not wanted to be a mother at seventeen but, unless fate intervened, she would be.

Alexander had been thrilled when their suspicions were confirmed and quickly wrote to his mother. Any moment they expected her reply.

But what about her own mother? It didn't bear thinking about. She could hear Alexander on the phone in the salon talking to his office. She knew he was dying to get back. While they'd been touring there had been a lot to occupy him, marvellous things to see. They'd been to the opera in Venice, concerts at the Caracalla baths in Rome. But beautiful though the bougainvillea-covered Villa Scritori was, it wasn't enough to occupy Alexander's mind. One could live on love, but for not for ever.

Mary often looked back to the summer: her last days at school, her refusal to return, the suggestion, no the command, that she should go to a finishing school in Switzerland. The escape to her grandmother, the appearance of Alexander like some white knight dashing to her rescue, and the flight. The night in Dover where they consummated their love, the bumpy Channel crossing, which she spent being sick all the time. The trip to Paris, staying at a hotel near the Louvre, journeying down to the Riviera, then Genoa, Pisa, Venice, Rome and, finally, Milan.

It had been a very heady brew for anyone, but especially for a girl so young that she had never left her native Dorset, never mind crossed the Channel or stayed in grand hotels on the continent. Almost instantly she had felt herself transformed into a woman.

Mary heard the doorbell ring. After a few moments the maid entered with an envelope which she handed to Mary who glanced at it. Her heart jumped.

When, moments later, Alexander finished his call and came into the salon she handed it to him.

"I think this is from your mother."

Alexander snatched the letter from her. Going over to the balcony he opened it and stood there for some moments reading. Finally, his face showing no emotion, he handed it to Mary and sat down studying her face as she read it.

My darling,

I don't know how to reply to the news you have just given me except to say that my heart is full. I think you are quite capable of becoming a good father, but the position of

145

little Mary concerns us all.

I have talked to Eliza and Carson and we all feel that, of course, you must come home at once. She must have the best possible care and although we have not yet given the news to Elizabeth, we can't envisage that there will be any objection to a speedy marriage.

You will have from me, my dearest son, a loving welcome which of course will be extended to your bride. Please cable or telephone me the date of your arrival.

Your very loving
Mother

Mary leaned against Alexander's shoulder, her eyes on the landscape through which the train was passing. Now that the time was finally upon them it felt good to be going home, but she was frightened. For three months, she and Alexander had lived in a dream, in another world, and reality would soon banish that dream. In every way the adventure, undertaken without much thought, had been perfect. Perfect understanding of each other, perfect love.

Alexander, who had been asleep beside her, stirred, opened his eyes and squeezed her arm.

"Happy darling?"

"Very happy." She smiled up at him. "But I wish..."

"What?"

"I wish we were still in our pretty little villa and that we didn't have to go back."

"But you said you wanted to go home?"

"In a way, though I'm scared of Mother."

His arm gripped hers reassuringly. "There is no need to be frightened of your mother now you're with me."

It was so wonderful and comforting to have him beside her. To know that he would always be there.

"When we are married, we can return to the villa again."

Mary sighed. "You'll be so busy with your work."

"We can have holidays and when baby is born, we can take him with us." Suddenly a gleam came into his eye. "Tell you what, if you like I'll try and buy it for us. I think they'd be willing to sell it. Would you like that darling? It will be my wedding present to you."

Mary gulped and suddenly everything seemed to overwhelm her. A whole villa as a wedding gift! Alexander could give her everything she wanted. It took some getting used to. He could and he would, loving and generous to a fault.

But then that was Alexander: impulsive,

positive, decisive, so sure about the future. Mary was less sure. She wondered how long a man so dynamic and talented would be satisfied with a woman like her? She was unsophisticated, poorly educated, with nothing to offer but her love. What would happen when love waned, as people said it did? Could she live up to his high standards, to the glamour of his life? Why now, when everything should be so perfect, did she doubt that the future could be anything but bright?

Alexander tightened his arm round her and looked at her questioningly as if puzzled by the slowness of her response.

"Are you pleased, darling?"

"Very pleased. Thank you, Alexander."

The sixteen-year-old woman, a mother-to-be, who in many ways was still a child, smiled, or tried to smile back, in an effort to conceal the sense of foreboding she felt: that somehow, despite her great love for Alexander – and she loved him with all her heart – the good times were over and would never return.

Seven

January 1934

The three people sat as statues, silent and still. The only sound was the crackle of logs in the great hearth of the drawing room at Pelham's Oak as a huge fire roared up the chimney. Outside, although it was only early afternoon, it was nearly dark and flakes of snow drifted down from the louring sky.

Finally Alexander spoke, "I can't believe what I'm hearing." He paused and looked from Carson to Lally, whose eyes were downcast. "You waited all these years to tell me. Why?"

Lally, her handkerchief crumpled in her hand, shook her head slowly from side to side. Every now and then she dabbed at her eyes. Carson sat upright, his face grim and unsmiling as if somehow his thoughts were miles away.

"I was so afraid of losing you." Lally's voice was scarcely above a whisper. "You were so precious to me."

149

"Besides," Carson interrupted, addressing Alexander, "no one knew until I brought Nelly – your natural mother – back to Pelham's Oak. I certainly speculated about it many years ago when certain characteristics you had as a child seemed to resemble mine."

"Yet you said nothing." Alexander's eyes bore into those of the man he must now call Father.

"I had no proof. I didn't *know* that Nelly was having a baby. I tried to find her but I couldn't. We all wondered why you had been left on the Martyn family's doorstep. To a certain extent you also resembled your mother, your real mother." Carson looked apologetically at Lally. "You had her colouring. But nothing was confirmed until I brought poor Nelly back here to die."

"Even then I should have been told."

"No question, now," Carson said with a rueful smile. "But then we can all be wise with hindsight."

"You would have found out when you saw your birth certificate," Lally said in a small voice. "You need that for your wedding."

"Have you my birth certificate?" Alexander demanded. Lally shook her head. "You came with nothing except the crib you were in and the clothes you wore."

"Do you know where I was born?"

Lally looked across at Carson who replied. "At the Lady Frances Roper nursing home in Clerkenwell. They will have a record of your birth."

"And Massie knew all this?"

"Massie was with Nelly when you were born. She knows everything about your first few days of life."

"And yet she told me nothing, because I now realise she was frightened of you." Alexander's tone became angrier and angrier.

He rose and strode across to the window, his mind in a turmoil. Of course Massie had been afraid. One couldn't blame her. Carson had fathered him in the year 1909, when he had been having an affair, in London, with a barmaid called Nelly Allen. Carson, working unhappily for the family business, had been dismissed abruptly for alleged wrongdoing and sent home, and when he tried to find Nelly, she had gone. Many years later circumstances had led him to find her dying of tuberculosis, and he had brought her back to Pelham's Oak. She had died in the spring of 1931 and had been buried in Wenham churchyard.

Lally's voice seemed to come from a distance as Alexander gazed broodingly over the landscape upon which the snow was now falling freely. He thought of Mary waiting for him at Forest House. Maybe she would be anxious. She would certainly want to know what this mysterious meeting that had been called so soon after their return home was all about.

"Carson did want to tell you, Alexander, but I was afraid."

"Afraid of what?" Alexander turned and faced her. He couldn't bring himself to use the word 'Mother', although he knew that after all these years it would be very hard to think of her as anything else.

"Afraid of losing you."

"Well, I'm afraid you have lost me now. I'm dumbfounded by what I've heard. It seems to me that I have been deceived all my life about my origins." He pointed a finger at Carson. "And you, a man I revered. I am now to look upon you as my father."

"There is no doubt of it." Carson managed to force a smile. "I am your father, and I am very proud to acknowledge you as my son."

"And what will your 'other sons' say about this?" Alexander's tone was sarcastic.

"I'm sure they'll be pleased. We are all pleased now that it is out."

"Well, I am not pleased. I don't see why you should think you can claim me that easily. How am I to forgive you for the fact

152

that I could have met my poor mother while she was alive instead of seeing her standing at the window gazing at me? I could have given her some comfort, eased her last days."

"She never stopped loving your father," Lally murmured. "He was with her constantly. That was a great comfort to her. You see, darling, we all thought it was for the best. Even she did."

"Well, she was wrong. You all were. It was not for the best. It was grossly deceitful and hurtful to her, and until I can compose myself about this matter I prefer not to see either of you again. I shall take Mary up to London today and stay there."

As Alexander crossed to the door, Carson hurried after him and seized him by the arm. "Alexander! Please don't leave in this way. I beg of you not to do something you might regret. We have said we are sorry; that what we did was wrong."

"Nothing can put it right."

"Except that you can forgive us and understand why we did what we did. You were a young man at university and we did not want to cause you distress, because we thought it *would* distress you. We underestimated the strength of your feelings."

"Lally knew how much I wanted to know about my origins." Alexander looked across at Lally who, eyes averted, didn't reply.

"I did not know for sure that I was your father until three years ago and Lally did not know either, or that Nelly was your mother. We didn't know how you would respond to the news that a sick and dying woman was your natural parent. Even Nelly did not ask to meet you. She left you on Lally's doorstep all those years ago because she knew she was a good woman and would bring you up well, which she has. You have turned into a splendid young man and we are all proud of you. We love Mary. We are overjoyed you are to become a father. Please, Alexander, show that magnanimity of mind, that breadth of vision we have come to expect of you and let us make a fresh beginning. Let us be a united family, as before."

For a moment Alexander seemed to hesitate. Then he roughly removed his arm from Carson's grasp, opened the door and raced across the hall and down the front steps to his car.

Mary was indeed worried. When Alexander returned it was dark and the snow lay thickly on the ground. When she heard the car she ran to the door and hurried down the steps.

"I was so *worried* about you," she cried as

Alexander emerged. Then, seeing he was alone, she looked into the interior of the car. "Where is your mother?"

"She is not with me." He took her arm and walked with her up the steps. "She is not my mother. Now pack your things as quickly as you can. We are going to London."

"But Alexander ... look at the snow."

"The main roads will be clear. If necessary we can spend the night at a hotel en route but I can't stay a second longer than is necessary in this place." He gave her a swift kiss. "As soon as we're on the road I'll tell you everything, darling. Now hurry."

Alexander Martyn and Mary Sprogett were married at the parish church of St Marylebone by special licence, the consent of Mary's parents having been obtained without difficulty. Alexander got a copy of his birth certificate from Somerset House which stated that his mother was Nelly Allen, servant. The name of his father had been left blank. The witnesses at the wedding were Pieter Heering and Jeremy and Nora Sydling, the financial director of the Martyn Heering Corporation and his wife. They were the only people present except for a few onlookers who had come into the church mostly to get away from the cold.

Pieter took the small wedding party to lunch at the Ritz Hotel. It was rather a solemn gathering, more like a funeral, and seemed an inauspicious start to married life.

Eliza felt they were being paid back for being so secretive about the birth first of Elizabeth, and now of Alexander. The family had managed to alienate two people they loved but, in many ways, Alexander seemed the worst loss of all.

He had been so loved, so lovable. His reaction, even if it was understandable, had stunned them. It seemed extraordinary for one normally so full of compassion and understanding. It was somehow quite out of character.

They knew about the wedding, but none of them had been invited, not even Agnes who had aided and abetted their elopement. She managed to let it be known she was very hurt. The effect on Lally had been devastating. She had grown pathetically thin and had even stopped dying her hair which was slowly reverting to grey. She seemed to have lost all will to live and had no interest in life or the world about her.

Dora, on a visit to her mother, was concerned about Lally. "People do die of a broken heart, you know," she said.

"Oh, don't say that!" Eliza looked appalled.

"Maybe I should go and speak to Alexander?"

"You could try."

"I was always close to him."

"Yes you were. But be prepared to be snubbed."

March 1934

Mary Martyn, as she now was, felt lonely and miserable in London with Alexander away all day. Her heart fell when she heard the front door close after him in the morning and his car starting outside. Sometimes she would hurry to the window and watch it drive away and vanish out of sight. She counted the hours until his return.

Alexander was off to the bustle and excitement of work that he enjoyed, which occupied him all day, and sometimes all night, as he wrestled with a problem which prevented him sleeping. She knew he was anxious to make up for the time he had had off and, in a way, she felt guilty and blamed herself. Events had happened so quickly. They had got out of control and she knew that if she hadn't threatened to run away none of this would have happened.

But then they wouldn't be married either. She would be languishing in an expensive finishing school in Switzerland, and he would probably be doing pretty much what he was doing now, only his mother, or his 'adoptive mother' as she was now coldly called, would be here looking after him. She might never have captured Alexander's heart.

As it was, she was now a married woman expecting a child and he was alienated from the family that he'd loved.

In many ways, rather as she'd feared, Mary hadn't felt happy since her return to England. Too much had happened. At the beginning it had been all right: Lally and the Woodville family had welcomed them home (but not of course her mother), and Grandma Agnes had come over to greet them, rather proud of her part in their flight. But that had only lasted a few days. Even as Alexander had made preparations for the wedding in Wenham Church the truth about his birth had come out, and everything had changed.

In her opinion it had changed for the worse.

Mary knew that her attitude was unreasonable. She had everything she wanted, could possibly want. She had only to ask for something and it was hers. But money couldn't buy you family and friends and, except for Alexander, she had neither.

In the morning after a leisurely toilet she would consult with cook about dinner. Of course, she had no ideas of her own and always left it to cook. She knew that cook despised her because she was always dropping remarks about Lally and how good she was at everything, how skilled in all the ladylike arts.

Having been snubbed by cook she then cooled off with a walk in the park, came back for a light lunch served usually by Gladys, with whom she enjoyed a chat. Mary would have liked to tell Gladys to take off her uniform, or put a coat over it and come to window-shop with her in Oxford Street. But, of course, she didn't dare, so she went on her own. Down the length of Oxford Street and then Regent Street, though sometimes she would cut down along Bond Street where there were all the marvellous little boutiques selling jewellery, perfumes, shoes and couture clothes. Sometimes there would be just one dummy in a window showing off some gorgeous garment, usually with a fox fur draped over one shoulder, with a long cigarette holder in its hand.

Arriving in Piccadilly she would go to

159

Swan & Edgar on the corner of the Circus where she looked around and had a cup of tea. Then it was time to wander home again, her spirits soaring at the thought that, in a hour or two, Alexander would come home and they would have that precious time together until he left again in the morning.

This particular, chilly day in early spring they were having a dinner party that evening: something she dreaded. She felt so useless, so out of place with Alexander's business friends and their wives – older, sophisticated people – who she was sure were so nice to her because they despised her; despised her youth, her inferiority, her poor dress sense, her shyness and her general awkwardness. She would have prefered to have stayed upstairs and had a tray in her room, but of course, it was out of the question. She had to be the hostess because Alexander wanted her there, and she was so anxious to do what he wished.

She wanted to be a credit to him. She had had a long session with cook that morning, understanding nothing, approving everything without question and had then spent some time with Gladys discussing what she should wear. Now she was getting bigger nothing fitted or looked nice. So she hadn't gone to the park in the morning but had a stroll there after lunch before visiting her hairdresser in George Street. She got home a little after four in time for tea.

To her surprise Roberts opened the door as soon as she began to mount the steps and held it open for her.

"Is there anything wrong, Roberts?" she asked.

"No, madam." The butler gave her a reassuring smile. "Mrs Parterre arrived a few minutes ago. I asked her to wait in the drawing room, madam."

"Oh, that's lovely," Mary exclaimed excitedly, as Roberts helped her off with her coat. Throwing her hat and gloves on the chair in the hall, she flew into the drawing room where Dora, arms outstretched, came to greet her.

"It's *wonderful* to see you," Mary said as Dora hugged her and, for a few moments, the two women stood locked in a close embrace. Then they drew apart and gazed at each other.

"You look marvellous," Dora said.

"You do too."

Dora, the customary cigarette in her fingers, wore trousers and a cashmere sweater over a man's open-necked shirt. Her blonde hair was cropped and the little make-up she wore subtly applied. Mary thought she looked wonderful: vigorous and strong, as she wanted to be.

"How's Louise?"

"She's fine." Dora sat down as Mary pointed to a chair.

"And Jean?"

"He's fine too."

"Are they with you?"

"No, I came over to see Mother and do a bit of shopping in London. I'm staying at Brown's for a few days and thought I'd look you up. I hope you don't mind."

"Of course I don't mind. I'm thrilled." Mary turned to Roberts who stood hovering in the doorway.

"I'm sure Mrs Parterre would like tea, Roberts."

"Of course, madam."

"And is everything all right for the evening?"

"I think everything is in order, madam."

"We're having a dinner party," Mary explained. "I do hope you can stay."

"Well..." Dora looked down at her trousers. "I'll have to go and change. Are you *sure* it will be all right?"

"Of course. Pieter Heering is coming and some nice friends of..." Mary hesitated for a fraction of a second "...of Mrs Martyn's called the Schwartzes. He's an art dealer. Then Jeremy and Nora Sydling. Jeremy is

162

the financial director of the group and they were witnesses at our wedding. Oh, Dora," Mary held out her hands again, "I can't tell you how good it is to see you. I miss ... well, I do miss family."

Dora nodded understandingly as Roberts and Gladys appeared with the afternoon tea.

"This is Gladys." Mary pointed to the young maid. "She's a great friend and advises me on my clothes. Gladys, this is my cousin Dora." Gladys coloured and bobbed in Dora's direction.

"Afternoon m'm."

"Good afternoon, Gladys." Dora smiled.

Gladys, covered with confusion, scuttled out of the room.

Roberts, his face expressionless, said, "Should I pour tea, madam?"

"I think we can manage, Roberts, thank you."

"Milk and sugar?" Mary asked standing by the teatray.

"Milk, no sugar, thanks." Dora looked up as Mary brought her cup over to her.

"Have you no other friends, Mary?"

"Not yet." Mary gave a rueful smile. "The wives of Alexander's business colleagues are so much older than me, though everyone is very nice."

"So what do you do all day?"

"I don't do very much, frankly. There's not very much for me to do. I go walking in the park or window-shopping along Oxford and Regent Street, and I wait for Alexander to come home. That's all."

"I see." Dora paused for a moment to drink her tea. "And how is Alexander?"

"He's very well. Very busy."

"Delighted about the baby?"

"Oh, yes.

"And are you well?" Dora looked at her keenly.

"I am very well. The doctor has been a few times to check me over."

"Will you have the baby here, or in a nursing home?"

"It's not decided. Dora." Mary hesitated and then suddenly the words came tumbling out, "I am *very* sorry about the rift between Alexander and his family. I didn't want it and I don't think it's necessary."

"It *is* very sad," Dora agreed and put her cup and saucer back on the small table by her elbow.

"Is that why you've come? To try and build a bridge?"

"Not at all. I was in London and I wanted to see you and Alexander. I'm very fond of him."

"And he of you. He often talks about the way you taught him dressage. And, Dora, I *do* see the family's point of view, but Alexander is very stubborn, he won't see it."

"The family did behave—" Dora began, when the door opened and Alexander walked in. He stood for a few moments on the threshold taking in the scene. Then he gave a broad smile.

"Dora, what a lovely surprise." She rose and he crossed the room to kiss her.

"How long have you been here?"

"Not long." They remained holding hands as she went on. "I'm visiting London for a few days and came on the off-chance. I hope you don't mind?"

"Of course I don't mind. You must stay for dinner. We're having a few people round. You know Pieter Heering, don't you?"

"Of course." Once again she looked down at her trousers. "I shall have to go back to the hotel to change. In fact," she glanced at her watch, "I think I'd better do that now. What time do you expect your guests?"

"Seven thirty."

"That will give me time to bath and change. You're sure I shan't be in the way?"

"Of course you won't. It will be lovely to have you."

Dora could remember many dinners at this house in Montagu Square. It seemed very odd not to have Lally presiding at one end

165

of the table, a consummately gracious hostess quietly overseeing the serving of the dinner while taking full part in the conversation and contributing to it. She was an intelligent, cultured woman who took a great interest in current affairs. She read *The Times* daily and was interested in the theatre and quite passionate about art. Dora had heard of the Schwartzes, but had not met them before. Tonight they had brought their daughter, Irene, an interesting-looking woman of about twenty-two or three with short black curly hair and piercing dark eyes. She wore a lot of make-up, a flamboyant, short, brightly-coloured dress and a number of pieces of chunky costume jewellery.

Alma Schwartz, had obviously once been a beauty and had the quiet dignity of advancing age. Her hair was softly waved and greying. She wore a long-sleeved black velvet dinner dress with a double choker of pearls at her throat.

The talk at the dinner table had mostly revolved round Germany and the threat posed by Hitler, which some people took very seriously indeed, Pieter Heering among them.

"Germany is re-arming at a much greater rate than was agreed under the Treaty of Versailles. She is also increasing the number of troops she is supposed to have."

"When I last saw you you talked of pulling out of Berlin altogether," Alexander said to Reuben Schwartz. "Have you done that?"

"I have transferred most of my assets, but while Irene is at art college there I have to have a home for her. I am hoping that she will come and settle in London with us, maybe finish her studies at the Slade school."

"I have all my friends in Berlin." Irene, who like her parents, spoke fluent English, shrugged. "I don't want to leave them."

"You will soon make friends in London." Her mother tried to sound persuasive, but there was no hiding the concern on her face. "It would make us very happy, Irene, if you would agree to move here. Then we can leave Germany for ever."

"But I don't want to leave Germany for ever," Irene said indignantly. "Berlin is my home. I can't believe that Hitler won't be overthrown soon."

"That is not the view of my business colleagues." Pieter Heering sounded solemn. "Many of them are shutting down their businesses in Germany."

"Then what will happen to the German people if everyone deserts them?" Irene protested. "They will be poorer than they are now, and that will give more power to

Hitler and those who support him."

"But you must take this anti-Semitism seriously." Jeremy Sydling had been silent for most of the conversation but had listened carefully. He was a quiet, rather solemn man who, as director of financial affairs, had enormous influence in the Martyn-Heering business. Beside him, his wife Nora took an intelligent interest in the conversation without contributing very much to it.

Mary, however, in Dora's opinion, appeared lost, quite out of her depth, as the conversation progressed. She gave no silent directions to the staff, as Lally used to, but left everything to Roberts whose many years of experience meant that he was perfectly capable of dealing unaided with the situation. Courses came and went with almost military precision: soup, hors d'oeuvres, the entrée of roast English lamb, a variety of cheeses and finally dessert. The carefully selected wines – a Chablis with the first course, a fine claret with the lamb and a Sauternes with the pudding – were impeccably prepared and served.

Alexander seemed anxious to draw Mary into the conversation, but he was unsuccessful. Her unease was almost palpable. At her side Pieter Heering also made many attempts at conversing with her, but was met either with monosyllabic replies or blank stares. Alexander appeared increasingly uncomfortable at her obvious inability to cope with her guests or simply relax and enjoy the evening. Her food remained mostly uneaten. He dispensed with the custom, which had been continued by Lally from the old days, of leaving the men to their port and after the meal all the guests went into the drawing room where the men lit cigars and Dora and Irene smoked black Sobranie cigarettes. Coffee and liqueurs were served and the conversation continued, on a more or less serious level, until Mary suddenly excused herself, saying she felt tired.

Everyone looked apologetic as if somehow this was their fault. Alexander solicitously accompanied her from the room, returning after a few minutes.

"I'm afraid Mary is terribly tired. She is five months' pregnant, you know."

"Quite an ordeal for her," Pieter said expelling cigar smoke. "All these people."

"Oh no, she enjoys them," Alexander insisted. "It is just that ... well," he looked around, "she is not used to entertaining. But she will learn in time."

"Anyway we must be going." Reuben looked at his watch and glanced at his wife and daughter. "Irene, too, is very tired."

"I do hope I see you again," Dora said as they got up. "I enjoyed our conversation." She was referring to a talk she and Irene had had before dinner about German art and how everything was being driven underground by the Nazis.

The Sydlings too called it a day. Roberts was summoned and the guests escorted to the door by Alexander while Pieter remained behind finishing his cigar.

When Alexander returned he looked tense and unhappy and immediately poured himself a brandy.

"That was a difficult evening," Pieter said. "I thought Mary was going to faint halfway through dinner."

"She will get used to it," Alexander replied brusquely. "She will have to. She knows quite well that I have to entertain."

"But she is *very* young," Dora insisted, also rising and pouring a brandy. She wore a long-sleeved couture evening gown of heavy gold satin designed on a slip-over princess line. With her cropped blonde hair and tall, slim figure she looked poised and elegant, the very antithesis to her young cousin. "After all she should still be in the schoolroom."

"I wish you wouldn't say that," Alexander looked annoyed.

"But it is true."

Pieter suddenly threw the butt of his cigar into the fire.

"I really should go and have an early night." He looked affectionately at Alexander. "Your wife is a very sweet little lady, and I am sure that in time she will learn to be the perfect hostess, but I can't help thinking of the splendid occasions Lally used to host here, and I miss her."

"What a perfectly *beastly* remark," Alexander said angrily as he came back to the drawing room after seeing Pieter to the door. He went over to the table and poured himself another brandy.

"I don't think he meant it unkindly."

"Well what do you think he meant?" Alexander lit a cigarette and threw himself into the chair opposite Dora.

"Well, I think he misses Lally, naturally. He's very fond of her and she had some marvellous parties here."

"In time so will Mary. Don't forget Lally was young once. I shall protect Mary by not having these dinners again for a while. They're clearly an ordeal for her. It's not fair."

"Then your business will suffer."

"No it won't. I can take people out."

"It's so nice to entertain at home." Dora finished her drink and went and perched on the arm of Alexander's chair, tentatively placing a hand on his arm.

"Alexander, you know I love you."

"Yes, I do." He reached out and took her hand. "And I love you."

"I love Lally too," Dora went on. "All this has made her very unwell. She's changed a great deal in the last few months. She's even let her hair go grey. I really fear for your mother, if..."

"She is *not* my mother, Dora, don't forget that!" There was a distinct note of warning in Alexander's voice.

"You have thought of her as your mother since you were a tiny baby. I don't know how much closer a mother can become."

"And what of my *real* mother? That poor woman whose only glimpse of me, her own son, came as I rode by her window? How would *you* feel Dora if you never knew your mother? If someone told you Eliza was your real mother and you had been brought up by someone else?"

"I can't compare—" Dora began but Alexander interrupted her savagely.

"Because you're a Woodville too, Dora. You can't begin to put yourself in another person's place. I saw you tonight looking pityingly at Mary."

"I was *not* looking pityingly at her." Dora's voice rose heatedly.

172

"Yes you were. She didn't talk, she didn't understand what was going on. She didn't tell Roberts when to serve. She just sat there. Don't think I wasn't aware of it. But I love her. Mary gives me happiness and stability. I used not to know who I was, and now I know all too well and, believe me, sometimes I wish I didn't. But for the unselfish love that Mary gives me, I would go to pieces altogether. She is a sweet, good, wonderful person; she is simple but not simple-minded. You devious Woodvilles could learn a lot from her."

"I object to being called 'devious' Alexander," Dora said stiffly. "Every family has its skeletons. Maybe we have more than most, I don't know. All I *do* know is that my mother acted for the best over Elizabeth, and Lally and Prosper certainly acted for the best over you."

"Well, sometimes I wish they hadn't." Alexander almost spat out the words. "Sometimes I wish that I had grown up with my *real* mother, the mother who bore me, whatever the hardship, and that I had never been turned into the sort of person I was obviously not meant to be."

"But you're happy, surely?" Dora looked around her. "You have a beautiful home, money, work you like and a lovely wife. You're going to be a father. What more could you want. I ask you Alexander what more?"

"I would like to have known my real mother and to have kissed her and helped her through the disease that killed her, Dora, when she was a younger woman than you are now.

"I find it very hard to forgive the Woodvilles for denying me that."

Part Two

A Great Tradition

Eight

April 1934

"Ah, Sir Carson, how very nice to meet you."

Carson bowed slightly and shook hands with the tall, grey-haired, distinguished-looking gentleman who, casting aside the copy of *The Times* he'd been reading, had risen to greet him.

"How do you do, Count?" Carson said in a rather formal manner, as Paolo Colomb-Paravacini pointed to a chair. He sat down and crossed his legs.

"Did you have a good journey, Sir Carson?" the count enquired as he, too, resumed his seat.

"A little stormy, but I enjoyed the train."

"Yes, train journeys are fun," the count mused, his English almost without accent. He looked towards the door. "I believe the children are nearly ready. My wife is with them now. They will be delighted to see you."

177

Carson winced at the word 'wife'. He had not been looking forward to this visit, but it had to be done. If he wanted to see more of his children he had to go and get them. Yet it meant facing Connie and the man she had recently married, Paolo Colomb-Paravacini, seventeen years her senior.

How, he wondered, could Connie have married this elderly gentleman with grey hair, thin on top, wrinkly, liver-spotted hands and parchment-coloured skin?

There was no doubt that he looked like the aristocrat he was: a scion of one of the oldest families in Venice. He was wealthy too, but wealth didn't count with a woman as wealthy as Connie.

At that moment the door opened and three small bodies hurled themselves at Carson, who took them in his arms one by one: Toby, nine, Leonard, eight and little Netta, his darling, his pet, just seven years old.

His eyes filled with tears as he kissed them. When he put them down, Netta clinging on to one hand and Leonard to the other, he raised his eyes and saw that Connie had silently entered the room. She had tucked her arm in that of Paolo's in a close, proprietorial gesture that was not lost on her ex-husband, who wished paradoxically at that moment that he had done more to try and keep her.

Connie, elegant and dignified, had also acquired a kind of beauty in her middle years that she had not possessed in her youth. She was dressed in a white linen suit and white calf shoes. There was a jewel of some kind in her lapel, otherwise nothing but the gold wedding band whose shining newness told Carson what he knew already. It was not the one he had placed on her finger ten years before. No longer Lady Woodville, she was now Contessa Colomb-Paravacini.

Her skin was brown and vibrant. Her glances towards Paolo were loving, but when she looked at Carson he saw only indifference in her eyes. Releasing the children Carson went over to Connie. She freed her hand from Paolo's arm and politely shook his, as though she was greeting a stranger or, at the very most, a mere acquaintance, not a man she'd been married to and by whom she had three children. It was very mortifying, very wounding.

"How are you Carson?" Her expression was polite, impersonal.

"Very well thank you, Connie. And you?"

"Wonderfully well." She glanced lovingly again at Paolo. "We had the most marvellous honeymoon in the Balkans. Have you been to the Balkans, Carson?"

"No," Carson said stiffly, unable to resist

the feeling of jealousy and resentment that swept through him at the idea of his wife sleeping with this old man.

He wanted to be gone from the exquisite Venetian Palazzo Colomb-Paravacini which was now Connie's home, as quickly as he could. He glanced at his watch.

"If the children are ready, Connie?"

"Oh, so soon?" Connie looked surprised. "We hoped you'd stay for luncheon."

"I'm afraid I can't. I have other plans."

"Oh, very well. Nanny is ready. I'll tell her you want to leave at once. Come along children." She held out her hand, and obediently the little group trotted after her as she left the room, only Netta looking fearfully behind.

"See you in a minute, darling," Carson said giving her a little wave, a smile of reassurance. "Run along and get your things."

"Don't forget dolly," Paolo called out with a smile. "She's a darling." He turned to Carson after she'd left the room. "They all are. I couldn't be more fond of them if they were mine."

"But you have children of your own I believe?" Carson said thickly.

"Two, and they both have children. I am a grandfather four times over."

"Fancy." Carson looked out of the lofty

windows of the palazzo across the waters of the Grand Canal.

Fancy, he thought, Connie marrying a grandfather.

And then he realised that very soon he would be one himself.

"I found I deeply resented the fact that Connie had married someone so much older than she was," Carson said a week later. He was sitting on the terrace with Dora as the children played on the lawn. "It seemed to reflect on me."

"Did you feel jealous?" Dora looked at him with concern.

"Yes."

"Do you think you still love Connie?"

"Well," Carson stroked his chin, "I don't know that I love her exactly. I'm quite bewildered by my emotions. I don't think I expected her to marry so soon after the divorce. Of course, this chap wanted to marry her before."

"Do you think she loves *him*?"

"She was certainly looking very fondly at him. Whether it was to annoy me or not, I don't know. Anyway, no use crying over spilt milk. It's over and done with and that's about all one can say. I hope she will be very happy."

Dora reached out and Carson slipped

181

his hand in hers.

"Poor old thing," she said. "I believe you do still love her."

"Oh, the whole thing was such a mess." Carson found that, to his embarrassment, tears were pricking the backs of his eyes. "If Connie had been more understanding about Nelly none of this would have happened."

"But you did let her go." Dora tried to make herself sound reasonable. One could see Connie's point of view. If Carson had behaved charitably towards a former mistress he had certainly been misunderstood by his wife.

"I was angry. I felt guilty. Was it too much to ask my wife to understand me? No, she took off, with my children, left me. Then, before any time had passed at all, said she wanted a divorce. I was still grieving for Nelly. I don't think Connie ever really loved me, you know. I think she hankered after this Colomb-Paravacini chap all along. She says they have an awful lot in common: opera, art, antiques. They were off to Egypt the day after we left." Carson rubbed his chin again feelingly. "No, on the whole I think I am well rid of Constance, but I miss my children."

Two of the grooms from the stables had joined the two boys in a vigorous game of ball on the lawn. Netta was sitting on the edge with her English nursemaid, Harriet, who was reading her a story. Harriet was a brisk, sensible, capable young woman of about twenty-five or six who had been invaluable on the long journey back to England where the children were to stay with Carson over the Easter holidays. In the end, the divorce had been amicable, both parties having in mind that the main thing was the welfare and happiness of the children.

It had been agreed that for the time being they should stay with their mother and go to school in Venice, and spend the holidays with their father. When the boys were eleven they would go first to a prep school, then a public school in England. They would then divide the holidays between their mother and father. Connie had not wanted any money for herself, but Carson would pay the school fees and contribute to the upkeep of the children.

"I feel in a way I have lost everything," Carson continued. "These children are no longer really mine. We get used to one another and then it's time to part again. They talk quite fondly of the count. Of course, I am glad they like him, and he's good to them, that's obvious, but it's not the same as having your own children in your own house with you.

"And then there is Alexander. Sometimes I wonder if I will ever see him again or if he is lost to us for ever?" He looked despairingly at his companion. If there was anyone in the world he could confide in it was Dora – cousin, friend, contemporary. She was only three years older than he. They had always shared a bond, a love of horses, of the countryside, the family. They had both served in the war and then, and at various other times in their lives, suffered physical and emotional hardship.

"It's been a tough year for you." Dora still held his hand tight. "Connie, Alexander..." She sighed. "I can't say what will happen about Alexander. He was certainly very bitter when I saw him in London. I think he will take some time to come round." She looked anxiously at Carson. "Maybe, after the baby is born, things will be better. Perhaps as Mary gets older she will have a softening effect on him. I got the impression she very much misses the family and she is sure to want to mend bridges. After all they have had a very hard year too."

Dora was interrupted by the sound of a car horn and, looking across the lawn they saw an open tourer driven by a striking fair-headed woman sweep up the drive. A hand fluttered as the car came to a halt a few yards from where they were sitting. Dora shaded her eyes.

"Well, I'm blowed. I do believe it's Sally. Sally Yetman," she said jumping up.

"Remember me?" the blonde called gaily, getting out of the car.

"Of course we remember you." Dora, seeing that tall, vibrant goddess-like creature dressed in slacks and a loose sweater, a canary coloured scarf at her neck, experienced a completely unexpected *coup de foudre*, a sense of excitement, as she walked towards her. And when Sally clasped her warmly in her arms and kissed her cheek Dora felt a raising of the spirits, an elation she hadn't felt ... well since she'd fallen love with May, and that was many years ago.

"How lovely to see you again!" Sally exclaimed.

"And you." Dora hoped that the overwhelming emotion she felt had escaped Sally's notice.

Carson stood behind Dora, an amiable smile on his face, and also embraced Sally, though with a cousinly peck on the cheek rather than a hug.

"I do hope you don't mind. I just happened to be passing." Sally began apologetically and Carson vigorously shook his head as he drew up a chair.

"Of course we don't mind. I have been meaning to get in touch with you ever since Eliza's party."

"And I you." Sally looked at him. "But it's been such a busy year."

Carson looked at the ground murmuring, "For me too."

"What have you been doing?" Dora asked eagerly.

"I went to South Africa to visit my cousins, Uncle Robert's children, and stayed for months. I came back through Africa, Egypt and the Middle East. It was marvellous."

"What an adventure," Dora said, a little enviously.

"And you? Is your husband with you?" Sally looked around. Dora shook her head.

"No, he and Louise stayed in France. I came to see Mother who has been nursing Lally Martyn, a great family friend who has not been well."

"Oh, I remember her at Aunt Eliza's party. I'm so sorry. She was a lovely-looking woman. I remember her very well."

"You would see a change in her." Carson shook his head. "She had pneumonia and nearly died."

"She now looks like an old wizened lady," Dora said sadly.

"And that handsome son Alexander? We

had a dance together. He was a charmer."

"Well, temporarily we hope, they do not get on and that is partly the reason Lally has been ill."

"But she *adored* him! It was so obvious."

"Oh, she does."

"Then why ... ?"

"Could we leave this subject for the moment?" Carson said quietly. "It's something we can't go into now."

"I'm sorry." Sally looked rebuffed.

"I'll tell you later," Dora said *sotto voce* as Carson's attention was temporarily diverted by David, the butler, who had appeared on the scene.

"I'm sure Miss Yetman will stay for lunch?" Carson looked across to Sally.

"I'd love to. And, of course," she leaned forward noticing for the first time the children playing on the lawn, "these must be your children."

"They're over from Italy to spend their holidays with me. Their mother has just remarried." Carson rose to his feet and cupping his hands around his mouth called, "Children! Come and meet Miss Yetman."

The stable lads disappeared. Netta and Harriet got up from the lawn and joined the two boys, who moved shyly towards the new arrival.

"This is Miss Yetman. She is related to Cousin Dora and your Aunt Eliza. Say, how do you do? children."

"How do you do, Miss Yetman?" the children said, one after the other, queueing up politely to shake her by the hand.

"What beautiful manners!" Sally exclaimed. She stooped to greet them, kissing Netta, who bore a strong resemblance to Carson. The boys favoured their mother. Netta had curly ash-blonde hair, and the same intense blue eyes as her father. Round her hair was a blue bandeau, and in many ways, she resembled a character from one of the story books she might have been reading. She was a grave little girl, which seemed to add to her attraction.

"Why are you not related to Daddy?" Netta asked wriggling up on to an empty chair next to Sally to whom she appeared to have taken a fancy. Toby and Leonard went back to the lawn where the stable boys had been lurking, anxious to resume the game.

"Well..." Sally looked up to Dora for assistance.

"Sally's daddy was the brother of Aunt Eliza's husband who was called Ryder Yetman."

The relationship angle seemed to appeal to Netta who announced with an air of pride, "We have got a new daddy."

"Oh!" Sally looked amused. "Do you like him?"

"The new daddy is very nice. But we like our daddy best," Netta confided. "Only we don't call the new one 'Daddy'."

"What's his name?"

"Paolo. He's Italian."

"And do you speak Italian?"

Netta nodded. "We go to school and everyone there speaks Italian."

David appeared on the terrace and hovered by Carson's side.

"Will the young people be lunching with you, or separately, Sir Carson?"

"Oh, I think we'll all eat together." Carson looked around. "Is that agreeable to everyone?"

Everyone nodded and Netta seized the hand of her new-found friend.

"Are you going to stay and keep Daddy company?" she asked in her solemn, childish voice. "He'll be very lonely when we've gone."

"But he has Dora." Momentarily Sally looked embarrassed.

"Dora has Uncle Jean and Louise. Daddy has no one."

"Poor Daddy." Carson, amused, stood up and ruffled her hair. "Go on you little matchmaker and wash your hands before luncheon."

Over lunch Sally was the object of everyone's attention. Carson admired the way she entertained the children who were captivated by her. Obviously she had a natural gift. Dora, as well as admiring this skill, was taken by her looks, elegance, above all by her youth. Dora was fifty and Sally was thirty-two, yet in Sally she saw much of herself. Somehow the age difference gave her a pang.

She felt she wanted to know more about Sally. After lunch, they sat on the terrace drinking coffee while Carson joined the children for games on the lawn.

Dora said, "Is there a man in your life?"

Sally looked taken aback by the remark.

"I'm sorry," Dora went on noting her expression, "it's no business of mine. I just wondered."

"Not at the moment," Sally said. "Why? Do you think I'm after Carson?"

"Oh, not at all." Now it was Dora's turn to feel embarrassed. "Although he is quite a good catch, and very lonely. On the other hand, I think he's still half in love with his wife and regrets losing her, so he may not be such a good catch after all."

"Tell me about Alexander." Sally seemed anxious to change the subject and Dora launched into the long tragic story which left Sally looking thoughtful at the end. She gazed across to Carson, who was acting as wicket-keeper in an improvised game of cricket in which even Netta and Harriet had been persuaded to participate to make up the numbers.

"He does look very sad, also much older than when I last saw him. This explains a lot."

"What angers me," Dora said, fiercely protective of him, "is that he's such a nice man. He's a good man, always thinking of other people. He doesn't deserve all this."

At that moment Carson came over to them, wiping his face on a towel, before he sank on to the grass at their feet.

"I think I'm too old for this caper. I've had enough."

"I've just told Sally about Alexander," Dora said and he grimaced.

"I'm terribly sorry," Sally murmured. "I'm sure that, as Dora said, after the baby..."

"You don't know Alexander," Carson said tersely. "Underneath all that charm he's a very determined, stubborn young man. Even if he thinks he's wrong he'll be too proud to admit it. Oh well..." his voice trailed off. Leaning back on his hands, he gazed across the countryside. On this late spring day it was at its best; the tender young leaves beginning to unfurl on the trees, a carpet of daffodils on the borders surrounding the lawn and the heads of the tulips beginning to peep above ground.

"I really must be going," Sally said, suddenly jumping up as if she'd only just become aware of the time. "I've been enjoying myself too much."

"Oh no," Carson looked dismayed. "I thought we might persuade you to stay the night."

Sally smiled down at him. "I am on my way to Bath to attend a function and I better hurry or I'll be late."

"Well," Carson got to his feet as Dora rose too, "don't let it be so long before we see you again."

"I won't," Sally promised as she led the way to her car. At that moment the children saw she was about to leave and abruptly abandoning their game ran towards her.

"Oh, no!" Netta said. "We thought you were staying for days and days."

"I'm afraid not," Sally stooped to kiss her.

"Come back soon," Leonard said, "before we have to go back to Italy."

"But you'll be here in the summer." With a smile Sally turned to Dora. "Why don't you come to Bournemouth? It's not all that far away."

"I may," Dora smiled back, "but not this visit. I have to return to my husband and daughter. One day I promise I'll try." As she leaned over to kiss Sally, her hand fell lightly on her shoulder, but she didn't let it linger.

Carson shook hands and then kissed her lightly on the cheek. Sally got into her car and prepared to drive away. They all stood back watching her.

She reversed the car smartly and, with a carefree wave of her hand, disappeared down the drive and out of sight in a cloud of dust.

"She was ever so nice," Netta said skipping beside her father, her hand tightly clutching his. "Why don't you marry her Daddy?"

Carson laughed. "Because I hardly know her."

"But she's your cousin."

"She's Dora's cousin."

"But she is family."

"Kind of family," Carson agreed.

"Does that mean you can't marry her?" Toby wanted to know.

"Oh no, I could marry her. I mean, if she wanted to and if I wanted to, and I'm not sure if I do, or if she does. Now look, this is getting complicated." He patted Toby lightly on the bottom. "If you're to get your hundred by teatime you'd better be smart about it."

Dora and Carson stood watching as, with

Harriet, the children hurried back to the lawn. The stable lads had now been joined by off-duty staff from the house, supervised by the majestic David who had taken over from Carson as wicket keeper.

"It's amazing that we didn't know about Sally's existence for so long," Carson said as he and Dora slumped once more into chairs.

"Well, we knew of her existence. We just didn't know her. I mean I remember visiting Uncle Hesketh a couple of times when I was very young. But he was quite old when Sally was born. She was a late arrival. Of course, my mother was not enamoured of her in-laws as, after Daddy died, they didn't behave very well towards her. I think there was a bit of a rift in the family."

"She *is* awfully nice," Carson said reflectively. Then, "She a nice age too."

"What do you mean by that?"

"Well, you know ... oh, nothing."

Carson leaned back, hands behind his head, gazing at the sky. Dora observed a half-smile on his face and it seemed to her that suddenly the years had slipped away and he looked younger and more relaxed than he had for ages.

Alexander had made up for lost time. In the six months he'd been back he'd managed to impress the members of the board with his diligence and business acumen. He had been given an office of his own next to Pieter Heering, a secretary, and was now obviously being groomed for the succession. He knew, however, that he was very young and this would inevitably be a long time coming.

On this particular day in summer he had gone over to the warehouse where both Carson and Guy Woodville had once worked unwillingly and unhappily in a small office preparing dreary bills of shipping. Neither of them had been at all equipped for business and both had hated their days cooped up in this small room where Alexander now stood. It was high up in a warehouse, overlooking the river in Lower Thames Street, and contained spices imported from the Far East for further shipment to America and other parts of the world. The whole building smelled deliciously of spice as did the streets around.

Alexander found business fascinating. He liked nothing better than a ledger full of figures, or examining orders from all over the world. He stood by the diligent young clerk who sat where his uncle and father had once sat doing very much the same kind of work. It had hardly changed with the passage of years.

"Do you enjoy your work, Smith?" Alexander asked the eager young man who had risen to his feet as he came into the room.

"Yes, Mr Alexander, very much."

"Good." Alexander turned over the pages of the ledger that had been filled with a fine italic script. "Your work is good. You will be due for promotion."

"Oh, thank you, sir." The clerk blushed and Alexander realised that he was only a little younger than Smith, and yet here he was with a seat on the board, being groomed for the chairmanship, whereas this capable young man would probably never progress beyond the ledger department, though one day he might rise to being chief clerk.

"Are you married, Smith?"

"Yes, Mr Alexander. And my wife is expecting our first child."

"Mine too," Alexander said, brightening, and held out his hand. "Good luck to you and your wife, Smith."

"Thank you sir." The young clerk gratefully shook Alexander's hand.

"And let me know when the baby is born. I think some sort of bonus might be in order."

"Oh, *thank* you, sir."

Alexander left the room and completed his inspection of the rest of the building reflecting on Smith's deference towards him and on the inequalities of life: the fact that some people were born to power and position, while others would never achieve it, however hard they tried.

He left the building and in the fine summer sunshine strolled along Lower Thames Street towards the spanking new offices of the group at the side of London Bridge. He stood for a moment gazing into the river and thought that his life, in many ways, was an anomaly.

He was the illegitimate son of a baronet and a London barmaid whose father had been a porter in Covent Garden. One day, not long ago, he had stood beside the former Lady Frances Roper Home in Clerkenwell where he had been born only to find it boarded up and looking for a new owner. Outside there was still a board proclaiming in faded letters that it had been founded in 1860 by the charitable woman who had given it her name. It was a large Dickensian building built of red brick, now derelict, and discoloured by the smoke and grime from London's streets and chimneys.

It looked a bleak, desolate place and Alexander had turned from it, his horror compounded by the knowledge that his mother lay in a grave in Wenham church-yard, after a life of poverty and deprivation.

And now here he was, only twenty-four years of age, the possessor of a fortune, a lovely young wife who was about to give birth to his first child. He had a comfortable, luxurious home in the best part of London. He was due to inherit a business to which, he now realised, he had a legitimate claim. The Dutchman, Willem Heering, one of the founders of the business, was his great-grandfather, the father of his grandmother, Margaret, who had married Sir Guy Woodville. He now had a right to the business by birth, which he hadn't had before. He *was* a Woodville, a member of the family he professed to hate and despise because of the way it had treated his mother. And, by accident of birth, he was a descendant of the great Heering family of Dutch burghers who had brought it wealth.

Why, now that his claim to the business was not merely as an inheritance from an adoptive father, was he so resistant to the astonishing change of fortune that had come his way?

As if Pieter Heering could read his thoughts, it was the first thing he brought up when, later that morning, the two men went for lunch to a City chop-house on the edge of Smithfield market. Usually they ate with other executives in the dining room at head-quarters but, occasionally, when they wanted to discuss something in private, they took themselves off to one of the many restaurants catering for businessmen. Today, Pieter had suggested the lunch and, after they had ordered, he sat back waiting for his uncle to say what was on his mind.

"How was the warehouse today?" Pieter asked. "How's young Smith?"

"He is coming on very well." Alexander smiled. "His wife is expecting a baby. I said a bonus would be in order when it is born."

"Quite right." Pieter drummed his fingers on the unpolished table. Around him, earnest diners were engaged in discussing share prices, shipping news, the effects of government policies on the City, and other weighty matters to do with commerce. "How is Mary?"

"Well," Alexander inclined his head, "but uncomfortable. The baby is due any day."

"You must feel very excited."

"I am." Alexander looked across at his uncle and smiled. "I am very excited."

"Alexander—" Pieter paused and resumed his little tattoo again as though he didn't quite know how to say what he had in mind, "it is a great source of pain to me, as it is to your family, that you persist with this vendetta against them."

"I don't have a vendetta," Alexander said coldly.

"Oh, but you do. It is not only painful to my old and dear friend Lally, but to Eliza, Carson your father, and..."

"I would rather you didn't talk about it, Pieter, if you don't mind." Alexander bent over the plate of rare English beef that had been set before him.

"Alexander, I feel I have to talk about it, especially with your baby due any day. You know that I love you and I respect you. I was overjoyed to know that we were related by blood. I think it should have been a happy time for you and not a sad one. I think you have behaved unreasonably, and I think it's time I said so."

"Thank you. Now can we discuss something else?"

"If you wish." Pieter took up his knife and fork, admitting defeat once again. It was not the first time he'd brought up the subject.

After a while, like the many merchants and men of business around them, they started to talk about share prices, shipping news and the state of the economy, a subject always pressing on their minds. England, in common with other European countries, continued to make a slow recovery from the consequences of a war that had ended sixteen years before.

"They say we will have another war," Pieter said gloomily. "Hitler is re-arming at such a rate. Here we have our heads in the sand. No one will listen to Churchill, who is trying to warn them. He says we must re-arm too, and quickly."

"My God." Alexander put down his knife and fork. "I dread a war."

"Most of us dread wars," Pieter said grimly. "Unfortunately some people, and I think Hitler is one, seem to relish them."

They walked back to the office enjoying the sunshine. On the way Alexander told his uncle about the progress of the purchase of the villa in Italy which was now going through.

"I am looking forward to taking Mary and the baby there as soon as he is able to travel. So please God, we don't have a war," Alexander said as they turned the corner towards London Bridge.

"It won't be as soon as that." Pieter looked fretfully up at the clear blue sky. "I would say in three or four years' time. Of course, it might be averted. Please God it will be, with commonsense all round."

The two men ran briskly up the steps to the main door, smiling at the uniformed commissionaire on duty who saluted them. As they got into the lift which would take them to the top floor Pieter said, "It's a 'he' is it? The baby? You said you would take 'him' to Italy."

"Oh, definitely. Mary says she knows it is a boy. Not that I would mind a girl."

"Next time," Pieter suggested.

"Exactly." Alexander smiled. "I hope for a large family. Mary would like one too."

As the doors of the lift slid open on the top floor, the outer door was pulled open by Alexander's secretary, a young woman called Norma. He was at once struck by the look of concern on her face and said anxiously, "What is it Norma? Is something wrong?"

Norma put her hand to her mouth and looked from Alexander to Pieter and back again.

"Mr Roberts rang you from your home, Mr Alexander. He is most anxious that you should get there as soon as possible."

The room seemed very still, very quiet. In an effort to make it less clinical it had colourful chintzy curtains, and two easy chairs. But it still had that all-pervasive air of a hospital, with a single bed in the middle, a locker by the side, and a corner washbasin.

Alexander shivered.

If he looked out of the window he could see along Harley Street as far as the trees waving in Regent's Park. He had tried to read the paper but it was useless. He was too restless. They had brought him tea and the doctor had visited him twice and given a report.

The baby was a bad breech case and was stuck fast in the birth passage.

Labour had come on very suddenly. One moment Mary had been resting and the next minute her waters had broken and she had been ringing frantically for her maid, who had at once called the doctor. The doctor, just around the corner, had come within minutes, realised Mary needed hospitalisation and had sent for an ambulance which took her to the private clinic.

Time passed so slowly, so heavily. Alexander had never before been conscious of the fact that time actually weighed. It crept. It was heavy, leaden. He thought of his darling struggling in the the labour ward and he wished with all his heart he could be with her.

Time continued to creep by. The door opened again and the obstetrician, Mr Whatmore, reappeared, gowned, a mask round his neck. He was perspiring and grim faced. Alexander rose and went anxiously towards him.

"I am afraid it is not good news, Mr Martyn, and there is no easy way to tell you this. I have to operate and, in doing so, I may lose either your wife or the baby, or both. I'm afraid I have to ask your permission to go along with this."

Instead of beating fast, Alexander felt his heart creeping along with the slow motion of time.

"Is there no other way?"

The consultant shook his head, and behind him a nurse produced a pad on which there was a piece of paper. Alexander signed it.

Alexander stood by the window as the evening drew on. There had been no news for an hour except a visit from the nurse to offer him food and drink, both of which he had declined.

"Any news?" he had asked. She had shaken her head.

The cars passed up and down Harley Street, people on their way home, or to an evening out in the West End. A day was ending, night approached. He had never felt so alone, so vulnerable, in his life. He longed for Lally or Carson or Dora, or someone near and dear to him, to comfort him. He realised the meaning of family, and how foolish he had been to reject them: people he had known all his life and who loved him. There and then he vowed that if Mary and the baby lived, the first thing he would do would be to effect a reconciliation.

The door opened and he spun round. The consultant appeared dressed in his suit. His weary expression told Alexander everything.

"I am very sorry, Mr Martyn, to tell you we have lost your wife. It was impossible to save her. I thought I'd succeeded, but she was too weak and too distressed. Her heart failed. But," momentarily he paused, "I must give you the good news that you have a fine, healthy baby daughter. There is no need for any concern about her at all."

And then that good, compassionate man took the weeping Alexander into his arms and tried to comfort him.

Nine

"Man that is born of woman hath but a short time to live, and is full of misery. He cometh up and is cut down like a flower; he fleeth, as it were, a shadow, and never continueth in one stay.

"In the midst of life we are in death..."

A solitary wail eerily broke the stillness as Mary Martyn's coffin was lowered into the grave beside that of the mother-in-law she had never known.

The churchyard was so full that the wailing mourner was hard to see, but the sound came from the back of the crowd and not from the immediate family who, supporting Alexander, gathered by the side of the grave.

Carson recalled that on the day Nelly had been buried the sun had also shone, giving an awful sense of incongruity to the solemn proceedings. Then it had been spring. Now it was midsummer and the earth was ablaze with the bright colours of flowers and the

206

variegated greens of the trees in the churchyard. The lime tree that had been about to burgeon the day Nelly was buried now had myriads of little pods which fluttered and danced, embodying the very spirit of life, in the soft breeze. It was as though everything in this place of death was vibrantly alive, giving some sense to the belief that the soul of the departed rises from the dead to rejoin the Creator in heaven.

Beside him Alexander stood quite still, his head bent, his face utterly impassive as if he too had no life left in him. Tentatively Carson put a hand on his shoulder and briefly Alexander raised his head flashing him a grateful smile. In that moment an intimacy between father and son was born that made Carson rejoice even amidst the gloom, the awful all-pervasive sense of loss at the cutting off of the life of a young girl of such tender years. Out of such evil good might yet come.

Even the rector, Hubert Turner, veteran of many a funeral, had been hard put to offer consolation to the mourners who flocked into the church. Several times he had faltered in his sermon to blow his nose loudly. There had been a lot of snuffling and coughing among the large congregation that filled the church and overflowed outside.

The whole of Wenham had closed its doors and come to the funeral, not so much to honour Mary, who they hardly knew, but to support the Woodville family of which she, by however devious a route, was a member.

The gravediggers finished lowering the coffin, withdrew the straps that had secured it and stood back beside the mound of earth they had dug the previous day. Hesitantly Alexander stepped forward, picked up a lump of soil and threw it on the coffin. He stood for a long time gazing at it and at the simple words inscribed on the brass plate:

Mary Martyn
1917–1934

She was just a few days short of her seventeenth birthday.

He stepped back and then the members of the family approached the grave, each one casting a handful of earth upon the coffin. Lally, supported by Dora and Eliza with Pieter Heering close by, didn't go to the graveside but remained where she was in the shelter of the church. Grey-haired and frail, she looked like a little pale ghost, who might not long survive the girl who was being buried.

Agnes Woodville stood a little away from the main body of the family – after all it had always made her feel an outsider – clad in black from head to foot, grim-faced. She had perhaps suffered more than others because, in many ways, this had been her doing. It seemed amazing that so much drama could be played out and accomplished in a year.

Next to her was Sophie Turner and Ruth and Abel Yetman, behind her Sarah-Jane and Solomon Palmer, Deborah and Bart. Jean Parterre and Sally Yetman also formed part of the family group. Connie had sent flowers, preferring not to undertake the long journey from Venice at such short notice.

On the other side of the grave, and as far away from the family as possible, stood Elizabeth flanked by her husband Graham, Mary's sister Betsy and older brother Jack. All were dressed in deepest mourning. Betsy never stopped snivelling despite threatening glances and a few digs in her ribs from her mother.

Elizabeth and her family had arrived ahead of the cortège and most of the mourners, and had not addressed a single word to Alexander or to anyone else.

As the crowds began to drift silently away, and the gravediggers started to fill in the hole, Alexander stood in front of the cross that had been erected on his mother's grave:

Nelly Allen
Born 1889 Died 1931

This seemed to move him in a way the burial of his wife had not, although he couldn't have been more grief-stricken. It released the tears that he had so far held back and, producing his handkerchief from his pocket, he wept silently for a few moments. Carson remained by his side protecting him from the stares of the curious.

Alexander finally raised his head, blew his nose and smiled at Carson. The two men turned towards the church and the respectful crowd that remained behind, hands outstretched, to offer him condolences.

Suddenly Elizabeth broke away from the shelter of her immediate family and rushed across the grass to Alexander, administering a sharp blow to his face that sent him reeling. Instinctively he put his hands up to protect himself as Graham Temple, horrified, roughly seized his wife by the arm to prevent her from aiming another blow.

"You should be *ashamed* of yourself," Elizabeth bawled at Alexander. "You alienated my daughter from her family." She raised her hand and pointed a quivering finger at him. "You were the cause of her death. You should be put in prison, locked up and the key thrown away. You—"

"Come now, my dear," the red-faced Graham tugged agitatedly at her, "this is no way to talk." He looked up apologetically at Alexander, who had taken his hands from his face and was staring at Elizabeth, the imprint of her palm clearly visible on his cheek.

"I am very sorry, Mr Martyn. My wife is beside herself with grief."

"Beside herself with grief." Agnes snorted. "That's a nice one."

Agnes crossed over to Alexander's side. She confronted her daughter pointing an accusing finger at her. "You're a nice one to talk. If there was ever an unnatural mother it is *you*, Elizabeth. That poor girl eloped to get away from *you*. Don't blame Alexander. He was nothing to her but kindness and love, whereas you," Agnes's loud, bold voice began to tremble, "you have not a kind senti-ment in your body. Look at the way you have treated me, your own mother, a reflection of the way you treated your daughter. You—"

"Agnes *please*." Carson caught hold of her outstretched hand and forcibly lowered it. "This is no place for a brawl."

"She started it." Agnes tugged angrily at Carson's hand, but he held tight.

"Graham, please take Elizabeth away." Eliza commanded. "One can understand her distress, but this is not the time."

"Understand!" Agnes, nostrils flaring, retorted.

"*Please* Agnes," Eliza appealed to her. "Let us have a little decorum and respect for the dead."

Suddenly silence fell. The townsfolk who had stayed to gawp at this wholly novel and unexpected event, such as had never been witnessed in Wenham churchyard in living memory, began to slink away. They would talk about it for days, perhaps years, to come. It would be part of Wenham folklore, as was so much else of a scandalous nature to do with the Woodville family.

Graham Temple drew his wife, who was now sobbing loudly, towards the church gate and Sophie put her arm round Agnes who, her moment over, had also dissolved into tears. She led her to the bench by the side of the church where she sat her down and, producing a handkerchief, began to dab at her eyes.

"Are you all right?" Eliza looked up at Alexander who still pressed his hand to his face. He nodded and sat down beside Agnes and took her hand.

212

"Thank you, Aunt Agnes. What you did was very brave."

"What *she* did was atrocious." Agnes's whole body was quivering. "I never saw such a scene in my life. Coming from *her*." She looked towards the churchyard gate where Graham Temple could be seen bundling his wife and family hurriedly into his car.

Bart, accompanied by Deborah, came up to the group and held out his hand. "My condolences, Alexander. A terrible, terrible thing."

"Thank you, Bart. Thank you for coming."

"Will you come back to Pelham's Oak?" Carson addressed Bart. "We have a small luncheon laid on for family only. We didn't think it was the right occasion for a big wake, such as we have had in the past and to which we normally invite the townspeople.

"That's very kind of you," Bart said shaking his head, "but Deborah doesn't feel too well and, as Sarah-Jane and Solomon are staying with us, we thought we'd go straight back to Upper Park."

He shook Alexander's hand again. Deborah put her face to his cheek, as did her mother and sister. Solomon and Abel also shook hands murmuring words of sympathy.

213

"Where's Mother?" Alexander asked suddenly observing that Lally was nowhere to be seen. "Where's Lally gone?"

"She didn't feel well, either," Eliza said. "Dora and Pieter have taken her home. Perhaps you'll go and see her later?"

Alexander nodded, aware that, for the first time for months, he had instinctively referred to Lally as 'mother'. Was it possible, he thought, looking towards the grave, now being filled in, that a man could have two mothers?

He hadn't yet seen Lally alone. She had remained at Forest House while he had accompanied the coffin to Wenham church where it had lain overnight. He had then joined the baby and her nurse at Pelham's Oak.

"Ready old chap?" Carson put a hand on his arm and Alexander nodded as Eliza again inspected his face.

"I don't think she hurt you very much, did she?"

"She hurt my pride," Alexander said tenderly fingering his cheek. "I deserved it."

"You did not," Carson protested. "It is easy to be sentimental and forget what happened."

"But for you I have no doubt that Mary would have run away, as Deborah once did," Agnes said firmly, "and may well have been lost to us for ever. Her mind was made up, and when I get the chance I shall lose no time in conveying that message to my daughter, monster that she is."

"I think you've said enough, Aunt, thank you." Alexander looked up at her and, for the first time for many days, he managed the ghost of a smile.

At the end of lunch Alexander, excusing himself without explanation, slipped out of the room and made his way on foot to the cottage a mile or so away where Massie Smith, his mother's companion, lived. Alexander knew that when she was needed she worked up at the big house but, otherwise, she lived here on her own, dependent on the bounty and goodwill of Carson. This undoubtedly was why she had kept the truth from him the day he'd gone there with Mary in an attempt to find out more about Nelly. He hadn't seen her since.

Despite himself Alexander enjoyed the walk through the fields on this lovely day in high summer whose beauty was only spoilt by the fact that he had just laid his beloved to rest, an event which lay heavily on his mind. Without her he could feel no lift in his spirits.

It was a relief to be away from the family. Much as he appreciated their uncritical support, it was an unnatural situation in which to be reunited with them after the passage of nearly a year during which so much had happened. Everyone chose their words very carefully and there was so much that was left unsaid, so much that needed to be said. He and Carson had yet to have a long talk, but that supportive hand on his shoulder at the moment of interment had spoken volumes. It was rather as if Carson had been trying to say, "I am here, man to man, when you need me."

For a few seconds Alexander stood outside the pretty little cottage gazing up at the window where that day, four years before, he had looked up from his horse and seen this rather strange, beautiful woman standing at the window looking at him. The window was open, as it had been then. He was struggling to control the tears welling up inside him when the door opened and Massie stood there, her face creased with sorrow.

"Master Alexander," she said stepping back. "What a surprise it is to see you. Please come in."

As he crossed the threshold she shut the door after him and turning said, "I was so sorry to hear..."

Alexander nodded. "Thank you, thank you."

"Please sit down." Massie pointed to a chair and then took the one opposite him.

"I say I was surprised to see you, Master Alexander, but, in a curious way, I have been expecting a visit. I knew you would want to hear about your ma."

"I would have come before, but I couldn't," Alexander said. "I was so hurt and upset that it was kept from me, that in the last months of her life, when I could have helped her, I was not told. I felt it was very cruel and wicked of my family, and so I found it hard to forgive them. Impulsively I decided to have nothing more to do with them."

"That *was* very foolish, Mr Alexander," Massie said earnestly, leaning towards him. "If you will forgive me for speaking so bluntly. Nelly, your mother, wished for nothing but the best for you. She could give you nothing and she left you with that good lady in the hope that she would bring you up as a gentleman, which she did.

"Your poor mother never enjoyed very good health. If you had remained with her it would have been a miracle if you had survived your childhood, and if you had you would have had a terrible life. But her circumstances meant that poor Nelly couldn't have kept you. She had not the means, nowhere to live. She would never

217

have abandoned you, but she would have
lost you. Bad enough now but you've no
idea what conditions were like in those days.
She'd have had no choice. The Frances
Roper Home was already arranging for the
guardians to take you from her. You would
have been adopted by strangers who no one
knew.

"But Nelly knew you was the son of a
gentleman and she wanted you to be
brought up as one. She made the sacrifice
for you, and her thanks were that she
succeeded. She was very proud of you and
hearing your father, Sir Carson, talk about
you going to university and that, and seeing
you that day looking so handsome on your
horse, gave her nothing but joy. She died a
happy woman, I can tell you. Far, far
happier than if the son she had given birth
to had died in childhood, wracked by
disease, or turned to crime and wickedness
to support himself if he had lived to be a
man. I can tell you, Master Alexander, life
on the streets as we knew it was very, very
hard and you should be grateful to that
good lady who gave you a home and
brought you up to be the fine man you are
now."

Alexander sat for a long time looking at
the woman opposite him, pale and worn,
who had been his mother's constant

companion. She was a small, neat little person with an elfin face, badly pockmarked from disease. Although she was the same age as his mother would have been, merely forty-five, her hair was more white than brown, and her hands were gnarled and roughened from years of hard work. But she had a very fine pair of hazel eyes and a sweet, rather wistful smile.

Alexander felt at that moment that he loved and trusted her.

"One day, Massie," he said standing up and going over to take her hand, "you must tell me all about my mother and the life that you lived before you came here."

"It will take days," Massie said with a smile, "but I will do it."

"You will have plenty of opportunity if you like what I have to say. You see there is something you *can* do for me."

"Anything, Master Alexander, you know that."

"In the first place, I want you to call me Alexander."

"Oh, very well then. Nelly wanted you to have a fine name that would give you a good start in life, and she was right."

"The second thing is that my infant daughter is badly in need of a nursemaid who will be more to her than a nurse, and you immediately came to mind. I wondered if that is a task you might like to undertake?" He paused and looked earnestly into her eyes. "Now you don't have to, Massie. You have a happy, comfortable life here. My daughter will have every comfort money can bring. She will lack for nothing but that one precious thing: a mother's love. Is it possible that—"

"Oh, *Alexander*!" Overcome with emotion Massie seized his hand and, drawing it to her cheek, let it rest there. "Alexander you have no idea what happiness such a task would give me. I am fit and able and have not enough to occupy my mind or time. I sit around all day brooding about the past and thinking. I have nothing really to look forward to as the years roll by. Time hangs very heavily on my hands." She looked anxiously up at him. "If you really think me capable there is nothing more I would like to do in the whole world."

"It was very kind of you to come," Carson said as he and Sally stood on the steps watching the last of the family guests drive away.

"I was glad to." Sally turned eagerly to him. "I feel I know the family so little. I want to be part of it. I want the family to mean to me what it clearly means to you."

Carson stood for a while watching the

departing guests, pondering her words.

It had been a sad lunch but a cathartic one. With close family there Alexander had unwound a little and had spoken about the last days and Mary's totally unexpected death. He had also spoken of their happiness together, the joy they had given each other. He knew her short time on earth had been happy or, rather, he hoped it had. Only he knew she had been lonely in London, with few friends, and he knew that Dora knew it, but he didn't speak of this. Theirs was a relationship full of unfulfilled dreams that now lay in his baby daughter who was slumbering upstairs in the care of her nurse.

Alexander had abruptly left the room just before lunch had ended. Carson suspected he wanted time to be by himself and had made no comment. They had to talk, but there was all the time in the world to do that. He felt already that a tentative bridge had been built between them in their new relationship as father and son.

"Shall we have a stroll," Carson asked Sally, "and wait for Dora and Jean to come back?"

"That would be nice." Sally slid her arm through his in cousinly fashion and they walked along the terrace onto the lawn. They passed under the great oak tree that, legend had it, was the same oak planted by Pelham Woodville who had built the original house in the seventeenth century. Its trunk was about five feet in diameter and its circumference three times that number. It was a visible landmark for miles around.

Sally stood for some moments in its shade gazing up through its branches. She sighed deeply. "This place is steeped in history isn't it?"

"It is indeed. We nearly lost it several times, particularly under my father, who was atrocious at managing money. I was even made to propose to Connie with the purpose of saving it." Momentarily he bowed his head before looking up into Sally's disconcertingly clear, blue-eyed gaze. "It was a very shameful episode in my life."

"Oh dear." Now it was Sally's turn to study her shoes. "I didn't realise you had to marry for money." She raised her head. "Is that why the marriage broke up?"

"Oh no. That had absolutely nothing to do with it. I became engaged to Connie by the wishes of my father and her guardian when I was twenty-four. I didn't love her, but was told it was my duty. Then Agnes reappeared on the scene, ostensibly with money. My father had loved her in his youth, indeed they were Elizabeth's parents, as you know. By this time he was a widower and fell in love with her all over again. It was genuine enough, but it was also supposed that she had money. Consequently I felt I would be released from my engagement and I caused both Connie and myself much misery. Later, after the war, when I was older and much wiser, Connie reappeared and re-entered my life. We had both changed and we fell, this time, genuinely, in love."

"I see." Sally was striding ahead of him and Carson wandered along after her. In the distance they could see Jean and Dora galloping across the valley in the direction of the house.

Sally paused to let Carson catch up with her, watching the riders.

"She rides beautifully, doesn't she?" Sally said admiringly, turning to Carson as he drew level with her.

"She's an excellent horsewoman," he agreed. "First class. Jean is good too. He was a very old friend of mine from wartime days. They met here, you know."

"Oh did they? Interesting."

Carson studied her profile which, in so many ways, was like Dora's. There was a very strong family resemblance: both tall, capable women, with good bone structure, fair hair and blue eyes. He wished very much that Sally had come into their lives earlier on. He felt they'd missed a lot by not

223

knowing her but, perhaps, it was not too late to make up for it.

"And you? You have never married?"

Sally shook her head.

"I never met the right person. You never know, it may happen yet."

"Oh, certainly. You're not too old. Dora was quite old when she married Jean."

"I have also travelled a lot. I find it hard to settle. I'm thinking of going to the Far East next year. Spending some time in India, China, places like that."

"Oh dear," Carson grinned ruefully. "Just when I was hoping we'd see more of you."

"I'm not going until next year," she said. They both turned at the sound of a car travelling towards the house, and saw a flutter of childish hands waving frantically from the windows.

"They're back," Carson cried going to the car, which drew to a halt outside the house.

The children had been sent away for the day while the funeral took place. They got out of the car and ran, not to Carson, but to Sally, who seemed overwhelmed by the attention and, stooping, tried to greet them all at once.

"Did you have a lovely day?" she asked, hugging Netta.

"We went to the beach at Weymouth."

"Did *you* have a nice day?" Leonard asked gravely.

"Well, not very nice," Carson answered. "It was very sad to bury Mary, Alexander's wife. We miss her very much."

"Where has she gone?" Netta looked with interest at Sally. "Will you never see her again?"

"Some people think there is another world," Carson chose his words carefully, "and souls go there after they die."

"Don't you think that, Daddy?" Toby looked puzzled. "It's what we're taught at school."

"It's called heaven." Netta informed them. She was a bright, precocious child, sometimes unexpectedly witty.

"Well *I* believe in heaven," Sally said firmly. "And I believe that Mary went straight to heaven and that in time we shall all meet there and see her again."

"Come on children." Harriet called holding out her hand. "Nearly time for tea. You will see your father and Miss Yetman again later on."

The young people ran obediently into the house, Carson and Sally watched them.

"They're lovely kids," Sally murmured. "You're lucky."

"I only have them part of the year. That's the trouble. And, to return to what we were talking about before, I once *did* love my wife very much, but I don't any longer. Please be clear about that. She belongs to my past."

"Your past seems to have been very full," Sally said. "Nelly and Connie, and I suppose there were other women as well."

"When I was young," Carson acknowledged, "I had a reputation. But as one gets older one realises that these things are less important than family life, which I very much miss. I miss my wife and children or, rather, I miss my children. Look..." he hesitated "...why don't you stay on for a while if you've nothing better to do? The children love you and I would like to have you here too. We can have days out, go to the beach, that sort of thing. What do you say?"

"Well..." Sally appeared nonplussed. "I'd like to very much. But are you sure?"

"Sure," Carson said and, momentarily, his inner being seemed to flood with joy. "That's settled then. The children will be awfully pleased. Ah, here's Dora." Dora appeared round the corner of the house from the stables, Jean following her. "Did you have a good ride?"

"Excellent," Dora said, looking at Sally. "And what have you two been doing?"

"Just chatting."

"We thought we might come and visit you in Bournemouth on our way back to

226

France," Dora continued casually. "Will that be all right?"

"When ... ?" Sally hesitated.

"In a day or two, on our way home."

"I've persuaded Sally to stay for a few days," Carson said. "She's so good with the children."

"Oh, that's nice," Dora said acidly. Then, to her husband, "Perhaps we should stay on too, Jean?"

"Impossible, my dear. We have a lot to do at home. The vines."

"Oh, those vines," Dora erupted angrily striking her thigh with her riding crop. "They make me sick!" and she strode off in the direction of the house.

"Now, what brought that on?" Carson asked looking after her in surprise.

"I think life in France is a bit too quiet for Dora," Jean said sadly. "Sometimes I feel she's very restless. There's not enough for her to do."

An hour or two later as Dora and Jean were preparing to leave to drive back to Riversmead, where they were staying, Carson drew Dora aside and said, "You are very welcome to stay on you know. I think Jean understands."

"Understands *what*?" Dora asked heatedly, clearly still agitated.

"He says you find life very quiet in France. That you haven't enough to do. I'm sure he won't mind if you stay."

"He mentioned the blasted vines but he didn't mention our daughter," Dora said coldly. "I have a duty to her as well as to my husband and the dratted vines, which are treated like children anyway. Besides, I don't want to hang around watching Sally make sheep's eyes at you."

"Oh, that's not true," Carson protested.

"Haven't you noticed?"

"As a matter of fact, I haven't. Anyway what's wrong with it if she does?"

"Nothing." Dora flapped her hand at Jean who was calling impatiently to her from the car. "I only hope, if you fall for it, you're not going to make another terrible mistake like you did with Connie."

Carson watched her as she ran towards the car, puzzled and disturbed by her attitude. Dora was tempestuous, but she was not cruel or catty and, just now, he felt she had been both.

"Anything wrong?" Sally enquired as she emerged from the house and came to stand by his side. She had bathed and changed and looked cool, fresh, composed, and, Carson thought, rather beautiful.

"Nothing." he answered. "Just one of Dora's little moods."

"Pity she can't stay. I like her," Sally said conversationally. "I am sorry about Bournemouth. Perhaps I should have gone back?"

"Don't be silly. The children are thrilled you're staying. Dora comes over quite often. There will be plenty of other times to visit you in Bournemouth."

Carson took her casually by the hand as they walked back into the house. "Now, let's have a drink before dinner."

Alexander used his own key to let himself into Forest House, which was silent. He stood for some moments in the great hall from which rose a spectacular circular staircase, curving up around the three floors. The glass cupola in the ceiling allowed the light to flood the hall.

When it was first built, forty years before, the design of the house had been considered innovative, incorporating many ideas that were then thought of as extremely advanced, like underfloor central heating and a swimming pool in the basement, complete with a Turkish bath. It was a sumptuous dwelling, a beautiful house that had been Alexander's home since he was a tiny baby. Except for occasional visits to London, Lally preferred to bring him up in the country with its fine pure air and fresh, wholesome food. This obsession with

Alexander had alienated her from her husband and, for many years, they had lived virtually separate lives, although Prosper never stopped loving his wife. He had had the generosity, and the foresight, to make Alexander his heir.

Alexander loved Forest House and he'd missed it. His boyhood had been idyllic. In fact his life had been idyllic until this last terrible year, yet he did not regret marrying Mary and fathering her baby. All he did regret was that she was with him no more.

It was late afternoon, when the staff had a few hours off. Cook might be in the kitchen listening to the wireless and quietly getting on with her preparations for the evening meal.

Swiftly, Alexander climbed the stairs to the first floor and, stopping outside Lally's room, knocked softly on the door.

"Come in," she called.

He gently pushed the door open and found her lying on top of her bed covered by a light blanket. On her lap lay an open book, but she had obviously not been reading because her spectacles were on top of it and her head turned towards the window. Her appearance shocked him, as it had at the funeral, though she had remained some distance away. Her hair was completely white, her face ghost-like. Never a very tall or robust woman she had had an elegant, feminine figure, but now she was wraith-like. She had lost perhaps a stone in weight.

The realisation that he was the cause of this deterioration in a vigorous and beautiful woman increased Alexander's sense of shame. Perhaps she had been dozing, or thinking. As he reached her bed she turned her head and gazed at him.

"Alexander," she murmured.

"Mother." He smiled down at her and, as she put out her hand, he took it. "I am very, very sorry."

"It is I who should apologise. But I didn't mean to hurt you." Lally's voice faltered and she began to weep silently.

Alexander removed the book and spectacles from her lap and sat down on the bed beside her still clasping her hand tightly.

"I'm sorry," Lally spluttered, groping under the pillow for her handkerchief and vigorously wiping her eyes. "I am a very stupid emotional woman, but I love you very much, Alexander."

He leaned across and kissed her wet cheek. "And I love you. I behaved like a spoilt schoolboy."

"No, you were hurt. It was such a shock to you. You didn't understand."

"I could have *tried* to understand. Mother,

I just went to see Massie, Nelly's friend and companion, who told me how grateful I should be that she did what she did. She said there was no other way, unless I was brought up on the street, or carried off to the orphanage for adoption by a complete stranger. Massie said that I owed so much to you and, of course, I know I do. I wish I'd spoken to Massie before, because she said Nelly bore no grudge but was grateful for all that had been done for me."

Lally said nothing only nodded.

"It wasn't only Massie, Mother. Mary never approved of my behaviour. When she was fighting for her life in the hospital, though I did not then know it, I realised how much I missed the love and support of the only family I had ever known, and I vowed to repair the damage if I could."

Lally looked to him and her pale face was lit by a wan smile. "You have repaired it, darling, this very day. I have always loved you like my own son, and knowing you were Carson's flesh and blood gave me such happiness. I knew you had his strength and commonsense and, sooner or later, dearest Alexander, I knew that you would come back to me."

She raised herself on her bed and, leaning towards him, ran her hand tenderly across his cheek.

"Between us, your family, we shall do everything to support and help you in your terrible grief, and in the upbringing of your darling little baby girl. We shall do all we can to make up to her for the loss of her mother, just as I tried so hard to make up to you for the loss of your own dear mother so many years ago."

Ten

From the bedroom window it was possible to see undulating fields, interspersed with copses and stretches of woodland, almost as far as Salisbury. Upper Park was slightly elevated above the Dorset landscape giving it unsurpassed views for miles around. Yet the beauty of the scene did little to raise the spirits of Sarah-Jane Palmer as she sat by the window waiting for her brother and husband to return from their day's work.

It was a week since poor little Mary Martyn had been laid to rest and Sarah-Jane, never comfortable in her native county, was anxious to be gone.

She'd been slow at first to appreciate the delights of life in Brighton, but now she had settled down. There was a lot to be seen: the lanes with their delightful little shops, the extensive promenade with its wonderful view of the ocean, the pier, the grand hotels on the front where it was possible to have coffee, or even to take a drink in the lounge bar with some decorum, no one asking too many questions. Occasionally she was discreetly approached by a gentleman who would offer to buy her a drink, and that way she had cultivated one or two interesting new acquaintances. Nothing improper had occurred – well, anyway, not yet. They were gentlemen, usually retired after a lifetime in the colonies or in the army, with too much time on their hands, who were not after sex but companionship.

Like her, they were very lonely.

Sarah-Jane realised that her life had taken a wrong turning when she had fallen for the youthful charms of Solomon Palmer. It had not been love but infatuation, and it had soon passed. They had very little in common, and as drink became more important than physical passion to her, the fact that he was away so often quite suited her. It gave her a life of her own to do with as she pleased: to wander along the Lanes, drink in the hotel bars or, occasionally, take day trips to London.

Sarah-Jane had not wanted to go to the funeral – she hardly knew Mary Sprogett after all – but Solomon had dragged her along only, it seemed, so that she could be lectured to by Bart about the desirability of moving.

She turned away from the window and poked around in the wardrobe. She eventually found a green bottle and, unscrewing the cap, poured a little of the contents, neat, down her throat. They called it Dutch courage, to give one the strength to face the evening. And it worked. As soon as the liquid reached her guts she felt better, more in control, less afraid. Tonight she would tell them that she was not going to move. And that would be that.

Before returning the bottle to its hiding place she had another sip of gin, larger than the first. Then she went and brushed her teeth and rinsed out her mouth before changing her dress and preparing herself for the discomforts the evening was sure to bring.

Solomon watched the butler as he poured more wine into Sarah-Jane's glass. He tried to catch his eye to stop him giving her any more, but without success. He thought the butler knew what he was doing and, rather maliciously, enjoyed it, maybe in the hope that his employer's sister would make a fool of herself.

Solomon was quite sure that Sarah-Jane had been drinking before he got home. She had that kind of reckless gleam in her eyes that he recognised from past experience.

She had a couple of cocktails before dinner and grew more and more animated as the evening progressed casting Deborah, who appeared moody and withdrawn, into the shade.

Bart didn't seem to realise that his sister had an alcohol problem and Solomon didn't care to enlighten him. He knew that, despite their past differences, Bart was fond of Sarah-Jane and indulgent towards, her. He also might just conceivably lay the blame at Solomon's door and thus jeopardise their relationship.

"We saw a house today," Bart announced as they were in the middle of the main course, "that we thought might suit you and Solomon, Sarah-Jane."

"Oh?" Sarah-Jane sounded disinterested.

"It is not too far from Wenham, is a good size, and Solomon thought it would do quite well. You might like to see it tomorrow." Bart looked across at his sister, whose expression remained impassive. She continued to eat without raising her head.

"Would you like to see it Sarah-Jane?" Bart asked a little impatiently.

"Not particularly." She finally raised her head, putting her glass to her lips, eyes slightly glazed.

"Really, Sarah-Jane," Bart's air of impatience grew, "you can't go on living in one part of the country while your husband works in another."

"I don't see why not. I like Brighton. I like the air. And the sea."

"How about Bournemouth?" Deborah suggested, suddenly reviving. She had not welcomed the idea of her lover bringing his wife to stay in the same house as herself and she couldn't wait to see them both go. "Bournemouth is only an hour away. Weymouth is nice too."

"You'll have to be settled by winter, my dear," Bart said encouragingly. "You don't want Solomon traipsing across country in the snow."

"I'll see." Sarah-Jane took hold of her glass and drained the contents. Surreptitiously the butler sidled up to refill it once again.

"I think Mrs Palmer has had sufficient," Solomon said. "Haven't you dear?" He smiled at her sweetly.

"No dear," she said, smiling just as sweetly back, and looked up at the butler encouraging him to pour.

Bart seemed bemused by the exchange and frowned at Solomon.

"It's a terrible thing to be left with a little baby." Sarah-Jane waved her glass in the air. "I keep on thinking of poor Alexander and wondering how he'll cope."

"Cope!" Bart snorted. "He'll cope very well. He is not only wealthy enough to employ all the help he needs, but he is now reconciled with his family and staying, I hear, with Lally."

"She immediately made an appointment with her hairdresser to get her hair restored to its normal colour," Deborah said maliciously.

"Really, dear, you mustn't gossip." Bart's tone was gently reproving.

"I am not a gossip," Deborah replied defensively. "I admire Lally. I'm happy for her. They say that without Alexander she would have died."

"I also heard that in a very short time she has been transformed. Alexander is back living with her and the baby. It's a happy ending to a sad story. I, too, am pleased. But I still think he has a lot on his plate." Sarah-Jane beamed round at the table. She felt quite light-hearted, fully in control of herself and the situation.

Perhaps Bournemouth, after all, was not such a bad suggestion if it would keep everyone quiet. After all it had the same kind of amenities as Brighton – the sea, a pier, grand hotels – and there were sure to be a number of retired elderly gentlemen with enough leisure and money to keep her supplied with drinks at the hotel bars. Solomon would still be away all day and she could pass her time as she wished.

Bart cleared his throat. "Talking of babies." He glanced sideways at his wife. "Deborah informs me we are expecting again. A little brother or sister for Helen."

"But that's wonderful news," Sarah-Jane gushed, raising her glass a little unsteadily towards her hostess. "When is the joyful event?"

"Some time in the spring," Deborah murmured. "The doctor is not quite sure."

"A spring baby. Lovely. Isn't that lovely Solomon?"

But Solomon was looking at his plate, his face grim and unsmiling.

"I think congratulations are in order," Sarah-Jane swung her glass high again. "Solomon, drink to the health of Bart and Deborah. You're going to be an uncle once more and I expect you're very, very happy about it."

After dinner they moved into the drawing room where Bart usually put on the gramophone. He was in an expansive mood, possibly because of the baby, and lit a large cigar before going through the records by the side of the machine inspecting the labels, tapping his feet in time to the tune he was humming under his breath.

"How about 'No, No, Nanette'?" he asked, looking round.

"One of my favourites." Sarah-Jane sashayed up to the drinks table, but Solomon got there before her and placed a hand on her wrist.

"No," he whispered. "I forbid it."

"You forbid it," she mimicked and, firmly taking hold of the decanter, poured herself a sizeable measure of brandy. She then went across to Bart and began to wriggle her hips in time to the music, whereupon Bart turned, caught her and, taking her by the hand, began leading her swiftly round the room. In one hand he held his cigar while Sarah-Jane – with some difficulty and a lot more laughter – managed to cling onto her glass. Obviously in great good humour brother and sister threw back their heads and laughed uproariously. Maybe Bart was a little tipsy too.

"Would you like to go for a stroll in the garden?" Solomon turned to Deborah, who was tapping her foot in time to the music.

She shook her head. "I think I'd like to dance."

"It's terribly hot in here." Solomon ran his finger round the neck of his shirt.

"Oh, all right," she said, reluctantly getting to her feet. They strolled through the french windows onto the terrace. It was a beautiful evening, the air balmy and pervaded by the heady smell of roses brought to perfection by one of Bart's gardeners in the beds below them.

"I don't really feel like walking," Deborah said slumping in a chair. "I don't feel terribly well."

"How long have you known?" Solomon demanded sitting down next to her.

"Known what?"

"You *know*. I thought you weren't sleeping with him?" Solomon could hardly contain his anger.

"I had to say that, didn't I?"

"You're a bloody liar."

"And you're a bloody fool," she retorted, "if you think I could refuse a man like Bart. Anyway he's been away such a lot I'm not sure it is his. In fact," she glanced slyly at her companion, "I'm almost sure it's not. The doctor did say he thought I was three months' pregnant and Bart was away during most of May." She gave a nervous giggle. "I can always tell him the baby was premature."

"You've made a complete cuckold out of me," Solomon spluttered.

"*And* Bart. He's been cuckolded too and, after all, he's my husband." Deborah gazed at him coldly. "Come on Solomon. You knew it was a game that we both enjoyed."

242

"I love you," Solomon said thickly.

"No you don't." Deborah shook her head vigorously. "It's lust, not love. But lots of fun." She reached out and taking his hand, winked at him. "Didn't we have a lot of fun?"

"I think you're a perfect little slut," Solomon hissed, enraged by her attitude. "You'd go to bed with anyone just for a game."

Beside him Deborah stiffened.

"You'd better be careful what you say, Solomon. Remember you work for Bart. I could make things very difficult for you if I was so minded."

"And I could make things very difficult for you," he retorted, "if I told him the truth."

Deborah gave a hard, brittle, mirthless laugh.

"You wouldn't dare. He'd kill you." She leaned towards him, her eyes narrowing. "You be careful, my boy, and mind how you talk to me. If I say anything to damage your reputation, even hint that you behaved improperly – and he'll believe me, not you – he'll get rid of you, and you'd have difficulty in ever finding another job. Bart would make sure of that."

Deborah rose sharply to her feet and swept back into the drawing room where the dancers, apparently oblivious to their absence, were still bobbing energetically around in time to the catchy little tune.

Those weeks of summer were among the happiest Carson could remember for a long time. Of course the early years of his marriage to Connie had been happy, and there had been plenty of nice summers after the children arrived. But the last few summers he had been alone with the children and, much as he loved having them, as a single man he was often hard put to know what to do with them.

Watching Sally as she played with them on the lawn, peeping round doors as she entertained them inside on rainy days, or carefully guiding them when they went riding, he realised how much he'd missed the company of a woman. How much he needed a woman, and how important Sally was, not only to the children but, increasingly, to his own happiness and welfare.

He soon realised that Sally was attractive and desirable, and that they were perfect companions, sharing the same interests in a way he and Connie had not. Connie preferred the city to the country. Although she was a Wenham girl born and bred, she loved smart, fashionable cities like London, Paris and Venice. She liked the company of clever, cultured people, attending openings, going to the opera and theatre. She was artistic, bookish and read a lot.

It was unfair to say she had been a bad wife and mother because she had not. She was a very good housekeeper, had run a good home and adored the children. Nor was there anything to complain about the more intimate moments they'd shared. No, it had all fallen apart after he brought Nelly to Wenham and, he was sure, but for that that he and Connie would still be together.

However, he felt it had been a true test of the strength of his marriage, and it had failed. One took a solemn vow in the marriage ceremony for better or for worse, and as soon as a real crisis had blown up Connie had refused the challenge and gone off to Venice, probably the place she preferred best anyway.

But now, to his great good fortune, in her place had stepped, almost effortlessly, Sally Yetman, a woman who liked country pursuits. She was a cheerful, outgoing, relaxed sort of person. As the days of summer slid pleasantly and effortlessly by, they went on various outings to the coast, to Weymouth or Studland or Bournemouth, where Sally took them all to her home, or to the New Forest where the wild ponies roamed. Carson came to realise that he was coming to rely on her more and more.

Also that he was once again falling in love.

The days of the holidays came to an end. All too soon it was time to think of taking the children back to Venice.

"Next week," Carson said as, the children safely in bed, they sat on the terrace after dinner drinking coffee, "we shall be on our way." He looked across at her and saw that she had her head back, eyes closed.

"Tired?" he asked.

"I'm absolutely exhausted." Sally opened her eyes. "But it's been a lovely summer. I've enjoyed every minute."

"I can't tell you how I've appreciated having you here. I don't suppose..." Carson hesitated "...well, I don't suppose you'd like to come with us to Venice? I mean it would be wonderful to have your help on the journey, but I thought that as a reward for all you've done I could give you a little holiday afterwards, you know, saunter through Italy at our leisure. Or France and Switzerland if you prefer. How does it appeal?" Feeling nervous and fearing a rebuff, he looked at her anxiously.

"Do you know," Sally opened her eyes and gazed at him, "I can't think of a more perfect idea."

The two women embraced each other, though they had never met.

"It's *very* nice to meet you at last." Connie stood back and looked at Sally. "You know I'm your aunt."

"I know," Sally smiled. "Ridiculous, isn't it?"

As the children gazed at them, wonderingly, Connie explained.

"Sally's grandfather was my father. I was born when he was quite an old man."

"How did you never meet if you were Sally's aunt?" Netta wanted to know.

"Well, we lived a long way away. I'm older than Sally and the families didn't have much to do with each other."

"Sally's been of the most enormous help," Carson said. "I don't know what I'd have done without her."

"An excellent choice." Connie smiled again. "I can see how happy the children look." She turned and put her arm out as a gesture of welcome to Paolo as he walked into the room.

"Darling, this is Sally Yetman. Her grandfather, John Yetman, was my father. Isn't it a coincidence? We've never met before. Sally, my husband Paolo."

"How do you do?" Sally said.

After greeting Sally, Paolo turned politely to Carson and they shook hands.

"We do hope you'll stay for lunch this time, Sir Carson."

"Oh yes, you must stay for lunch," Netta insisted. "We wish you'd stay for ever."

"That would be lovely, but alas it's not possible." Sally laughed. To her surprise she felt amazingly relaxed and at ease with Carson's ex-wife. Well, after all, she was one of the family.

"Well," Carson said as, after a good luncheon and copious farewells, they walked away. "That went off awfully well."

"Were you nervous?"

"A bit." He smiled at her.

"I can't imagine you nervous. You didn't show it. I did think Connie was very nice by the way."

"She is."

"So is her husband." Sally paused. "I mean, I do hope you don't mind my saying it?"

"Of course I don't mind. They are both perfectly charming people. And we can have a very civilised relationship, as much for the sake of the children as anything else."

"I shall miss the children very, very much."

"I miss them too," Carson paused, "but now that I've got you, well, it helps."

He looked at her but she avoided his eyes

and he wished, not for the first time, that she'd give him just a little encouragement.

Despite the lack of intimacy, Sally was the perfect companion for the tour of Italy, going down one side and up the other as far as Como, where they were to meet up with Alexander. She was indefatigable, good humoured, eager to learn yet no ignoramus when it came to works of art or ancient monuments. She had, after all, travelled a great deal and this was by no means her first visit to the Continent.

But whenever Carson put his hand over hers at table, or took her arm in the street, there was no response. She seemed to be holding back as if she was afraid to give herself. If he lingered outside her bedroom door as they said good-night there would be a swift peck on the cheek rather than a kiss, and the door would be politely but firmly closed behind her.

He wondered if he did not press his suit hard enough or if it was simply that he did not attract her, preferred him to be what she had been to the children: a friend?

Carson had always been a very physical man, celibacy was hard for him, particularly in the presence of a woman he felt so attracted to. It was rather humiliating to be, in a sense, rebuffed. Without more encouragement, Carson, was nervous of declaring himself for fear of further humiliation.

This apart, it was a perfect holiday stretching over several weeks and towards the end of October they arrived at the villa Alexander had bought in Como as a wedding present for Mary, but which he had hardly ever visited since.

"I'm awfully glad to see you," Alexander said as, after greeting them and taking them into the villa, he stood with them on the balcony gazing over the lake. "It's rather spooky here without Mary. She so loved it. In fact, I think I'm going to sell it again."

"Oh, you can't!" Sally exclaimed. "It's perfect, it's heaven."

"It is lovely," Carson agreed. He gazed earnestly at his son. "Think about it a little more before you decide what to do."

"You must be tired." Alexander looked across at Sally. "Had a long day?"

"Exhausted!" Sally exclaimed. "I think I'll go to my room and have a long bath or shower.

"Of course. Let me take you." Alexander moved away from the balcony but Carson remained where he was. "Coming?" Alexander asked adding, hesitantly, "Dad."

Carson's heart turned over and he put an

arm round Alexander's shoulder, rather as he had on the day of Mary's funeral. But he said nothing as, picking up Sally's suitcase on the way, Alexander led them through the cool tiled hall up the stairs and into a large bedroom facing the lake with a double bed right in the centre.

"The bathroom's off here," he said opening a door. "I think you'll find everything..." He walked back into the bedroom and saw Carson and Sally looking uncomfortably at each other.

"Anything wrong?" Alexander enquired.

"I think Sally would like this room." Carson cleared his throat.

"Oh, I'm sorry. I thought..." Alexander covered his mouth in confusion.

"It's perfectly all right." Sally smiled. "We haven't quite got round to that yet."

"You do have another spare bedroom I suppose?" Carson asked him.

"Of course. I'll take you." Alexander turned to Sally. "Would you like to see it too?"

Sally shook her head.

"This is just fine. I'll relax and unwind in the bath and see you downstairs in about" – she looked at her watch," – an hour."

"Drinks on the terrace in an hour," Alexander agreed, and led the way out of the room. Sally came with them to the door and smiled as she shut it.

Alexander walked along the corridor and opened another door.

"This has no bath but the bathroom is just next door."

Carson inspected a smaller room with two single beds. "This is fine."

"It hasn't got the same view either." Alexander pointed to the window.

"That doesn't matter."

"Care for a drink? I'll bring your bags up later."

"Wonderful." Carson followed his son back the way they had come and onto the terrace where Alexander drew up chairs.

"What will you have? Whisky?"

"A glass of wine would be very nice. I'm fond of the stuff."

"Great. I'll go and get a bottle of Orvieto." Alexander disappeared, returning in a short time with a bottle of wine and three glasses. "It's not very cold, I'm afraid," he said feeling the bottle before opening it.

"Never mind," Carson said. "Don't you have any servants here, Alexander?"

"I would if I lived here but I only arrived yesterday to open the place up. I've arranged for someone to come in and clean, make beds, and get any meals. I thought we'd eat out mostly. How long are you staying?"

"A few days? Is that all right? This is the

end of our trip. We're catching the train back from Milan."

Alexander poured two glasses of white wine, handed one to Carson and sat down beside him. "I'm sorry about the bedroom. I thought..."

Carson grimaced. "I thought, too. I hoped. You know I'm half in love with her."

"Only half?"

"I feel I need some response from her before I fall completely."

"And nothing... ?"

"Not really. I mean, we get on awfully well. I know she likes me, but I don't know quite how much. As for me, I'm nervous, you see, after Connie."

"I think you ought to take the plunge, Dad," Alexander said. "She can only say 'no'. If it's what you want, that is?"

"Oh, it is. It *is* what I want without question. Perhaps she thinks I'm too old for her? There're fifteen years' difference."

"Nonsense, you're very youthful and a fine figure of a man. I like her too." Alexander stared across the water. "I'd like very much to have her as a stepmother."

Carson started to say something and then hesitated. "It's 'Dad' then, is it, Alexander?"

"If you don't mind."

"I'm delighted. You know that."

"I'm surprised it comes so naturally to me

after years of 'Uncle Carson', but it does."

"It seems right to me too." Carson held out his hand towards Alexander who took it. "I'm glad."

"I'm very sorry for everything, Dad."

"No need to say a word." Carson, feeling very emotional, pressed his hand. "I'm sorry, too, and the fault is more mine than yours. I thought, when you were very young, that you might be my son."

"Why was that?"

"You looked so like Nelly and we always wondered who the woman was who left the baby on the doorstep. Nelly, you see, knew about Lally though she didn't know her. She'd been to the house in Montagu Square with me. It wasn't until I met Nelly again that she told me the truth."

"It's an amazing story."

"It is."

"I'm awfully glad it had a happy ending, Dad."

"So am I."

"I do hope I'm not interrupting." Sally had glided into the room and both Carson and Alexander turned and rose to greet her.

"Not at all. We're just talking about the past."

Sally looked quite stunning in a short dress with straps that showed off her brown skin which, in turn, enhanced the colour of her deep blue eyes. Her hair, also bleached by the sun, was corn coloured.

Carson swallowed. He felt then that he was completely in love with her, not just half. What would he not have given to have got into the large double bed with her that night?

"Drink?" Alexander asked feeling the bottle again. "It's not very cold but it's drinkable."

"Lovely." Sally took the glass and also the cigarette Alexander offered from his silver cigarette case.

"We thought we'd go out to dinner. I have no staff and no provisions, but tomorrow it will all be different. Tomorrow, by the way, I have to go to Milan to see the lawyers about the house, all sorts of formalities which will take all day. I don't suppose you want to see Milan again?"

"Don't mind about us," Carson said, "I want to explore the mountains about here. They say the countryside is fabulous."

The jagged mountains behind Como, the foothills of the Alps, rose to a great height. This was not, strictly speaking, the pretty tourist part – that was in the Dolomites further on – but it had a majestic grandeur that was all the more sensational for being little known and almost inaccessible. Above its main town, Sondrio, through which they drove, there rose a very narrow, dangerously winding road to the top. Below them were deep valleys, and the sides of the cliffs through which they passed were sheer.

Finally they arrived at the place where the road ended in a cluster of houses, some of them quite large and used by prosperous Milanese as holiday homes. Dominated by the great craggy Monte Disgrazia, meaning bad luck, it had an eerily claustrophic air about it which made Carson and Sally disinclined to linger.

"I wouldn't like to live here," she said, feeling goose pimples on her arms. "Let's go back."

"I agree. On the way home let's find somewhere to eat. I'm starving."

Carson began the perilous journey downhill which seemed, in many ways, more dangerous than the way up. Fortunately they encountered little traffic except for peasants, on foot carrying huge bundles of twigs on their backs, and standing aside to glare at them as they passed by.

Halfway down they came to a trattoria from which emerged a wonderful smell. It was with same relief that they inspected the terrace at the back which, perched on the edge of a cliff, had a truly spectacular view of the mountains for miles around.

They ordered pasta and a bottle of red wine, and as they waited for their meal sat for a long time gazing at the view.

Carson was aware that somehow the mood between them had changed. He couldn't say why or how. Maybe it was relief at being away from the shadow of the bad-luck mountain.

Sally, in a shirt and slacks, with a sweater which they'd needed further up tied round her neck and sunglasses disguising her expression, seemed meditative. He thought how lovely her profile was as, hands round her knees, she sat gazing up the way they had come. It was as though there was electricity in the air. Carson was suddenly overcome by a feeling of sadness that the holiday of which, perhaps, he'd had too much hope, was coming to an end.

He sighed deeply and Sally, roused from her reverie, turned to him.

"What's the matter?"

"Nothing."

"It was a big sigh."

Carson, emboldened by her expression, by the subtle change in mood, put a hand over hers.

"I'm just sorry."

"Sorry, for what?"

"Sorry it's coming to an end."

"Me too."

"Are you?"

"Yes of course. It's been wonderful."

Carson swallowed. "When will you go abroad again? To the Far East?"

Sally ran her finger round the edge of the table.

"I haven't decided. Some time in the spring perhaps."

"I suppose you have to go?" Carson, who had never really been physically afraid of anything in his life, was suddenly frightened. Now he would know.

"No, I don't have to." She looked at him and he could see her expression changing.

"I mean, we could go together, if you wanted. Sally, what I want to know is," he paused and took a deep breath, "will you marry me?"

"I thought you'd never ask." she said.

"I wanted to but ... I was afraid."

"What for?" She looked at him with surprise. They were lying side by side in the big double bed in her room, the evening sun casting its gentle rays on the lake, all the inhibitions gone. It was so much easier to talk, to let the words flow.

"I was afraid you didn't love me."

"And I was afraid that you still loved Connie."

"I told you I didn't."

"I wasn't sure and you seemed ... a little shy. I didn't want to throw myself at you, you know."

"Throw yourself at me?" Carson scoffed. "I wish to God you had. I mean, we've spent all these weeks misunderstanding each other. What a waste."

"A waste of what?"

"Precious time," he said bending to kiss her. She looked so eminently desirable, her face shiny from the vigour of their love-making, that, at that moment, she seemed to him the most beautiful, most precious thing on this earth. He felt ten times more in love with her than with any woman he'd ever known, certainly Constance, even, he had to admit, poor Nelly.

When Alexander got back that evening from Milan he found them sitting on the balcony, hands joined, gazing out across the beautiful lake whose shimmering waters were dappled, now that the sun had gone in, by moonlight. Sally had on the white dress she'd worn the evening before, and Carson a crisp white shirt and grey slacks. It was not just the joined hands that gave them away, they seemed to have an aura, an air of apartness, as though they'd been translated onto another planet.

Alexander, who also had known great

259

love, saw them then for what they were, had been from the beginning: a pair. The signs were unmistakable. He looked at them and they looked at him, smiling mysteriously. There was absolutely no need for words.

Eleven

June 1935

Carson put his arm round his bride as they stood in the great hall of Pelham's Oak welcoming their guests. Because Carson was divorced they had married quietly in a register office in Bournemouth in January attended only by Eliza, Lally and Alexander, and Sally's mother Judith. After a luncheon in a hotel they had gone up to London, embarking a few days later on a liner in Tilbury which took them to Calcutta.

There had followed a tour of the Far East so that Sally got her wish to travel far afield only accompanied, as he had suggested when he proposed, by her husband. It had been a dream time, the stuff of which all good honeymoons are made. They had found on their tour of Italy how compatible their interests were and, as lovers now as well as companions, their expectations had not been disappointed.

In April they had returned to Wenham and

had a private service of blessing in Wenham Church. Since then they had been settling down and planning this first of many receptions to introduce the new Lady Woodville to the community. They had avoided having it in May as England was *en fête* with celebrations for the Jubilee of King George the Fifth.

"How do you do?"

"How do you do?"

"May I present my wife?"

Smiles all round.

"How do you do?"

The line of family and local notables passed slowly by, each pausing for a few minutes' chat so that the time taken seemed interminable. It was past one o'clock when Carson and Sally came into the main reception room where the buffet had been prepared in case it rained, a wise precaution because the day was overcast and cold.

Not quite like Hong Kong. Sally shivered.

"Are you all right my love?" Carson looked at her with concern.

"A little nervous. A bit cold." She rubbed her arms. "I think mainly it's all these people."

"You know so many of them." Carson reassured her, taking her hand and drawing her forward. "You will get to know the others in time. It's part of being a Woodville."

That was it, Sally thought, 'Part of being a Woodville'. Wenham might as well be called Woodvilleland. Everything revolved round the family and also, in her Uncle Ryder's day, the Yetmans, who had lived at Riversmead, almost in the centre of the town. But then she'd known that when she had lived here the previous summer and had realised at first hand what it was to be part of the family, however peripheral. Now she was at its epicentre. Lady Woodville, mistress of Pelham's Oak. Heiress to a great tradition.

Overcoming her nerves Sally moved away from Carson to greet Dora and Jean who had come over for the occasion.

"So sorry we missed the wedding." Dora sounded a little insincere. They had given no reason for declining the invitation. As it had taken place in January it was a bit early to be concerned about the vines.

"We were sorry you weren't there, although it was only very small. Carson didn't want a fuss."

"Couldn't have a fuss," Carson said, grimacing as he joined them. "Marriage of a divorced person in church is not permitted. However Hubert blessed us, so all's well." He tucked his arm in Sally's and smiled at Dora. "And I'm very happy."

Dora had abandoned her customary casual attire for a dress and coatee of crêpe de Chine with matching pipings. A wide straw hat was decorated with a broad band made of the same material. She looked very poised and soignée, almost aloof. She had an air of disapproval as though something about the occasion displeased her. It was a little unsettling: Dora not quite her usual self.

Sally, hatless and, of course, much younger, wore a pretty, very flattering afternoon frock in blue and white organdie with three-quarter length sleeves and a pleated skirt that fell to a few inches above the ankle. The full bodice, which emphasised her pretty bust, had a deep, square decolletage.

Dora and Sally seemed to appraise each other for a few moments, almost as though they were rivals. They were the most fashionable women in the room. Sally had bought her outfit in Bond Street, Dora in the Rue de Rivoli. They rather put to shade the other ladies, few of whom had ventured further afield than Yeovil or Blandford for their afternoon attire. Lally, as always the acme of elegance, favoured a style of another age: a long dress of floating chiffon, the bodice decorated with a large diamond clasp.

"The honeymoon was sensational, I hear. Ten countries in – how many weeks?"

"We were away twelve weeks altogether."

Sally decided to take no notice of the nuance in Dora's tone which seemed to suggest that no one could possibly take in so many countries in so few weeks. "It was the holiday of a lifetime. India was magnificent. And Siam – I never saw such a beautiful place. The war between China and Japan, and the upheaval there, meant we couldn't go to those countries, but we had so much to see elsewhere. I don't suppose we shall ever have another holiday like it."

"Oh, I don't know. I might get a taste for travelling," Carson said, draping his arm around her. "Sally has convinced me that there is more to life than working on my land, keeping books and accounts."

"You have always had to work very hard," Dora said reprovingly, "to repair the damage done to Pelham's Oak by previous generations."

"So doesn't he deserve a reward?" Sally said smiling sweetly. "And he shall have it."

"I have my reward," Carson kissed her cheek. "I have all I could ever ask for."

Lunch was eaten at small tables placed round the room, guests helped themselves from a long buffet that ran the length of one wall. Servants circulated with drinks, and Carson and Sally moved among the tables stopping to chat to the guests. Many eyes followed Sally as she drifted elegantly from one table to another, clearly now more at ease, though Carson, with a watchful eye on her, was not far behind.

Many people were surprised that Carson had married again. They had hoped that he and Connie would repair their differences. Connie was a local girl, and a popular one; she was the mother of his children; they had been a happy and united family. The community had felt very let down when the separation occurred; no Woodville had ever divorced before. Yet it was Connie who had remarried first, making a reunion impossible.

To some people it seemed that there was a curse on the house of Woodville. It was a family with more than its fair share of troubles which afflicted one generation after another. Maybe the new Lady Woodville would change all that. Hopefully, she would have children of her own to fill the long corridors and high rooms of Pelham's Oak with their happy voices.

After lunch the clouds gradually dispersed and the sun came out. Guests wandered out onto the lawn, some still clutching drinks in their hands while the servants moved chairs and tables swiftly onto the terrace. The atmosphere was of growing festivity.

Chattering became clamorous as Sally and Carson hand in hand continued to mingle with the guests.

All the family were there except Sophie Turner who would not attend any occasion at which her daughter and son-in-law were present.

Alexander, urbane as usual, elegant and charming, moved slowly with Lally on one arm, Eliza on another, pausing here and there to chat. Bart Sadler paraded with Deborah, Solomon Palmer tagging along behind.

Sally and Carson stopped to talk to them.

"How's the new baby?" Sally asked.

"Beautiful," Bart replied. "You must come and see him."

"We will."

Bart turned to Sally.

"You met my architect Solomon Palmer, didn't you Sally?"

"We met at Aunt Eliza's party," Sally smiled. Solomon inclined his head.

"Is Sarah-Jane not with you?" Carson looked around.

"She wasn't too well," Solomon mumbled. "Sent her apologies."

"I'm sorry. You must bring her to dinner soon to meet my wife."

"That would be delightful."

"I hear the new houses are beautiful.

Are they selling?"

"Not yet, but they will," Bart said. "You ought to come and see them."

"We shall," Carson promised.

They continued their leisurely stroll among their guests, the lawn and terrace now full of people who had come out to test the air. The afternoon promised to stay fair and Pelham's Oak was a picture in the sunshine. Its walls of Chilmark stone and its gleaming white paintwork were redolent of an earlier, more gracious, but less democratic, age when the lower classes would have been banished to the servants' quarters or a marquee on the lawn to quaff ale and eat hearty country fare, while the local gentry ate quails' eggs, lobster and haunch of venison and drank champagne in the house to the sound of a string quartet.

Those days had gone. Now there were fewer class distinctions, and local tradesmen, farmers and builders mixed as equals with people who, in former days, would have felt it demeaning to talk to them. Much of this was due to Carson who had grown up among ordinary people and felt at home with them. Had not his Nelly been a barmaid? Did he not retain a hint of the broad vowels of a Dorset accent? If ever there was a man of the people was it not he? For Carson, it was nostalgic to recall the number of occasions when his family had entertained the populace to celebrate some milestone in the life of the family: weddings, christenings, funerals, birthdays. One of the last had been the marriage of Ruth and Abel. The most recent celebration had been Eliza's seventieth birthday, when he had first met Sally.

There had always been family squabbles. It was still a fact that many members did not see eye to eye and avoided a meeting if they could. He had had to ask Elizabeth and her family, but only she and her husband had come. They turned their backs on Alexander, snubbed Eliza and talked almost exclusively with worthies of the town who were colleagues of Graham Temple's. Abel and Ruth avoided Bart. Since Bart had started his own building company he had stolen most of Abel's men. Sophie was not there, though Hubert was his usual affable self, very short-sighted now and overweight, but as Christian a man as you could find, the embodiment of his Master's virtues. Carson sighed. Family differences there were, and he supposed always would be, as in the past.

It was a joy to see Alexander and to know that between them such a good relationship had developed. In many ways he wished Alexander were his heir and could inherit Pelham's Oak, but he would be a very wealthy man when, in time, Forest House became his, and Toby – the future Sir Toby Woodville – had all the makings of being the sort of man who would make any father proud when he grew up.

In a huddle on the lawn were Pieter Heering, Dora, Jean, Alexander and Eliza deep in discussion. Lally and Agnes sat side by side, out of the sun, chatting from time to time but keeping a sharp eye on the crowd, always a rich subject of gossip. As Sally and Carson approached the group on the lawn, conversation appeared to peter out.

"Don't let us interrupt you," Carson said. "It seems extremely important, whatever it is you're discussing."

"Pieter is convinced there will be a war," Eliza's expression was deeply troubled.

"Oh, don't say that." Sally looked aghast. "Is it as bad as that? We've missed so much since we've been away."

"The German army is three times the size allowed by the Treaty of Versailles." Pieter Heering waved his cigar around in the air. "A move condemned by the League of Nations."

"Who are without power," Jean Parterre said contemptuously. "All sound and no substance."

Bart, who stood nearby, removed his cigarette from his mouth, saying politely,

"Excuse me, I couldn't help overhearing. Germany are not the only people re-arming, you know. We too have expansion plans for the services. The RAF will be trebled in size in two years. You can't blame the German Chancellor if he reacts in response to rearmament in Britain."

"That is nonsense." Pieter turned on him. "Hitler's plans are openly expansionist. Look what he has done in the Saar."

"I know what I'm talking about," Bart responded airily. "I go to Germany on business frequently. The Germans feel threatened and misunderstood. No sensible German wants war."

"I don't really see—" Pieter began heatedly when Carson put a restraining hand on his arm.

"This party is to celebrate my wedding, not to discuss the awful and, I hope, unlikely prospects of another war."

"Still it is prudent to be realistic," Pieter insisted, turning to Alexander. "You are worried about it, I know, aren't you Alexander?"

Alexander nodded.

"Italy concerns me particularly. Mussolini is in cahoots with Hitler and has his eyes on Abyssinia. An alliance between Germany and Italy could lead to conflagration in Europe."

"Stop, stop." Dora put her hands to her ears. "I find this whole conversation out of place. I refuse to listen to any more of it. Especially, as Carson says, on a day like this."

"I am inclined to agree." Eliza said gravely. She had been listening to the discussion with mounting distress. Having lived through one war she could not contemplate another.

Dora put her arm through Carson's and drew him away from the group.

"All this talk of war frightens me."

"Do you think it could happen?" Carson looked at her. "What is the mood in France?"

"They feel the same. They are worried about the extent of German rearmament. You know France signed a pact with Russia in case of attack? With so much sabre-rattling in Germany, where they have already introduced conscription, France does feel threatened. If there was a war, Carson, I'd come home."

"Please don't say that." Carson put his hand on her arm. "Don't even think of it. With my new-found happiness..." He paused uncertainly. "Dora, what's the matter?"

"What do you mean 'what's the matter'?" Dora looked at him wide-eyed.

"You seem to have developed a curious attitude towards Sally. I feel it. I can't understand why you aren't happy for me."

"I am happy for you," Dora insisted. "If it's what you want. I love you very much and I only want the best for you, you know that. I just feel you don't know Sally very well."

"But I do know her. I've known her for nearly a year."

"It's not very long." Dora ran her hand along the back of a chair, her expression thoughtful.

"My dear it is very long," Carson protested. "Most of that time we've been living together."

"I see. I didn't realise. Well then, as I say..."

Dora left her sentence unfinished and turned away. Carson gazed perplexedly after her. He couldn't understand the attitude of his favourite cousin, who he'd always been so close to. He thought that she liked Sally, the relationship had seemed warm. Why the change? It hurt him and he felt a kind of emptiness, a nagging worry. He looked round for solace and saw that Sally was still with the group on the lawn deeply engrossed in the depressing subject of the deterioration of the international situation.

Carson sat down on one of the chairs and lit a cigarette, smoking for a few moments in silence. He loved Dora and he wanted her to love Sally. As Alexander detached himself from his little group and wandered over to his father, Carson patted the chair beside him.

"You look out of sorts, Dad," Alexander said sitting down. "You shouldn't on a day like this."

"No, I'm not at all," Carson briefly placed a hand on his knee. "It's just that Dora seems to have taken against Sally and I can't understand why."

"Maybe she's jealous."

"Jealous?" Carson looked at him in amazement. "Of Sally? But she's got Jean."

"I mean of you."

"I don't think I understand you."

"Well, Dad, it's no secret, is it, that Dora lived for years with another woman. Maybe she feels that way about Sally."

"Don't be absurd," Carson said, in a rare burst of anger with his son.

But, nevertheless, the suggestion troubled him and he continued smoking in silence for a few seconds while Alexander deeply regretted making such a stupid remark.

Sally's mother Judith had never had much to do with the Woodville family, or the Yetmans for that matter. She had lived most of her life in Bournemouth, where she had her own circle of friends, and she felt rather out of place amid a crowd of strangers. However, the family kept an eye on her to ensure she was not left on her own.

She was a plump, rather jolly, grey-haired woman of about sixty. She dressed comfortably. Her ensemble of dress and coat was of patterned silk topped by a blue straw hat with an over-large bow. Her outfit had been bought in Dingles in Bournemouth, and it would serve her well in the future at her smarter bridge afternoons, whist drives or charity garden parties. She enjoyed the good things of life including her food and had taken a plate onto the lawn together with a full glass of champagne.

Dora went over to her, lighting a cigarette as she sat down beside her.

"Enjoying yourself, Aunt Judith?"

"Oh, very much," Judith Yetman enthused, wiping a crumb from the corner of her mouth. "It's a lovely place. Sally is so lucky."

"She is indeed." Dora gazed around her. "I often wished I lived here but I never did. My mother, of course, was born here. We all love Pelham's Oak."

"I wish I'd known your mother better." Judith sighed. "It seems such a pity we didn't see more of my husband's family. Of course there wasn't much love lost between your father and his brothers. I never understood why. Hesketh was a secretive man."

"I think it was something to do with money," Dora murmured, "it usually is."

"Oh?" Judith looked at her for enlightenment.

"It all happened so long ago I can't remember," Dora reassured her. "Anyway the main thing is that now that Sally is the new Lady Woodville you have an undoubted place in the family."

"I can't get over it." Judith Yetman's face crumpled with pleasure. "I'm so happy. I never thought Sally would marry you know."

"Really?" Dora gazed at her with interest. "Why was that? She's so attractive."

"Oh, it wasn't that. It was just that she never seemed interested in men. I couldn't understand it. Can you?" She looked at Dora whose eyes were on the elegant figure in blue and white organdie standing some distance away on the lawn.

"Yes I can," Dora said enigmatically, and again, "yes I can."

Judith prattled on. "She had a very great woman friend, Eileen. They used to go for holidays together. At one time they even shared a house in Poole. I didn't know what happened when she left but," she leaned confidentially towards the woman by her

276

side, "I'll tell you quite honestly, Dora, I was pleased to see the back of her. Shortly after that Sally came here to Eliza's birthday party and met Carson. You can't imagine how relieved I was."

"I bet you were," Dora said and sat back, a thoughtful gleam in her eye.

Solomon said urgently.

"I must see you again. Alone."

"Don't be so silly," Deborah hissed back. "All that's finished."

"You don't understand. Seeing you torments me. I can't stop thinking about you."

Deborah looked at him slyly. There were so many people on the lawn that they were lost in the crowd. Bart was still occupied, engaged in defending Germany, where he had so many business interests, to the group who persisted in discussing the situation in Europe.

Solomon had seen Deborah walk away and had followed her until they stood partly shaded by the overhanging branches of the great oak tree. He thought she looked breathtakingly lovely, tall and fair, her figure slight and still youthful. Never a great dresser, despite her marriage to a rich man, she wore a summery dress of blue taffeta with a high neck and leg-of-mutton sleeves, whose effect was to make her look about eighteen. Her fair hair was caught back by a matching blue band. The effect was disarmingly simple, contrasting with the outfits of many of the overdressed women.

"You once called me a slut." Deborah had an edge to her voice.

"You know I didn't mean it. You *know* I didn't."

Deborah hesitated. "Bart would kill us if he found out..."

Solomon's heart leapt with hope. "You mean – there *is* a chance?"

"There's always a chance," she said vampishly. "Why don't you give me a call when he goes away to Germany again? Then we'll see."

And as she eyed him she flicked the tip of her tongue round the outside of her mouth, as if in a gesture of anticipation.

Sarah-Jane made her way confidently into the lounge of one of Bournemouth's largest hotels and sat down on a sofa by a window overlooking the sea. It was important to show this confidence; to look as though you had a purpose, knew where you were going, what you were doing, perhaps meeting someone.

It was just after noon, her second call of the day. She usually walked along the front from the pleasant house they now occupied

278

in Allum Chine until she came to the promenade and made the first of her regular calls, though she varied the places a good deal. Hotel staff kept a careful eye on solitary women, and there were already a few places where she knew she wasn't welcome and would be politely asked to leave as soon as she stepped inside the door.

It was a long way down from her place as a respected member of the Wenham community, wife of one of its prominent citizens, allied to the great Woodville family. But she didn't see it like this. She thought that times were better now than they had been; that there was still a lot to live for, fun to be had, alcohol to be consumed, gentlemen to be met to pass the time of day with.

Solomon generally left for work early in the morning and then Sarah-Jane had the place to herself. Bliss. She liked this. She was glad he worked so hard, for having him around irritated her. Her time wasn't her own.

She wished now that she hadn't married him, that she'd taken note of what her children had told her. They'd warned her that this would happen. There was too big an age gap for the marriage to have any chance of succeeding. They had so little in common. At the time she'd put their reaction – particularly the girls' – down to jealousy and ignored it. It had been a heady time: to be desired by a man so much younger than herself. Wisdom was abandoned. Caution fled. But passion soon abated and recriminations set in. Inevitably she had found solace, strength and comfort in drink.

Often when Solomon came home she was in bed. She pretended to be asleep as he entered their bedroom, having had a drink or two himself. She knew he was unhappy. They both were, but it was difficult to know what to do about it. She now had no money left and was dependent on him. He probably would like to leave her, but he had that formidable alliance of Woodville and Yetman families to consider and, most important of all, the fact that his wife was the sister of Bart Sadler, his powerful employer.

Sarah-Jane usually got up around nine, listened to the wireless, had coffee and her first, and sometimes only, solid food of the day. She read the *Daily Mail* sitting at the kitchen table, smoking a cigarette or two. Then she had a bath, taking some time over her toilet and choosing her clothes with care.

For many years she had let herself go. After Laurence's death she hadn't cared if she lived or died. She had became depressed. She was a farmer's daughter and appearances had never meant much to her. When she was younger she was a bonny girl, sturdy and robust, uncomplicated, not a beauty but pretty enough to capture the heart of Laurence Yetman who had been such a promising, vital young man. He had been a loving husband, a caring father and they had had a good life.

She had been ill prepared for what happened. His death, so unexpected, had seemed cruel and unfair. One moment she had everything to live for, the next she had nothing. Suicide was a terrible thing; it destroyed not only the person who committed it, but everyone who loved them. It had changed her and it had changed her children. Increasingly she had withdrawn into herself and found it difficult to communicate with them. Nothing had ever been the same again. For many years, she had lived in a kind of limbo until the young Solomon Palmer had come along and swept her off her feet.

Sarah-Jane was now fifty-three, no longer young, not so robust, but she knew she had a quality that still attracted men, men a lot older than her husband, of course. She had a sort of faded prettiness, her brown hair not so luxurious but still brown, her eyes not quite as sparkling as they had been, or might have been had she drunk less, her skin a little withered and wrinkled, particularly round the eyes. They were not lines of laughter, but lines of age and hard living. Her figure was good, she had a neat bosom and legs that attracted men's eyes, and lesser thoughts. She had a quality of sexual allure that still stirred the loins. But she never went to bed with them. She led them on so far and no further. After that, when her meaning became crystal clear, she usually didn't see them again. No matter, there were plenty of other lonely men cast up on the Bournemouth shore, as in many other seaside resorts throughout the country, eking out their last days, desperate for a final fling.

As well as looking good, she now dressed well. She had bought a lot of clothes: pretty dresses and nice hats, well-cut costumes for winter, good leather handbags, shoes and gloves. Stylish. She was carefully made-up, smartly turned out, and ready to sally forth.

First she usually had a large brandy to steady her nerves and give her the courage she needed to face the day. Even with experience, it still did need courage to go by herself into a hotel for the purpose of drinking and, perhaps, meeting men.

Sarah-Jane liked Bournemouth. It had the edge on Brighton, with a better class of person, a nicer kind of hotel. The retired squirearchy, the army veterans and businessmen seemed, on the whole, less crude, better mannered, with more money.

Ensconced on the comfortable sofa within sight of the sea Sarah-Jane crossed her legs, lit a cigarette and when the waiter approached ordered coffee. "Oh, and brandy," she added as an afterthought, "make it a large one."

The waiter nodded and a short time later he was back.

The day had begun with clouds, but it was getting better. Solomon had gone off to Carson and Sally's wedding reception, but she hadn't been able to face it – all her family, the accusing looks, sly glances. She felt Wenham was no longer part of her life and she didn't care if she never saw the place again. She liked the sea, the shops in a smart resort and the large anonymous hotels.

Sarah-Jane lit a fresh cigarette and stirred her coffee. As she raised her cup to her lips she looked up and saw an elegant gentleman staring down at her, a deprecating smile on his lips.

"I wonder if I could trouble you for a light?" he said in a cultured voice indicating the cigarette in his hand. "I appear to have left my lighter at home."

"Of course." Sarah-Jane produced her

lighter. The gentleman took it, lit his cigarette and returned it to her with a smile.

"Thank you so much. In exchange might I be permitted to buy you a drink?"

"Well," Sarah-Jane went through the, by now, practised routine of doubt, surprise. "That would be very kind. Thank you."

"Colonel George," the gentleman said producing a card which he handed to her. "Late of the Tenth Hussars."

Sarah-Jane studied the card. Just a name, expensively embossed, no address.

"Colonel A.C. George MC." She raised her eyes waving the card across her face as if it were a fan. He was tall, over six feet, with sleeked back iron-grey hair, tanned, rather leathery skin as if he'd spent a long time in the colonies, and piercing blue eyes. He had a clipped moustache and a decided military bearing. His grey pin-striped suit was double breasted and he wore a blue striped shirt and some sort of military or club tie.

He seemed to her the real McCoy. No doubt about it. She moved along the sofa.

"How do you do, Colonel George?" Sarah-Jane raised her hand and politely shook his. "Sarah-Jane Palmer. *Mrs* Sarah-Jane Palmer."

"How do you do Mrs Palmer?" The Colonel carefully creased his trousers and perched gingerly on the sofa next to her.

"Do I take it you're waiting for your husband?"

"Not today," Sarah-Jane said. "As a matter of fact, he's away on business. He frequently is."

The Colonel shook his head and said with a roguish smile, "Silly man, leaving a lovely young woman like you."

The waiter appeared, took a fresh order for drinks and when he returned the colonel raised his glass towards her.

"Chin chin, Mrs Palmer."

"Chin chin, Colonel," Sarah-Jane replied gaily, raising hers. "Happy days."

Twelve

March 1936

Bart Sadler, Alexander thought, had every reason to be a very happy man. He had a young, beautiful wife, two handsome, flourishing children, a fine home and a business, it was said, that had made him into a millionaire many times over.

Yet in this relatively modest building on the outskirts of Wenham, to which Bart had mysteriously invited him, it was difficult to see where his fortune came from. It was an old stately home that had fallen into disuse and disrepair. He had bought it for a song and Solomon had transformed it into offices in the guise of a gentleman's country house. In many ways it seemed like the strange whim of an already rich man. There was a short drive leading up to the discreet double-fronted door beyond which was a large hall with a parquet floor. Reception rooms and domestic offices opened off it.

Upstairs Bart's own office ran the width of

the building. Walls had been pulled down to create enough space and light to satisfy the most inflated ego and Bart's, certainly, was of a considerable size. It had a vast mahogany desk on the top of which was a single blotter, an inkstand and writing implements, and two telephones. The floor was carpeted in thick soft woollen pile, probably woven at Wilton or Axminster. There was a long table around which were several upright chairs, and scattered about the room were comfortable armchairs and a sofa facing the garden with a view of Ham Hill rising above the trees. On the walls were original paintings, mostly of foreign scenes where Bart might have gone on his travels. It was very different from Alexander's office in London which, although comfortable, had nothing of the opulence and luxuriousness of this.

Alexander, one arm flung over the back of his chair, looked curiously across at Bart who had gone to a safe by the side of his desk and was in the process of extracting a bulky lever-arch file from it. When he had checked that the contents were what he wanted he carefully locked the safe again. He placed the file, with the greatest care, as though it were an object of great fragility, on a small table in front of the chair occupied by Alexander.

"This," he said in reverential tones, his hands still on the file as if he were touching the Bible, "is worth millions."

"Really?" Alexander, looking amused, put his chin in his hands and regarded Bart as he opened the file and leafed carefully through the contents.

"Now, Alexander." Bart looked earnestly up at his young companion. "I know you're a businessman through and through."

"Well..." Alexander gave him a deprecating smile.

"Pieter Heering told me you would be chairman by the time you're thirty. He can't get over the grasp you have developed for the business. He feels it is as though you really were the scion of a Heering and not a Woodville, few of whom ever showed much talent for making money."

"Except my father," Alexander interrupted him. "He has restored the family fortunes by his own hard work."

"Well, that's as maybe." Bart assumed an expression of wisdom. "Connie was a very rich woman."

"Connie had nothing to do with it." Alexander became heated. "My father insisted that her money was kept separate."

"Well, we shan't argue. I certainly have a great respect and admiration for Carson, and I certainly don't wish to offend you.

The point I am making is that Pieter Heering tells me he will be quite happy to retire early and leave the organisation in your hands."

"He said that, did he?"

"Oh, yes. And I can believe it. There is something about you Alexander, young as you are, that inspires confidence and trust which is why I have invited you over to see me today." He glanced nervously towards the door. "I must emphasise that what I have to say must not go beyond these four walls."

"You have my promise." Alexander, intrigued despite his distrust of Bart's cloak-and-dagger procedure, nodded.

Bart returned to his chair and folded his hands, his brows knotted, his expression grave.

"I am aware of what you feel about Germany, Alexander."

"Ah, this is about Germany." Alexander began to understand and sat up. He knew now that it was very important for him to pay careful attention. Bart Sadler would not have invited him here in conditions of such secrecy for nothing. With his reputation for intrigue, it was hard not to smell a rat where Bart was concerned.

"I can assure you I am not anti-Semitic. I have nothing against the Jews. I do business

with them here and, although you might not
believe it, in Germany."

"Really?" Alexander looked surprised.

"Oh yes. Despite all Hitler's laws against
them there are many still operating quietly,
and the field in which they are operating
might amaze you," Bart leaned forward,
"armaments." He finished dramatically.

"I do find that hard to believe."

"Nevertheless, it is true." Bart flicked
open the file again. "Rosenberg, Cohen,
Grutzberg, Feinstein ... all Jewish, all im-
porting armaments."

He handed Alexander a sheaf of bills
which, although they were all in German,
enabled Alexander to verify that the signa-
tories did, indeed, appear to have Jewish
surnames.

"A Jew will sell you anything," Bart said,
"or buy, if it is to his advantage. He is no
different from the rest of us. Of course I
don't only sell arms. I export all kinds of
goods. They're very partial, as we know, to
Scotch whisky, woollen goods, fine
leathers."

"All Jews?" Alexander looked incredulous.

Bart shook his head. "Oh no, by no means
all Jews. There are a few Jews, as I have
indicated to you, but the majority of my
customers are gentiles and doing very nicely
too, I can tell you. You see, contrary to what

you hear, Hitler has done much to improve the German state, to restore to a defeated and downtrodden people a sense of identity. Look, let's face it, the Jews in many ways have only themselves to blame. They control the law, the banks, the medical profession. People resent them. Whether you like it or not, that is the truth. Hitler may have gone too far, and I personally think he has, but he has also completely rid the country of the menace of communism." Bart threw his hands in the air. "Who can do business with communists? They don't believe in it. My enterprises in Spain have crashed to the ground in the short time that the left-wing government has been in power. No my money is on Herr Hitler and..."

Alexander held up a hand.

"Bart I don't know what this is about, exactly, but I cannot agree with you about a man who has just marched into the Rhineland in strict contravention of the Treaties of Versailles and Locarno."

"But my dear man the Rhineland is part of Germany. It is Hitler's own back yard. He is only restoring to the fatherland what belongs to it. The people there have greeted him with rapture. Moreover has he not proposed a treaty to the western powers to guarantee peace for twenty-five years?

Expansionist he may be, ruthless, yes, but you must be assured of his good intentions. I am."

"Well, I quite firmly am *not*." Alexander stood up. "And if you are trying to interest us in your business, and I imagine that is your aim in inviting me here today, I'm afraid it's out of the question. Pieter Heering is fanatically anti-German. He did a lot of business with Germany in the past before Hitler came to power and he will not hear of it now."

"He doesn't need to hear of it," Bart said silkily. "*I* shan't tell him. But I assure you, Alexander, if you were to entertain the proposition I am offering you, you would become an enormously wealthy man. Now, I am aware that you are not exactly poor. But I can tell you in the past two years my profits have expanded tenfold. And who can say 'no' to money so easily come by? Only a fool, and I know you are not one. There is an enormous amount of money to be made in the export of small arms not only to Germany but all over the world. Believe me, this left-wing government in Spain will have trouble on its hands, and as for Italy..." Once more Bart threw his hands in the air in an expression of disbelief.

Alexander, who had been standing by the window looking out, turned. "And what do you need from me, Bart? I'm sure you're not undercapitalised."

Bart shook his head. "On the contrary. There is no shortage of money, but I am hampered by shortage of transport. I can't get enough ships or lorries to transport my goods, and I know you have a world-wide network whose reputation is above reproach. No one would question anything carried by the Martyn-Heering organisation, whereas some of the dubious transporters I am forced to employ..." He shrugged his shoulders. "You know the transport of arms is not illegal. It is just, well, shall we say, not as simple as other kinds of produce. There is so much red tape. It can also lead to theft and crime if the goods are not secure."

"Nevertheless, it is in contravention of the peace treaties. Pieter would simply not tolerate it."

"But if I said..."

Bart stopped as he saw Alexander shaking his head vigorously.

"Bart, I am very sorry. Even if I was interested in your scheme, which I am not, I could not authorise anything without the concurrence of Pieter."

"Then don't tell him the purpose. Just lease me the ships."

Alexander shook his head again.

"I can't. I won't. It is against my principles. But thank you Bart for thinking of me." He held out his hand. "I appreciate it. Now," he looked at his watch, "Lally is expecting company for dinner. I promised not to be late."

Bart's expression of hope gave place to one of resignation and, rising, he put his hand on Alexander's shoulder.

"No hard feelings?"

"None at all. I assure you."

"And you will keep this confidential? I can rely on you, as a member of the family!"

"What family?"

"Why, the Woodville family. In some way or another are we not all connected? Your father is a Woodville and I am married to one. We are all Woodvilles, to a man." He slapped Alexander on the back again. "I like you, Alexander. You're honest and straight. One day I hope we can do business together. I'm sure we shall. In the meantime how's the little girl?"

"Wonderful."

"No problems coping?"

"Oh, none at all. Lally is a devoted grandmother, as you might imagine. Catherine has given her a new lease of life and I could not wish for a better nursemaid than Massie. All I have to do is play the part of loving father, and that's not difficult.

294

Catherine – we call her Kate – is an angel."

"I'm delighted to hear it. I, too, am most fortunate in my family." Momentarily Bart looked solemn. "And I can tell you Alexander. These days that is no small blessing."

June 1936

Colonel George was now known familiarly as Arnold. He was a perfect gentleman. They didn't meet every day, or even every week, but it was a relationship that grew closer, more intimate with the passage of time. Sarah-Jane could almost say he was her regular beau. She was sure he would have been jealous if he saw her with another man.

From time to time Arnold went away. He said he had a daughter in Bristol, another in the south of France, and he would visit them each for several weeks at a time. But withal, he was a mysterious man, gave little of himself and never made any suggestion that was the least improper. Anyway, like her, he relied a good deal on drink, and she suspected he began the day, as she did, with a nip or two of brandy or maybe whisky, in his case, as he was very fond of it.

Sometimes she felt she would be better off

with Arnold than Solomon, but he never brought up the subject of marriage. She thought it was a question of money because, though not mean, he was careful. He always paid for lunch if they had it, but usually at one of the cheaper hotels. She would often insist on paying, at least for some of their drinks, and he would accept. Arnold always saw her home, sometimes by taxi if she was a little the worse for wear. He never attempted to cross the threshold and she never asked him in.

Sarah-Jane, therefore, reacted with some surprise, almost shock, when, one day after they'd been seeing each other more or less regularly for over six months – the pattern the same, never varying – Arnold said, "I wondered if you'd like to have lunch at my place today, my dear? I've asked my man to prepare something for us."

"Your man?" she asked looking surprised, her glass half raised to her lips.

"My servant."

"I didn't know you had a servant." Sarah-Jane had somehow imagined that this solitary man lived alone, or perhaps in a boarding house. The question of his domicile had never arisen.

She had a woman to clean but not to live in. She didn't want anyone keeping an eye on her all day.

"He used to be my batman in the war. Good chap."

Sarah-Jane felt a bit confused. When you were used to a routine it felt a bit odd to have it disturbed.

But perhaps she wanted it disturbed? She looked at Arnold who was stubbing his cigarette out in an ashtray. She had already had four large brandies and he had had an equivalent amount of whisky. She hadn't seen him for some time because he'd been with the Bristol daughter. She'd missed him.

"Well, Arnold," she said after a while, "I suppose it's all right."

"Of course it's all right, my dear." His hand closed over hers. "My man's a first-class cook and from the balcony of my flat there is the most beautiful view of the sea."

"Sounds lovely," Sarah-Jane said, draining her glass, aware of a surge of pleasure and anticipation running through her. After all, with the servant there nothing could possibly happen, unless, of course, one wanted it to.

It was dawn. Time to get up. Solomon lay for some time gazing towards the curtained window, aware of the glimmer of light beyond. He could have done with another two hours' sleep but he had to get up before the servants started to move round the house. Of course, they knew. He was sure they knew. Debbie's maid certainly knew, and he thought Helen and James's nursemaids knew, because one night there had been an emergency – one of the children had started to choke – and they'd opened the bedroom door without knocking. After that Deborah had locked the door but, nevertheless, Solomon was sure they knew.

He felt a hand touch his arm.

"Penny for them?"

"I was thinking about the servants, if they knew."

"What does it matter?"

"You know it matters." He felt a momentary sense of irritation. "Bart would fire me, and God knows what would happen to you if he found out."

"We could go away and get married," she said.

"I'm married already." He was annoyed by her casualness. It was so irresponsible.

Solomon threw back the bedclothes and sat on the side of the bed. He felt out of sorts, uneasy, and this was unusual after a night of love with Deborah. He normally felt elated, youthful, invigorated.

"Solomon?"

"Darling?" He looked around at her.

"Do you love me?"

"You know I love you." He leaned back on the bed and began to caress her. She settled into the crook of his arm.

"It's just that you seem so afraid of Bart."

"My darling, it's not that I'm afraid, but until I am independent – and that time seems a very long way off – I have to be very careful of Bart. He is talking of making me managing director."

"You mean you won't be the architect any more?"

"Well, I can still go on designing houses, but his business is expanding so much. All these trips to the continent means he wants someone in charge."

It was true. Bart was away almost half the year and it had enabled the lovers to resume their affair with, they thought, impunity.

To Sarah-Jane, Solomon pleaded business saying that he stayed at the office which, indeed, had a bedroom with a bathroom *en suite* for emergencies. He imagined that Sarah-Jane didn't care very much. Half the time she probably wouldn't be aware if he was there or not. He thought her drinking was getting heavier. She'd end up in a home.

Solomon kissed Debbie's breasts, the little cleavage between them, her neck, her cheeks. His mouth lingered on her lips.

Suddenly he let her go and gazed earnestly into her eyes.

"I must go before the servants get up."

He rose rapidly, dressed quickly and was standing in front of the dressing table doing his tie when she said, "Do you think we shall ever be able to live together? You know, all the time?"

Solomon shrugged on his jacket, ran his hands through his hair. He perched on the bed and took her hand.

"Don't even think about it."

"But it is what you want, Solomon?"

"Of course it is."

"It's what I want too," she said. "I can't envisage spending the rest of my life with Bart."

Solomon pressed her hand to his lips.

"Darling we must be thankful for what we have. Neither of us is in the position at the moment to change things. Let's live for today. I love you." He bent and kissed her.

"I love you too," she called after him, blowing a kiss.

Solomon always left by a side door on the lookout for staff about their business in the early morning, and then skirted the grounds to the lane about half a mile away where he left his car in the trees.

But of course they knew, the servants all knew. In many ways, he thought, it was just a matter of time before Bart found out. And what then?

The body lay, face upwards as though the sightless eyes were gazing at the first rays of the sun. The sea gently washed over it. It was impossible to know whether it had been brought in by the tide or had lain on the beach overnight.

The early morning runner gazed at the body in shock as the water lapped over it. At first he had thought it was a swimmer out for an early-morning dip. The nearer he got the more apprehensive he had became at the stillness.

The woman was about forty-five, maybe fifty. She could have drowned at sea and been brought in by the tide, or she could have collapsed in the sand, the victim of a sudden seizure, perhaps, a heart attack.

But no. The man, despite his horror and confusion, couldn't fail to see that her face was a curious purplish colour and contused, the tongue protruding from her slack mouth – a ligature tied tightly round her neck.

Solomon got to the office early, had a bath, changed into a clean shirt and ruffled the bed to make it look as though he'd slept there all night. When the secretaries came in they could draw their own conclusions.

He still felt unhappy and uncomfortable, as though the day had got off to a bad start.

He worried about Debbie because he thought that one day she might do something foolish and betray them. Despite being a daughter of the rectory she had a reckless streak, as her past had demonstrated. She seemed unaware of the value of money or the penalties of not having any. She also didn't seem to take quite seriously enough the threat posed by her husband should he discover their liaison, or the fact that he, Solomon, was possibly James's father.

But what to do? He couldn't give Debbie up and he didn't want to. Yet to meet in a hotel room was sordid. Besides she was very well known locally so it would have to be some distance away. It couldn't be Bournemouth, for obvious reasons. He felt they'd got careless with Bart being away such a lot. The fact that the servants knew could also make them open to blackmail.

Yet they couldn't run away because they hadn't any money. Knowing Bart, Solomon was certain they would be pursued to the ends of the earth and a terrible vengeance extracted. Solomon really feared Bart's wrath.

When he'd had his affair with Sarah-Jane the servants had also known. They always found out, servants did. Only then neither of them were married, they were both free and it didn't really matter what the servants saw or thought. What *had* mattered in the end was what her children and local society thought. That had banished them into exile, caused their foolish marriage and precipitated the eventual collapse of their relationship.

Solomon spent all day wrestling with this problem, this fear. In the afternoon he had to go to Dorchester and, at the end of his meeting, instead of going back to the office he decided to go home. In the car he turned from the problem of Bart to the problem of Sarah-Jane and what to do about their disastrous marriage.

What could he do about her, a helpless alcoholic? He felt a kind of pity for her, and remorse. He had ruined her life; because of him she had turned to drink. Without him she could still be living in Wenham, at Riversmead, surrounded by her family and friends, although she'd always told him she wasn't happy until she met him, that he had made her come alive again.

Solomon had been, still was to some extent, a shy, quiet, withdrawn young man, the victim of a rather unhappy home life as a child with a remote father and a mother who didn't know how to show love. He had craved love and when he met Sarah-Jane he thought she was as wise as she was sexually attractive – that she could be at the same time a mother and a mistress to him.

But it hadn't worked out that way. Now, well, frankly, life was a mess.

Solomon got home at about five. The house was empty. He wasn't surprised. He didn't know what Sarah-Jane did with her day, only that when she came home she'd been drinking. She used to talk about a bridge club and meeting friends at various charity functions. He didn't ask too many questions. He wasn't really interested what she did with her time or where she went.

The cleaning woman had been and the house was tidy. It usually was. Yet it had an uncared for, unlived-in feeling as though its occupants spent little time there. Sarah-Jane, who had once been proud of her domesticity, her abilities as a homemaker, took little interest in the new house, possibly because, like the last, it was rented until something better came along. If Solomon had cared about saving their marriage he supposed he would have designed and built them a house, but he had neither the interest nor the time, nor the money to pay for it.

He looked in the Frigidaire for some food and found cold pork which they'd had for lunch on Sunday. If he was at home Sarah-Jane would cook a meal. She was a decent cook, but he often came home late or not at all, pleading business appointments, trips to London and so on. Sometimes they were genuine and sometimes it was when he stayed with Debbie. Altogether they didn't have much of a home life and, really, in many ways it was high time it was ended. But how? That was the problem.

Solomon made himself a drink. He switched on the wireless to listen to the news.

Nothing much. France had followed the example of England in lifting sanctions against Italy over its conquest of Abyssinia. After all, the King of Italy had now been declared Emperor of Abyssinia. It was a *fait accompli*. International politics was a very cynical business. One moment they were all condemning Italy for crushing poor little Abyssinia, the next everything was forgiven. The same was happening to Hitler. Excuses were being offered for every aggressive act perpetrated by him, whether against neighbouring countries or the Jews.

Solomon switched off the news and read the evening paper. By seven o'clock he began to wonder where Sarah-Jane was. He helped himself to cold pork, had a beer and then wandered out into the garden. The neighbour was mowing his lawn and Solomon went over to the hedge that divided them, and asked if he happened to have seen his wife.

The neighbour, who was not very friendly, shook his head and went on mowing.

Eight o'clock came, nine and then ten.

Maybe she'd gone to stay with somebody? Shouldn't he call the police? No, that was fanciful, stupid. She was possibly paying him back for all the nights he spent away from her. Only he always let her know that he wasn't coming home. Spiteful of her not to do the same.

Solomon slept fitfully. He woke up constantly, thinking that he'd heard something. But there was nothing, no one there. He fell into a deep sleep just before dawn and woke at eight, realising that he had a meeting at nine and he had an hour to shower, dress and get to Blandford.

He turned on the radio as he shaved. He listened to the morning news and was just about to switch off when the newsreader said, "The body of an unidentified woman has been found on the beach at Bournemouth. The police file of missing persons is being scrutinised..."

Sarah-Jane looked very peaceful, as though she'd fallen asleep, although her flesh was discoloured and her mouth swollen, as if she'd been in an accident.

306

"It is my wife," Solomon said.

"You're sure, sir?"

"Quite sure." Solomon looked at the policeman who was staring at him rather than at the corpse. "How did she die?"

"She was strangled, sir, with a ligature."

At a sign from the policeman the attendant lowered the sheet covering the body to reveal an ugly, deep purple mark that made it seem as though an attempt had been made to sever her head.

Solomon felt a surge of emotion that was partly grief and partly revulsion and turned away, covering his face. The policeman put a hand on his arm and gently steered him out of the room.

All Wenham was in shock. Disasters, scandals, misfortunes of all kinds had afflicted the Woodvilles and families connected with them, but never murder.

Sarah-Jane had been found dead on the beach at Bournemouth and the police wasted no time in arresting Solomon for her murder. He had no alibi but had an apparent motive, as it was known that the marriage was not happy. What was more plausible than a discontented husband, shackled to a much older woman, strangling her and dumping her body on the beach, then reporting her missing?

Bart Sadler drove home after seeing his sister's body. He was shocked and saddened at what had occurred in his absence in Germany. He arranged for a solicitor to represent Solomon, but had no desire to see him. Like the police he couldn't think of anyone else who would wish to kill his sister, although he found it extremely difficult to envisage the gentle, cultured Solomon as a murderer pulling that ligature, a length of piano wire, tightly round Sarah-Jane's neck, probably as she slept, and carrying her body to the beach in the dead of night. The time of death was estimated at late afternoon or early evening when Solomon would apparently have, on his own admission, been home alone with his wife.

The police would not release her body for burial. Already Martha and Felicity had come down from London, but Bart didn't wish to see his nieces either. They'd done their mother few good turns in recent years.

Bart felt a wave of pity for his sister. He knew what it was like to feel rejected by the community, to be an exile. That, probably, in the end was what brought them together, and now that she was no longer there he wished he'd done more. He'd known she drank too much, and he should have tried to find out why. Instead he had tried to pretend that it wasn't a problem and had pushed it under the carpet, out of his mind. He pleaded business pressures as an excuse for everything, even the little he saw of his children except to kiss them good-night. He neglected Debbie. He was away far too much and he took an acceptance of his lifestyle for granted. He adored his family. But, in truth, it was from afar.

It was an angry and bitter, but also chastened, man who arrived back at Upper Park. But as he entered the house a chill wind seemed to greet him and, imagining it still to be the influence of the morgue, he hurried upstairs calling for his wife.

"And the children? Where are the children?" he asked, seeing Harold standing in the hall below.

"They have gone out with their nurse I believe, sir. Madam had a headache and is lying on her bed."

"I won't disturb her then."

Harold gave a discreet cough. "May I say, Mr Sadler, on behalf of the staff, how distressed we all are..."

"Thank you," Bart said curtly. "You could bring me a whisky and water in the drawing room please, Harold."

"Yes, sir."

Bart hesitated outside the drawing-room door, wondering if after all he should go and see Debbie. He was aware of an emotion he seldom felt: loneliness, desolation, a need to be comforted. He knew he had few real friends. He thought Solomon had been one, his sister another. Most people pandered to him because they were afraid of him. None of the Woodvilles liked him, Abel wouldn't speak to him. Eliza avoided him. Alexander, though polite, wasn't a friend. The immediate members of his own family, many of whom he had helped financially, had little to do with him. They received but they did not give. There was no love for him, no warmth.

He was overcome by self-pity, and felt desperately in need of the love and comfort of his wife, the one person on whom he felt he could really depend.

He went into the drawing room and after Harold had brought him his whisky he stood by the window looking out across his land. All of it was his, as far as the eye could see, mile upon mile of lush Dorset countryside which, one day, his son would inherit.

A sense of peace and joy began slowly to infuse him. After all, the future did lie in one's children. The mistakes that one had made in the past would be obliterated by the generations that came after him. He would leave land, property, a colossal fortune to make the name 'Sadler' one, not only to reckon with, but to be proud of. He was the first Sadler – farmers for generations in Dorset – to achieve something, to make real money.

Bart replenished his glass of whisky just as the door opened and Debbie came in, or rather she crept in. She looked terrible, her face ashen, and he thought he detected signs of tears.

"My dear," he said anxiously, going up to her, "you look ill. You should not have got up on my account. You must go straight back to bed." He put a hand on her forehead. "Have you a fever? Shall I call the doctor?"

Deborah shook her head, then taking Bart by the hand, drew him down on to the sofa, sitting him next to her.

As he gazed at her in alarm she put her other hand over the one that she held. Bart could feel how cold she was, in a contrast to her burning brow and, remembering that sad corpse in the morgue, the awful chill of death, he was suddenly filled again with fear.

"Debbie, my darling, what is it? You're afraid of something. What?" He wanted to stroke her head again, but fear held him back.

"Bart." Debbie pressed his hand between hers and, somehow, found the courage to gaze straight at him. "It is not easy to tell you this. I have wrestled with my con-science, but there is no way out for me. Even if it ruins my life I can't let a good, an innocent, man die."

"What *is* it Debbie?" Bart asked urgently. "What are you trying to tell me?" For one of the few times in his life Bart suddenly felt real terror, an awful premonition that disaster was about to strike.

"Bart ... Solomon did not kill Sarah-Jane. He couldn't have. He was not with her the night she died. He was with me."

Thirteen

August 1936

"Man that is born of woman ... ashes to ashes, dust to dust."

As the rector's voice echoed round the churchyard Carson thought this sad and familiar phrase from the burial service had occurred too often in the past few years – Nelly, Mary, now poor Sarah-Jane laid, finally, to her rest.

There had been some dispute about the funeral as Bart had wanted to have her body cremated at a private ceremony in Bournemouth, but family wishes had prevailed. Her son and two daughters were strongly of the opinion that she should be buried beside her first husband who had so long predeceased her.

Eliza, who so seldom cried, found it hard to restrain her tears. Sarah-Jane had been her son, Laurence's, wife, and though she had changed after his death, Eliza recalled the many happy years the couple had together early in the century. Then the sun had always seemed to shine on the healthy, handsome, loving couple with their three happy children who now, dressed in deepest mourning, stood next to her watching in silence as the coffin was gently lowered into the grave.

What were their thoughts, Eliza wondered? She stole a look at Martha, who was trying with difficulty to hold back tears. Eliza surreptitiously took her hand. Solomon, a little apart from the rest, was a lonely figure apparently ostracised by everyone. The townspeople were divided about his release from police custody because of Deborah's evidence that he had spent the night with her. Half of them thought she was trying to cover up for him and that he probably had murdered the wife with whom everyone knew he wasn't happy. The other half gave him the benefit of the doubt, but they still regarded him with suspicion. So little was known about him: where he came from, who his parents were. His effect on the small community in a short time had been devastating, first for having run off with Sarah-Jane and then for having come under suspicion of killing her. For a mild-mannered, soft spoken, almost self-effacing young man, this was no mean achievement.

His former employee having been

summarily dismissed from his service, Bart stood well away from him, even turning his back on him as the coffin sank out of sight.

When, at last, it came to rest the rector stepped forward, took a handful of earth from the mound by the side of the grave and let it fall upon the coffin. Then he looked around him. No one moved. Solomon had his eyes cast to the ground; Bart seemed to be studying the sky. Then Eliza bent down, took up some earth and gave it to Abel who, as the first-born, impassively threw it on his mother's coffin. He was followed by his wife, Ruth, then his sisters, Martha and Felicity. Eliza stood for a moment, thinking of that year in 1912 when Laurence had been laid to rest, reflecting on the awful irony that husband and wife had both met death by violent means: one by his own hand, the other by that of someone else.

The family formed a small queue to perform the last rite before the ground closed over Sarah-Jane's earthly remains. First came the many members of the Sadler family, Sarah-Jane's sisters and brothers, the last of whom was Bart. They hurried about their task, not lingering by the coffin. The Woodville family came next: Carson, Sally, Alexander, Lally, Sophie Turner, her sons Sam and James, Dora, and Agnes. Last of all, belonging to no one really, Solomon.

He stood for several minutes, his eyes closed as if he was saying a prayer – perhaps asking for forgiveness? Then he moved away. After him sporadic members of the public came to cast earth upon the coffin, mainly to see as much as they could before it was covered up for ever.

As the gravediggers set about their melancholy task, the churchyard slowly emptied. Everyone moved towards the gate, some stopping in little groups *en route* to chat.

Sarah-Jane had never been very popular in the town. Few had memories as long as Eliza and could not recall the happy, laughing, wholesome sort of girl she had been when she was a young married woman full of energy and laughter. They could only remember the rather bitter widow she had become. Although a member of the large and well-known Sadler family, prosperous farmers in the locality, she had withdrawn from the community after Laurence's death and taken no part in the life of the town, unlike her mother-in-law, Eliza who was into everything. Sarah-Jane had then achieved notoriety by having an affair with a man twenty-three years her junior, and running off with him. Some of the more censorious might have unkindly thought that she deserved her fate though, if they did, they were careful not to say so.

Few came genuinely to mourn her. The majority of the townsfolk turned out to gawp, to observe the behaviour and demeanour, above all the expressions of the members of Sarah-Jane's family who had been stricken yet again by tragedy, by scandal and, finally, by mystery. If Solomon hadn't murdered his wife, who had?

Sally stood by the gate with Dora and Eliza. There was to be no family gathering. It didn't seem appropriate, somehow. They shook hands with many of the townsfolk who stopped in the hope of gathering a bit more gossip. But they had none to give. They could tell them no more than was public knowledge. Eventually they were joined by Sophie and Lally, with Agnes dawdling along behind talking to Hubert Turner.

"I'm taking Abel, Martha and Felicity back to Riversmead for a drink or a cup of tea. Would you like to join us?" Eliza asked Sally, who nodded.

"That would be nice, but I think Carson has some business with Bart. I don't think he'll come."

"Did anyone see Solomon go?" Eliza looked around, but he was nowhere to be seen. "I feel rather sorry for him." Everyone shook their heads.

"I think he slipped out by the side gate,"

Sophie said. "Poor man. I feel sorry for him too. He once saved my life, you know. I wish I could do more for him but, in view of what has happened..." she left her sentence unfinished.

"We know, we know," Eliza said. "I think Carson is going to talk to Bart today about the situation."

She was referring to the fact that Debbie had been ejected by Bart from the house after her confession and sent home to her mother.

"I must get back to Debbie," Sophie murmured. "She is really in a terrible state."

Eliza nodded understandingly. "Would you like me to come in too? I can, the others can go on without me." But Sophie shook her head.

"Perhaps later. Maybe Carson will have some news for us."

Eliza beckoned to Sarah-Jane's children and, with Lally, they set off along the path across the fields to Riversmead leaving Sally and Dora to wait for Carson and Alexander, who had moved on to two graves where they now stood silently, oblivious to the rest of the mourners, heads bowed.

The tombstones now bore the legends:

Nelly Allen
Born 1889 Died 1931
Mother of Alexander

Mary Martyn
1917–1932
Beloved wife of Alexander and mother
of Catherine Mary

"You know I think he still loves Nelly," Sally murmured sadly, and Dora put a comforting hand round her shoulders.

"He may still love Nelly, why not? But I'm sure he loves you."

"You think so?" Sally shook her head. "I think if only I'd known what a complex character Carson was I should never have married him."

"That's what makes him so appealing," Dora said. "But don't forget you're complex too." Her grip on Sally's shoulder tightened as if in an expression of solidarity, as well as understanding. "Come on – let's go and have a drink with mother."

"Whisky?" Carson asked.

"Thank you," Bart said. He remained standing while Carson poured the drinks and handed him his glass.

"Do sit down," Carson pointed to a chair. They were in his study off the main hall.

Carson sat opposite him, but before he could speak Bart said, "I suppose this is about Debbie?"

"Naturally, I feel some responsibility for her."

"Well, I'm not taking her back."

Carson studied his glass.

"That, in the circumstances, may be excusable, but to deprive a mother of her children is not."

"Debbie is not fit to be a mother, you know that."

"On the contrary, every time I have seen her with the children she has struck me as a very good mother."

"You're forgetting the bastard son in Bristol. She has never set eyes on him almost, I think, since his birth."

"That is very sad but understandable. It was a very traumatic time for Debbie. She was very young. The boy is well looked after and cared for."

Bart sat back in his chair and stared at Carson, the expression on his face severe. Carson had never had anything against Bart, hadn't shared the hostility of the rest of the family towards him. But he knew he had an uphill task to ensure that Debbie got fair play. Bart was the sort of man you deceived at your peril and he thought Deborah should have known this.

There was a very irresponsible streak in his niece and she had caused a great deal of trouble in her life. However, she was flesh and blood, the daughter of his brother George and he would act for her *in loco parentis*. It was no less than his duty.

But for a proud man, what Debbie had done was inexcusable, and Bart was not only proud but powerful, and violent too. Not for nothing was he feared by people who knew him.

"What is it you propose, Bart?"

"I propose to divorce Deborah and apply for custody of my children. I have no doubt I shall succeed. I shall try and prevent her having anything more to do with them, but I may not be as successful in this. I shall try and keep contact between them to a minimum. I may, as a matter of fact, even sell up and move out of the area. It's not something I want to do as I have my business interests here, and I love my house, on which I've spent a fortune. But I may. I may even move abroad or live there for much of the year. I haven't decided. Germany is a place that appeals to me. Not the cities, but somewhere like the Bavarian mountains or the Black Forest."

"But what about the situation there?"

"That has no terrors for me. I'm convinced there won't be a war. Once Hitler has what he wants he will settle down and make friends with everyone. You'll see."

"I wish I shared your confidence."

Bart finished his whisky and stood up. "I think that has taken care of things, Carson."

"Not really." Carson rose too. "You can't expect Deborah to want to stay with her mother. She's not a child. For the moment she needs Sophie but, eventually, she will want her own house. I am not satisfied that the court will grant you sole custody of the children. It will be vigorously opposed. But what Deborah needs right now is financial support from you to find her own home. And I can assure you that if it is not forthcoming, Bart, things will be made very difficult for you.

"You may consider yourself a powerful man, but I am not without influence and I shall do everything in my power to protect the interests of my niece."

"Thank you for the whisky," Bart said stiffly. "I'll see myself out."

After Bart had gone Carson remained where he was for some moments watching his car speed down the drive. He reflected sadly on the fact that neither of them, in the course of conversation, had once referred to poor Sarah-Jane, as though now that she was dead she was no longer a person of consequence. Reluctantly he had been drawn into Bart's selfish determination to rid himself as quickly as he could of his wife, so that he had forgotten Sarah-Jane too.

When Sally got back to Pelham's Oak in the early afternoon she found Carson waiting for her in the hall.

"I wondered where you were." he said.

Sally smiled. "I went back to Riversmead for a drink with Eliza. We all felt we needed it."

Carson grunted and the reason for his missing her soon became clear. He was in a melancholy mood, and wanted to talk. He told her about Bart's visit and admitted his guilty thoughts about Sarah-Jane, and his concern about his niece.

"After all," Sally said when she'd heard about Bart's determination to wreak vengeance on his wife, "you cannot really *blame* him. Debbie should have thought of all this before she got into bed with Solomon. I think you're too ready to forgive her because she's your niece."

Sally turned towards the hall mirror and began to take off her hat. Black depressed her and unrelieved black had been the order of the day. She shook out her hair and immediately felt better, groped in her bag for a cigarette and then gave her full attention to her husband.

Carson, arms akimbo, leaned against the great oak chest, carved with the Woodville arms, that had stood in the hall for as long as he could remember. Legend had it that it was carved from the oak which had preceded the one planted by Pelham. Maybe, therefore, the present oak was the progeny of the one that had been made into the great hall chest – an unbroken succession for hundreds of years, rather like the Woodvilles.

"I don't want to make excuses, but I'm concerned about Debbie. I mean, she can't be cast off without a penny. And she does love her children. Besides, it's very unfair on Sophie who has had quite enough hardship in her life. I thought," he paused, remembering the furore his behaviour had caused when Connie was his wife, and went on hesitantly, "I thought we could have her here for a while. I mean, we've plenty of room."

Sally puffed on her cigarette and gazed thoughtfully at the ceiling, saying nothing.

"I mean, would you mind?" Carson went on, "It would only be until we had a settlement. But Debbie doesn't get on too well with her mother and—"

"You can't help coming to the aid of the underdog, can you Carson?" Sally's smile this time was a little forced. "That's one of the things that Dora warned me about you."

"Oh really?" Carson's expression was impassive. "And what else did she warn you about?"

"She said you were complex." Sally, extinguished her cigarette, went up to him and put her arm around his neck. "And that I was too. Look, why don't we get changed and let the wind blow the cobwebs away, go for a ride?"

It was a good idea. The morning had been dull, but now the clouds had dispersed and the land around seemed to sparkle in the sunshine. Carson felt his good humour and his equilibrium returning. Sally was really expert at defusing situations. She had an innate common sense that Connie had lacked. Whereas Connie would have made a fuss about offering a temporary home to Debbie – she also had accused him of always supporting lame ducks – Sally would think about it and when she had, give a measured response. Connie flew off the handle and sulked. He had never seen Sally sulk. She just became thoughtful which was more positive.

They cantered down the meadow leading from the house, gathering speed as they jumped the hedge and galloped across the fields to where Ryder's white-washed cottage gleamed with a recently applied coat of fresh paint.

As they neared it Sally slowed down and Carson, behind her, slowed too.

"Are you going to let it again?" she asked.

"Oh no. It is Massie's home for as long as she wants it. I mean she's going to need time off from looking after Kate." By now they had stopped and Sally was gazing at the cottage.

"Is it open? Can we go in?"

"You've never seen inside?"

Sally shook her head.

Carson jumped off his horse, tethered him to the post by the gate and, walking up the path, tried the handle of the door. It opened and he beckoned to Sally who followed his example, joining him in the pleasant main room of the cottage with its pretty chintzy covered chairs, long shining table and large inglenook with fresh logs ready to be lit for a fire.

"What a lovely place," Sally murmured looking round.

"It belonged to Uncle Ryder.

"I know," Sally nodded. "That's why I wanted to see it. He died before I was born. Do you remember him?"

Carson shook his head.

"I was only young when he died. About eight."

"He had an accident didn't he?"

Carson nodded. "Fell off the roof of the cottage at Forest House, which was why Julius Heering would never live there."

"It must have been awful for Aunt Eliza."

"It was." Carson's sombre mood returned. "We've had a lot of bad luck in the family."

"No more than most." Sally put an arm around Carson's waist. "Show me upstairs."

"Why do you want to see upstairs?" He looked down at her.

"Because I do." And removing her arm, she ran up the stairs ahead of him and into the main bedroom which had pretty blue walls and a narrow single bed with a white counterpane. Through the window it was possible to see Pelham's Oak a couple of miles distant on the top of the hill. Sally went over to the window and, unfastening the catch, threw it wide open.

She was aware of Carson behind her and when she felt his breath on her neck she suddenly turned.

"Was this Nelly's room?"

As if taken aback, he could only nod.

"Was it where she died?"

Carson nodded again, and suddenly his features seemed to crumble and his eyes filled with tears.

"Oh, my dear," Sally cried, flinging her arms around him again. "Forgive me. I didn't mean to upset you." She gazed into his eyes and saw the tormented expression on his face.

"You still love her, don't you Carson? I saw you standing by her grave today and I knew then how you felt. You were miles away." Carson didn't reply and Sally went on. "I think Nelly was the love of your life. For her you sacrificed your marriage to Connie. The only thing is," she paused as if struggling to find words, "I don't really know why you married me. I don't think you've ever really loved me, Carson."

"I did. I do." Carson's voice sounded strangely unlike his own. "I can love you and Nelly too. I don't want to forget her."

"That's what Dora said." Sally drew away from him and sat on the bed.

"You have been talking to Dora a lot, haven't you?" Carson said scathingly.

"It's just that, well, she knows you, and I don't. You're a very hard person to know, Carson. I don't think I understand you at all."

Carson went over to be bed and sat down beside her.

"I'm sorry." He put his arm around her shoulder. "I will try and do better."

"You can't show affection you don't feel. It's," Sally's tone grew bitter, "not something you can manufacture."

"But I do feel it. I do love you, not as I loved Nelly, not as I loved Connie. Different but still love. I want you to believe that Sally." He turned her face towards him and gazed earnestly into her eyes.

She returned his gaze wishing hard that she could believe him, here in Nelly's room, where she'd died.

September 1936

Martha Yetman looked round the sitting room of the house where her mother had spent her last days. It was a large, though rather impersonal dwelling, with little sign of having been lived in, few intimate possessions.

Solomon had asked her to clear out the house, as he felt himself unable to go back there. He had left for an unknown destination – at least unknown to the family. The police who had released him so reluctantly would know where he was.

Martha worked on a newspaper in Fleet Street; one of the few successful women journalists of her day. She had started as a typist and worked her way up. The stories she was given were largely women's issues and she neither wished, nor had the strength to report on the murder of her mother. She was grateful they did not have the same name, so she could preserve her anonymity. Not that the murder had provoked much comment in the national dailies. At first it had seemed an open and shut case of a disgruntled and dissatisfied husband killing his wife. But now Martha knew there was more to it than that. She was quite convinced that Solomon was innocent because a disquieting picture had emerged of her mother as a sad, lonely woman with a drink problem who frequented Bournemouth hotels and picked up men, any one of whom could have killed her.

It was an image so alien to the woman she had known that, at first, Martha could hardly believe it. It was so unlike the strict, mother who had brought them up, not exactly with a rod of iron but with discipline and little outward affection. Martha had only been five when her father died and it was an event she could not recall. There was a hazy recollection of a catastrophic event, before which she had a faint recollection of a jolly childhood with lots of laughter and, at the time, love bestowed on her, her sister and brother by their parents.

Sarah-Jane had never been very tactile, she did not kiss and hug but she had been warm and when Laurence died that warmth and spontaneity went with him. Perhaps she had loved him too much.

Martha wandered around the house and thought there was very little to do here, a few scattered objects, nothing really personal. It was a rather chilly autumn day and the cold seemed to permeate the house, making it even less welcoming. She would be glad to be done by nightfall. Then she could close the house and restore the key to the solicitors who would see about the disposal of the contents and the furniture.

Her mother had not left a will, at least none could be found, but then she had little to leave and what there was would go to her husband. Martha thought how sad it was not to have any mementoes of the woman who had given birth to her and when she walked into the bedroom she picked up a cardigan that had been thrown over a chair and pressed it to her face. She fancied she could smell the very essence of her mother, the faint fragrance she'd worn, the familiar, not unpleasant, body odour. The close sense of bonding that an infant has at the breast.

Martha's eyes filled with tears and she sat on the chair hugging the cardigan as if it had been her mother's body last seen in the funeral parlour a few days before her funeral. The face had been made up and, except for traces of swelling that remained, she had looked very peaceful. A scarf had been tactfully arranged round her neck, disguising any sign of visible injury.

Martha had not wept then or at her funeral, but she wept now. After Laurence's death, Sarah-Jane had become remote, fault finding, a bitter woman who took her sorrow out on her children. The girls, who perhaps had suffered more than the only boy, left home as soon as they could, Felicity to train as a nurse, Martha as a shorthand-typist.

It had been a terrible shock when they had learned about Solomon; but why should it have been? It was unreasonable of them not to wish her happiness. But at the time, a woman of fifty sleeping with a man twenty-three years her junior had seemed obscene, made worse by the fact it was their mother even though she had been a widow for twenty years.

Martha rose, putting the cardigan to one side, and opened the long mahogany wardrobe. One section, where Solomon had kept his suits, was clear. The other showed a collection of dresses and ladies' costumes for all occasions.

On the top shelf were hats of various descriptions: pill-box, ones with rolled up brims, a Russian-style fur toque, several berets, a fez, turbans with draped bands. Some looked as though they'd never been worn.

Next she went to the dresser and opened the drawers one by one. Everything was very neat. Underclothes pressed, folded and ready to wear: neat petticoats with lace tops, cami-knickers in crêpe de Chine with lace bodices and lace edging, satin panties and brassières, nightgowns of flowered chiffon still faintly perfumed. In the lower drawers were handbags and gloves, some of which also looked as though they had hardly been worn.

All this was an eye-opener. Her mother had certainly got smarter, taken more care of her appearance, in recent years.

The dressing table told the same story with a variety of cosmetics: creams, powders, lipsticks and rouges. Martha never remembered her mother wearing a hat or using make-up at all until Solomon came along.

She wandered back to the dresser and began inspecting the selection of handbags, some in fabric for evenings, some in leather, many scarcely used. Some were wrapped in their original tissue paper. The one she must have taken the day she died had never been found. Discarded, perhaps, on some rubbish tip by the murderer.

Murderer. Martha shuddered. It was a horrible word for a horrible deed.

She took a selection of the bags and went

and sat on the bed inspecting each one. She marvelled at this revelation of a woman who she felt she had scarcely known.

She paused in the act of opening a bag made of fine black calf and gazed out of the window. Maybe they had been unfair to their mother. They should have tried to understand her better. But when she drank too much she had became an embarrassment, an object of pity and contempt rather than someone they should have tried to help and understand. Instead they had wanted to distance themselves from her. She remembered her mother falling over at Grandma Eliza's party and having to be carried out of the room. On the few occasions she'd visited her in Brighton her mother appeared to have fortified herself beforehand for the visit.

Initially, Martha supposed, there had been a hint of jealousy of their mother when she had remarried. It seemed a bit unfair that she had been married twice and neither of her daughters had married at all. She'd had three children, but Abel and Ruth were unable to produce any. Martha knew that Abel badly wanted a family. Sometimes she thought theirs was the legacy of bad luck, the suicide of their father followed by their mother's years of depression, and now the awful fact of her murder.

Felicity had had an affair with a doctor, but Martha had never had anyone. Her virginity weighed heavily upon her. She didn't know why it was that she didn't attract men, whether she was too cold or not flirtatious enough, but so far love had passed her by. It wasn't that she didn't like men. She did. She had quite liked Solomon when she first met him, and had wondered if perhaps he was interested in her when all the time it had been her mother.

She wanted to love and be loved, to be married, to have children, a nice home, all the things that so many other people had. The sort of jolly, noisy, busy bustling place, with animals and people coming and going, that she dimly remembered from those days before father died. The sort of homes that her Uncle Carson and her grandmother, Eliza, and so many other people had, or used to have. Why not her?

She looked up and gazed at herself in the mirror of the dressing room, facing the bed. She didn't think she was bad-looking. Tall, but not too tall, slim but by no means thin. Quite a nice bust, she thought, not too big, not too small. She had brown curly hair, brown eyes and a rather olive skin like her grandmother. Martha smiled at herself in the mirror to reveal even teeth, a well-shaped mouth with an orangey lipstick which matched her colouring. She wore a beige linen suit and had left her hat and bag in the hall.

Why was it, then, that at the age of twenty-nine she, a good looking woman and earning good money, appeared to be on the shelf?

Martha bent her head and opened the bag still on her lap. It was empty as she had expected it to be, like the others, except for a clean handkerchief and comb and a little pillbox which, when opened, proved to be empty too.

She was about to shut the bag and return it to the drawer when she saw something tucked in one of the side pockets and drew it out.

It was a white visiting card and engraved on it in impeccably good style was a single name:

Colonel A.C. George MC

The police were excited by Martha's discovery. They thought that 'Colonel George' could well answer the description of the tall, distinguished-looking man of military bearing with whom Sarah-Jane had been seen during her last weeks.

A hunt began for a man of that name in the bars, the hotels, the boarding houses and apartment blocks, as well as residences of all kinds in the smarter parts and less salubrious areas of Bournemouth. Hotel registers were examined, electoral lists, hundreds of shopkeepers questioned. Further afield the help of the army was sought, the roll of the holders of the Military Cross inspected. Other unsolved murders of women in the area and beyond were scrutinised for clues. Similarities in the method of execution were compared and assessed.

Nothing. Another Colonel George proved to have no common characteristics with the one they sought.

As time passed the police became convinced that the elusive Colonel George was their man but his name was false and his whereabouts remained a mystery. The murder of Sarah-Jane Palmer stood on the files of the Dorset police, unsolved.

Fourteen

January 1937

For a modern man Bart Sadler had very Victorian ideas about parenting. For one who had been so determined to keep them, he had little to do with his children. When he was at home he saw them twice a day, spending a little more time with them at night than in the morning, when he visited them after breakfast before setting off for work. In the evening he would sit and watch them at play, or occasionally read them a story as they huddled round his knee.

He still had a deep sense of grievance about Deborah, a feeling that he had been very badly wounded, a desire to do her harm, to get even with her. Deborah had never got on well with her mother particularly since her elopement with Bart, who had been her mother's lover. He understood she was staying with Carson at Pelham's Oak now. Meanwhile, he was proceeding with the divorce although, acting on

Carson's instructions, the solicitor was putting every difficulty he could in Bart's way. Deborah was making counter claims for the custody of the children on the grounds of Bart's suitability as a parent and his many absences abroad.

Helen was Bart's favourite child. She was golden-haired, bright-eyed, good-tempered, good-natured – a happy, laughing child. She was not at all in awe of Bart whereas little James was, clearly ill at ease when his father entered the nursery rather ominously shutting the door behind him. Although still a baby, James missed his mother more than Helen who was Daddy's girl. She had been told Mummy had gone away, but even she eventually began to ask when she was coming back. Bart had hoped that with the passage of time they would forget their mother, but they didn't. They seemed to miss her more, especially James.

On this particular evening towards the end of January Bart had read them a story and he now sat in a deep armchair in front of the nursery fire watching them at play. Helen was very sweet and protective of her little brother. The children could not have been more different. James, in contrast to Helen's fairness, had curly brown hair and brown eyes. He was an extraordinarily lovable and docile child, but so shy and nervous that he often made Bart wonder how a son of his could be so unlike him.

As he looked at James playing quietly with his toys, while his sister skipped noisily around with her nurse, Bart was suddenly struck by something that had never occurred to him before. He leaned forward and stared intently at James for several seconds before calling his nurse over. She dropped what she was doing and came immediately.

"Yes, sir?"

"I want to ask you something," Bart said, indicating that she should come nearer.

"Yes, sir?" Obediently Jemima bent so that her ear was very close to Bart's mouth.

"Who do you think young James resembles? Me or his mother?"

Jemima looked up, a smile of relief on her face at this seemingly innocuous question. Bart was greatly feared by all the staff, most of whom had at some time or other had received the sharp edge of his tongue. The nursery staff were no exception, particularly since Deborah had left and they were answerable only to him.

Nevertheless, anxious not to be caught out, Jemima took some time in a careful appraisal of James before delivering judgment. Fearing a trap she decided to err on the side of caution.

"Well, sir. It's hard to say, but he don't

favour either. He is not like you, neither in looks or temperament. And the same with his mother."

"Exactly!" Bart said solemnly stroking his chin. "I don't know why I didn't see it before."

"What's that, sir?" Jemima asked nervously.

"Never mind," Bart snapped. He jumped up and, without saying 'good-night' either to her or to the children, he peremptorily left the room.

Jemima, hand to mouth, stood and watched him, her heart thumping anxiously, wondering with consternation what on earth she had done wrong.

Sophie Turner hadn't spoken more than a few words to Bart Sadler since their brief and, in her self-critical eyes, sordid affair had ended in the year 1912. Sophie was the daughter of a parson. She had also married a parson who had died while working in the far-off mission field. All her life she had been of a deeply religious disposition, devoting herself to God and His work, only to succumb to a temptation of the flesh for which she despised herself ever afterwards and felt the most enormous guilt. Shortly after their disastrous relationship ended Bart had gone abroad and Sophie had married the rector's curate, Hubert Turner, who had long courted her. The son who was born to her in the course of the next year was not her husband's, as he knew. He was a kind and compassionate, as well as loving, man.

Bart Sadler's undoubted son, Sam Turner, now twenty-two years of age, looked very much like his natural father. He was a tall, saturnine young man, with fine brown, hooded eyes and a mass of dark, untidy hair. His general impression was unkempt, his manner buccaneering. Although he had been well educated he had never taken to scholarship. He was clever with his hands and, on leaving school, had become apprenticed to a builder in Taunton with whom he also lodged. His parents were glad to have him so far away because when he was at home he was disruptive, and a bad influence on his younger brother, Timothy.

Sophie awaited Bart with apprehension having been informed by her maid, Polly, that he had arrived on the doorstep and wished to see her on a matter of some urgency. She turned at the sound of a knock on the door of her sitting room and her voice weakened as she bade him come in.

Bart stood for a moment on the threshold looking at Sophie before he turned and shut the door.

"I can see you're not very pleased to see me, Sophie," he said, as he walked towards her.

"I am *never* pleased to see you, Mr Sadler. Less now than ever. You know that. You almost destroyed my life and now you have destroyed my daughter's. I would like you to state your business and be gone."

Momentarily Bart appeared uncomfortable and looked around for somewhere to sit.

Sophie remained standing and in the end he stood where he was, facing her.

"I think you do me a grave injustice, Sophie – and, by the way, I insist on calling you 'Sophie' as I once did."

"You may call me what you like," she said frostily. "I shall never address you in any way but by your surname. I would prefer not to address you at all, not even to see you. However," she shrugged, "I have my daughter's welfare at heart and I suppose you have come to see me about her."

Bart shook his head.

"Do you mind if I smoke?" he asked, producing a cigarette case. "I don't suppose there's any point in offering you one?"

"Thank you I don't smoke," Sophie replied. "Do I understand you are not here about Deborah?"

"That is in the hands of the solicitors."

Bart lit his cigarette with a gold lighter which he tucked back in the pocket of his waistcoat. He sat down, indicating to Sophie that she should do likewise.

"Make yourself comfortable Sophie. I am not here to seduce you, you know. We have a lot to talk about."

"Such as?" Sophie's face flushed with anger at the impertinence of his remark. She perched gingerly on the very edge of a chair and gazed across at him.

"Our son, Sam."

"You want to talk about Sam?" Sophie asked, amazed.

"He is my son is he not? Everyone says so."

"Oh, do they?"

"There is no point taking that attitude with me, Sophie. You were pregnant when you married Mr Turner, pregnant with *my* child. I did not know it because you did not tell me, for reasons of your own, doubtless. But since I have returned to this area a number of people have told me in what haste you and Mr Turner were married. Even then he could not have fathered the child born to you a few months after the wedding unless of course he and you..." Bart paused suggestively, giving her a sly smile. "I don't believe for a moment that a man of the cloth would transgress the laws of God by anticipating the marriage act, unless of course led on by *you*, Sophie." His gaze was so insolent that Sophie felt a fresh surge of blood rush to her cheeks. "I know what a temptress you were, what a hot-blooded woman, enough to stir the loins of any normal male, even a curate, you would imagine."

Sophie rose abruptly from her seat and walked towards the door. As she passed him, Bart caught hold of her hand and held it so tightly that she nearly cried out in pain.

"Just you stay where you are, Sophie Turner, and listen to me. I've had quite enough from the women of your family. First there was you with your provocative, virginal ways – although a widow with children – coupled with 'come-hitherish' glances, which drove a man wild. Then there was my poor, misguided sister Sarah-Jane who accused me of killing her husband. Next came her mother-in-law, Eliza, who tried to stop me buying her house, for the same reason. Last, but by no means least, was your flighty little daughter, no virgin when I married her, the mother of a bastard, who repaid my kindness and the love and affection I gave her – to say nothing of all the gifts I bestowed on her – by cuckolding me with a man I now believe to be James's real father."

"Oh no!" Sophie took advantage of a momentary lapse of attention on the part of her persecutor and pulled her hand away from his. She stood there rubbing the red weals his rough grasp had made and, gazing at him with hatred. She felt for the first time in her life that she would gladly have killed him had the opportunity and the means arisen. Appalled by the violence of her emotions she hurriedly sat down, aware that she was shaking violently.

"I see you have disturbed yourself, Sophie." Bart sneered. "And with reason. You say I have harmed your family, but look what they have done to *me*. Left me with the child of a cuckoo in my nest, a bastard who I am meant to feed and clothe."

"I don't see how you can possibly..." Sophie stammered, as Bart's wrath grew more violent.

"Have you ever *looked* at the boy? Studied him? No of course you haven't because you've hardly ever seen him. You don't know your grandchildren, Sophie, because you did not wish to know your daughter after she married me. A fine mother and grandmother you are, and Deborah takes after you! Well, James is a shy, timorous boy, neither dark nor fair. You will recall that Solomon Palmer, who bedded my wife and destroyed my sister, is of very similar appearance and disposition. For so mild a man he has done an enormous amount of harm. Appearances are important aren't they, Sophie? They give us a clue to our origins, who our mothers and fathers were. When I returned to Wenham, to my poor sister's funeral, I had the chance to observe young Sam from fairly close quarters, and I saw that he had the Sadler colouring and features – disposition too from what I am told – and I thought, 'Yes, he *is* my son. Of that there is no doubt.'"

"Then what makes you claim him now? You left it long enough."

"Because I want him back!" Bart thundered. "I want him to know *I* am his father. I want him to live with me, to make him my heir and, in exchange," he leaned forward jabbing his finger at Sophie like a madman, "*you* can have James. I want nothing more to do with him. Take him. Give him to his mother, do what you like with him."

Bart rose as if to signify that was the end of the matter, but Sophie no longer fearful, no longer trembling, stood up and faced him.

"You can't just discharge your responsibilities like that, Bart Sadler, and don't think you can," she said her firm, hard tone matching his. "Your name is on the birth certificate."

"That was before I knew..."

Sophie shook her head. "It doesn't matter. In law you are his father and you will have a hard job convincing anyone otherwise, whatever people say. As for Sam ... I don't know that he would want to acknowledge you as his father. There is no proof there either, except gossip, and Sam will have heard little good of you from people in these parts to make him wish to be your son. Few people I know, if any, have a word to say in your favour, Bart."

Sophie, her eyes glinting triumphantly behind the lens of her steel rimmed spectacles didn't realise that in her anger she had used his Christian name. For a moment the two protagonists stared at each other, breathing deeply. The atmosphere in the room was charged as if with static from an impending storm.

The encounter seemed to have exhausted him and Bart sat down heavily. Sophie, remaining standing, looking warily down at him. Finally Bart spoke. "I will bargain with you, Sophie. You and your daughter I know have little time for each other. Carson, good man that he is, can't keep her for ever and his new wife will object, as the last one did, at all the lame dogs he takes under his roof."

More at ease with himself Bart leaned back and joined his fingers, the tips of each one lightly touching. "My proposal is this. I will give Deborah a house, a nice one, one I built myself, together with an allowance generous enough to enable her to live in comfort and some style. Since she left the rectory she has got used to certain standards she didn't have before – took to them like a duck to water, I might say, for the daughter of an impecunious missionary widow.

"In exchange I insist that she must let the divorce go through without any further ado. I will not allow her to divorce me, as I am the innocent party, but I will divorce her. She will have James, who *is* her son, and visitation rights to Helen. I want things to be amicably agreed between us and not give the lawyers too much money.

"Now, in exchange for this largesse on my part, I insist that Sam be told the truth about his birth. After that I want him to come and see me, talk with me and then he can make up his own mind.

"Can't say fairer than that, can I Sophie?"

Sophie stood by the window for a long time after Bart had gone, looking out at the rain which almost obscured the view of the river in which she had nearly drowned herself in despair several years before. The droplets coursing down the windowpane reminded her of all the tears she'd shed then. She had not had an easy life, but a strong belief in God and His goodness had seen her through. He would not desert her now, as He did not desert her then when the icy water closed over her head and, weighed down by a heavy stone, she had felt herself sinking to the bottom.

She had been saved by, of all people, Solomon Palmer who had seen her jump.

If it was true that Solomon was James's father she could only say it wasn't as bad as having been sired by Bart. Sam, who had always been a difficult, rebellious youth, had all the characteristics of his father. That was why she had found it so hard to love him, why she and he crossed swords so often in a way that did not happen with Tim whose father she had come to love so much. Dearest Hubert, plump, good natured with none of Bart's fatal charm or sinister attractiveness, had been her mainstay in the years since she had married him. She only wished he were here with her now instead of at a diocesan conference in Salisbury.

Sam, on the other hand *was* here, at home for a few days to collect clean clothes and cavort with some of the local youths. He would probably still be in bed sleeping off the excesses of the night before.

Sophie went over to the mirror and looked

hard at herself to make sure that after all the torment of the past hour her hair was neat, her face not too pale.

Her hair of course, was neat. Swept back in a tidy bun, firmly secured with pins, it would be hard to displace a single strand. Her face devoid, as usual, of make-up was pale, her skin flaky and dry, her lips bloodless. She patted her cheeks to try and make them glow a little. Nothing could detract from her frosty expression, because that had become almost a habitual part of her appearance. The mask only came down when she looked at Tim or her daughter Ruth, her beloved Hubert, or her very few treasured relatives or friends. Then, from behind the steel-framed spectacles, which were like a shield protecting her from the world, emerged a gentler, kinder, more tolerant woman; a woman who had inspired the love of three men and who had, strange as it now seemed, loved passionately in return.

She stood back, pursed her lips, squared her shoulders and, going to the door, opened it with firmness. She walked resolutely along the corridor and up the stairs to Sam's room. She paused outside for a second before knocking. After a while a sleepy voice called 'Come in' whereupon she entered. For a moment or two she stood looking at the tousled head of the young man in bed.

"Sam," she said conscious of the old familiar antagonism against him welling up inside her yet again, however hard she tried to suppress it, "please get up, washed and dressed as quickly as you can and come downstairs. I want to talk to you."

Bart Sadler crossed the floor of the drawing room at Upper Park, hand outstretched. Sam, who had been sitting on the edge of a chair waiting, got up, looking very nervous. Bart clasped his arm as they shook hands and drew him over to a sofa where he placed Sam before sitting next to him.

"Would you like a drink, Sam?"

Sam shook his head, nervously cleared his throat.

"We'll have a little luncheon in due course. I thought a chat first. Eh, Sam?"

Sam nodded his head woodenly, avoiding Bart's eyes.

"Now Sam this is not a very easy meeting for either of us is it?"

Sam nodded again, saying nothing.

"Your mother has told you what this is all about?"

Once more Sam nodded, and now Bart began to feel uneasy.

"It's a difficult time for both of us, Sam. Me as well as you."

Sam looked at him, and in him Bart saw his young self. He felt an immediate surge of fatherly love, and a determination to protect and improve the life of this clearly difficult and disturbed young man.

"You may find it hard to believe I care for you Sam, but I do."

"Then why did you never say..." Sam began but stopped, clearly finding it hard to proceed.

"Because I wanted to be fair to your mother. I guessed from very early on that you were my son, the result of a love affair we had had before I went to South America. But she was the rector's wife. One had to consider her name, her virtue. It wasn't that I didn't care, but people have been very cruel and harsh to me since I returned to Wenham, jealous of my wealth. Now that I know James is not my son – and he clearly is not – I felt a desperate need to know you, Sam, and to hope that you, in knowing me better, might grow to care for me. I am not a bad man. I am not some ogre, but have feelings like other people. I have been very badly hurt, let down and deceived by your half-sister, Deborah, to whom I wished no harm, who I loved very much, and by her paramour who I set up in business, trusted as I did no one else and regarded as my friend.

"What vexes me is what people say about me..." Bart, in a gesture of exasperation, threw his hands in the air and when he looked at Sam again he saw that his taciturn, mulish expression had changed to one of surprise. His black eyes, instead of being clouded with suspicion, now glimmered with interest.

"Can you believe it Sam? That I should be the one to be maligned?"

Sam lowered his eyes and shook his head.

"Don't make no sense to me," he said in the rural accent he had, despite his public-school education, deliberately cultivated in order to annoy his mother.

Bart's eyes lit up with hope.

"Do you think then, Sam, that maybe, one day you might take to me? Think of me as your father?"

"Don't see why not," Sam said, the ghost of a smile illuminating his dark, brooding features. "Seems to me like you be a really nice man, much put upon by others."

Fifteen

September 1937

Alexander stood for a long time at the window of his sixth-floor office gazing at the small craft busily plying the river. It was dusk and some of the boats were illuminated so that they seemed to dart about like fireflies. The lights beginning to come on in the surrounding offices and buildings gradually lit up the skyline. It would soon be winter, a depressing thought.

His reflective mood was in keeping with the spirit of anxiety that was everywhere, despite the acccession of the new King, George VI, and the national rejoicing at his coronation and that of his popular queen. The terrible civil war in Spain showed no signs of ending, with atrocities being perpetrated by both sides. Germany was still making warlike and aggressive noises and, together with Italy, was openly helping the Fascists in Spain to test, some people said, its weaponry in case of a future

European war. There had also been the horror of Guernica.

At home the economic situation had improved, thanks largely to the arms race. A new Prime Minister, Neville Chamberlain, had replaced Baldwin who had been exhausted by the abdication crisis.

Alexander, however, had little cause to complain. The business was growing; his fellow directors were pleased with him, and he had his darling little daughter staying with him, just for a week while Lally visited friends in France.

Usually Alexander worked late and occasionally ate at a restaurant on his way home so as to avoid the loneliness of the evenings. But tonight he wanted to leave on time. Kate had just had her third birthday. She was at a delightful age and he loved nothing more than being with her at bedtime, tucking her up and kissing her good-night.

Instead of walking, as was his custom, he got a taxi and just before six arrived home in a mellow frame of mind. But, as always, his arrival was tinged with sadness. If only Mary had been there to welcome him. Not for a moment since her death three years before had he forgotten his darling young bride, so that Kate's birthday had been a time of sadness too.

Alexander bounded up the steps and put

his key in the front door. As he opened it Roberts hurried over to take his coat and hat and whispered in his ear: "You have a visitor, sir. A Miss Schwartz."

"Oh?" Alexander looked at Roberts with surprise, trying hard to place someone of that name.

"You may remember, sir, they were your guests about three years ago. Mr Schwartz is an art collector. His daughter is artistic."

"Oh, of course. I remember." Alexander nodded. "Mother's friends. Is Miss Schwartz alone?"

"Yes, sir. She arrived about a quarter of an hour ago, apologised for not letting you know in advance, but said the matter was urgent."

"Right." Alexander glanced at himself in the hall mirror to straighten his tie and smooth his hair. "I'll just pop up and say hello to my daughter. Offer Miss Schwartz a sherry, Roberts, and I'll be right down."

"Yes, sir."

Alexander ran up the stairs to the nursery where Kate, bathed and ready for bed, was sitting on Massie's knee looking at a picture book as Massie turned the pages, her head leaning sleepily against Massie's broad shoulder.

As her father appeared at the door the toddler scrambled off Massie's knee, the book fell to the floor. She ran over to her father to be lifted up high above his head and brought down for a kiss. Kate entwined her arms around him and hugged him in return. Alexander buried his face in her neck inhaling the enticing smells of baby oils and talcum powder. She was a lovely, cuddly little girl with blonde curls like her mother and the same cornflower-blue eyes. She had dimpled cheeks and a winsome expression and was so good natured and always full of laughter.

Massie doted on her and looked on with affectionate approval as Kate and Alexander indulged in their nocturnal greeting. Alexander put her gently down on the floor and, hand in hand, they wandered over to a chair where Alexander usually read her a story, or looked at a picture book with her.

Tonight however, was different.

"I have a guest downstairs," he told Massie. "I don't want to keep my visitor waiting and I don't think she'll be here for long. When I come up, if Katie is awake, I'll read her a story." He bent and kissed Kate again, his hand gently ruffling her hair. She put both plump little hands on his cheeks and planted a kiss on the tip of his nose.

"I'll be back soon, my darling," he said, picking her up and returning her to Massie who had retrieved the book from the floor and had it ready at the page to begin again.

Quite happily, little Kate settled back and waved to her father who, on his way down the stairs, reflected on his good fortune in having such a happy child to whom he was able to give the best of everything except, alas, a mother.

As Alexander entered the drawing room a tall slim young woman with curly black hair and arresting dark brown eyes jumped to her feet. She wore a pencil-slim black skirt, a red yoked blouse tied at the neck in a large bow and a black three-quarter swagger coat. She was hatless but a black calf bag and gloves lay on the sofa beside her.

"I'm not sure if you remember me," she said going towards Alexander, who held out his hand in greeting.

"Of course I remember you," Alexander said, smiling as he shook her hand and indicating that she should resume her seat. "Did Roberts offer you a sherry?"

"He did." She pointed to two glasses by the side of the sofa. "He brought one for you too. Dry."

"Ah!" Alexander took up the glass and held it towards his guest.

"Cheers, Miss Schwartz. How nice to see you again."

"Please call me Irene," the young woman

said, as she sat down placing the glass on the table beside her. "And I may call you Alexander?"

"Of course." Alexander produced his cigarette case and held it towards her. She took one and as he lit it he said, "And what can I do for you?"

"I do hope you don't mind me barging in like this." Irene looked apologetically up at him. She was heavily but skilfully made up; her soulful eyes rimmed with kohl, lashes mascaraed, her scarlet lips matching the colour of her blouse.

"Of course not." Alexander sat down, crossed one leg over the other and looked at her.

"I was very sorry to hear about your wife," Irene said suddenly, as though she had forgotten something. "A terrible tragedy."

"Terrible." Alexander nodded. "It was an indescribable blow for me, but I have a beautiful daughter, which is some small consolation. How are your parents?"

"Well," Irene sat up very straight. Her manner suddenly became agitated and she clasped and unclasped her hands in her lap. "They are why I am here."

"Oh?" Alexander, through the haze of cigarette smoke, looked puzzled.

"My father is missing in Germany. After I agreed to leave the country he returned to try and sell our apartment, finalise his business arrangements and transfer all his money to England. Suddenly he disappeared. We're afraid he has been arrested and sent to a concentration camp."

"But what on earth for?" Alexander stubbed out his half smoked cigarette.

"Because he is a Jew. Nothing more."

"I knew things were bad, but not as bad as that."

"I was told that, as a Jew, I could no longer attend art school. My father instructed me to come immediately to England. Jews are not even allowed to exhibit their paintings. I came to London in spring and father returned to Germany. At first we got letters and telephone calls, but they stopped abruptly. Neighbours told us of the Gestapo arriving in the middle of the night and of my father being driven away. Naturally we are frantic with worry, and have no one to turn to because all our friends in the Jewish community are in the same boat. We dare not return in case the same thing happens to us and that would be of no help at all to my father."

"Naturally." Alexander stood up and refreshed their glasses from the sherry decanter. "I am terribly sorry to hear this. You must be distraught. But," he glanced at her politely, "in what way do you think

I can be of help?"

"Through your organisation, the powerful Martyn-Heering concern. You must have representatives in Germany?"

"Well, yes, we do. At least, we have a representative in Berlin. It is not a very large office. Pieter Heering is very anti-Nazi and has curtailed our operations in Germany, so I don't really think there is very much I can do to help you. One man keeping a low profile – and our representative is German – will not wish to upset the authorities."

"Oh, well." Irene's tone was flat, her face suddenly showing vulnerability, the depth of her unease. "It was just an idea. I'm sorry I troubled you, Alexander."

"Look," he placed his glass on the mantelpiece and came over to her, "please don't think I am indifferent to the fate of your father."

"You hardly know us." Her voice now contained a note of resignation, tinged with bitterness, as she looked at him. "Why should you care?"

"But I do care. I assure you I do, and I would like very much to help you. I'm just saying the immediate outlook is not encouraging. But if I could have time to think, to consult with Pieter..."

"No, really," she flashed him a wan despairing smile, "you must consider me impertinent for having asked."

"I do not, I assure you Irene." He reached for her hand and looked into her eyes. "I am very concerned, not only about the fate of your father but about all Jews. I abhor the Nazis and what they are doing, not only to Germany but to Europe – filling the world with fear. As the father of a very young child I want peace not war, and I think Hitler is a menace. Now that you have brought this matter to my attention I assure you I will do everything in my power to help. Do you understand?"

Suddenly the tension evaporated. Irene relaxed a little and her smile was genuine.

"I think so. You're very kind. You see my mother and I are very worried, not knowing what to do. I remembered the evening we were here – I know it was a long time ago – and I said to my mother, 'Well it's worth a shot.'"

"And it is worth a shot." Alexander let go of her hand. "I promise you, Irene, I will give this matter my earliest possible attention. I do have contacts and I do have influence – I've just remembered a family member I can approach. Now go home and tell your mother not to worry."

Suddenly this upright, attractive, capable woman rose and leaned her head against him, the tears pouring down her face.

Startled, Alexander clasped her head against his shoulder in an effort to comfort her. He offered her the clean white handkerchief from his breast pocket and, after a few seconds, she took it, drew away from him and dabbed at her face, trying her best to smile.

"I'm terribly sorry," she said. "That was quite uncalled for. I feel very embarrassed. You see, it's the tension. When I am at home with my mother I have to be brave."

"Of course, of course," Alexander said soothingly. "There is no need to be embarrassed with me at all. My mother is very fond of your family. She would want me to do everything to help if I didn't want to myself, which I do. At the moment she's in France but when she returns I'll ask her to call on your mother."

Once more he put a hand on her shoulder and gazed earnestly at her. "I assure you, Irene, I shan't leave a stone unturned in my efforts to trace your father and, if possible, return him to England and his family."

Bart Sadler said, "Alexander, it is very good to see you. Are things going well?"

"I think so." Alexander sat down and looked round the office, recalling the last time he'd been here. "And with you, Bart?"

"Excellent." Bart sat back a smile of satisfaction on his face. "Couldn't be better." He waved a large cigar around in the air.

"I'm glad to hear it."

"I suppose you know that the divorce went through?"

"Yes I did."

"All very satisfactory. Deborah has a handsome house not ten minutes from here and I..." he put a finger on the bell by the side of his desk "...I have a bonus I could never have expected. You have heard about my son Sam? He's now my right-hand man."

"Ah, yes," Alexander began, thinking how strange it sounded to hear Sam referred to as Bart's son when all his life he had thought he was Hubert Turner's. He looked up as the door opened and Sam Turner walked in and, looking past Alexander, addressed himself to Bart.

"You wanted me, Father?"

"I want you to say hello to Alexander. I don't think you've seen each other for a long time."

Sam crossed the floor, a broad smile on his face and took Alexander's hand.

"How are you, Alexander?"

"Very well, Sam. Very well." Alexander continued to shake the young man's hand marvelling at the transformation since he'd last seen him. There had always been something rather shifty about Sam; shifty and evasive as though he was someone you felt you couldn't quite trust. He had a reputation in the family for bad behaviour. Certainly Alexander would never have given him a job as Bart appeared to have done now. "I hear you're Bart's right-hand man. Congratulations."

"Thank you." Sam's countenance, instead of being sullen and brooding, was now open and sunny. His hair, which had always fallen in an untidy mess about his face, was neatly brushed back, with a side parting. He always used to have stubble on his cheeks but was now freshly shaved, exuding a subtle but pleasant aroma of eau-de-Cologne. He wore a well-cut, double-breasted pin-striped grey suit, a crisp white shirt and a maroon-coloured tie.

Bart gazed at him with unconcealed pride.

"The best thing that happened to me, Alexander."

"And to me," Sam firmly echoed his father's words.

"Sam and I were made for each other. He is a chip off the old block. We are so alike, and Sam is a qualified master builder. Did you know that?"

Alexander shook his head in wonder. "Well I did hear that things had gone very well, and I knew that Sam was apprenticed to a builder."

"Who had a high opinion of him. An opinion I very much share. And I am not just saying it because I'm his dad. What's more, he is firm and decisive. We have Abel in the company now as well. Poor Abel had rather a raw deal I'm afraid, but I've made it up to him. Yes." Bart sat back drawing on his cigar. "I have a very good little team here. We are set to do big things, not only here but in Europe. Isn't it so, Sam?"

"Yes, Father," Sam replied eagerly.

"Sam has a remarkable grasp of business. He was completely wasted where he was. Thank heaven I discovered him in time." Bart beamed at his son who beamed back, obviously as pleased with this rapprochement with his natural father as Bart was with him. "Now, Alexander. You are here for a purpose I can tell, not just to pay a social call."

"You're quite right, Bart." Alexander settled back comfortably in his chair. "I have come to ask for your assistance and if you are prepared to help me, I will repay the favour."

"What is it?" Bart looked intrigued.

"I want, as a favour for a friend, to find someone, a man, who has disappeared in Germany. In return I am authorised to offer you any help you need in shipping your goods to Germany, or anywhere in Europe."

"Really!" Bart, his face alight with excitement, glanced at Sam who stood by his father's desk listening carefully.

"That's marvellous news. No questions asked?"

"No questions asked. The transport is leased to you to do what you like with it. There is, however, just one small proviso," Alexander also leaned forward as if to emphasise his point, "and it is this. You can take what you like to Germany, no questions asked. In return, I want you to bring back German Jews," he paused for a fraction of a second, "and one in particular."

Although he couldn't give a fig about the plight of the Jews, Bart enjoyed a challenge. He also loved any excuse to visit Germany, and once Sam was able to take sole charge of the business in England he intended to look seriously for a home there possibly in the Bavarian Alps or the Black Forest, and an apartment in Berlin.

Bart felt at ease among the Germans. He liked the robust, rather coarse, enjoyment of life among the businessmen and officials he associated with. He knew little about the ordinary person in the street or their views, although universally the population seemed to approve of the Reich Chancellor, with the exception of the Jews and their few supporters.

Germany had been humiliated by the Treaty of Versailles. The population had been ground down by poverty, unemployment and hyper-inflation. People had carried their money around in suitcases. All that was changing and Germany, under Hitler, was regaining its self-respect.

You couldn't blame them for crowing a bit.

When he was in Berlin, Bart usually stayed either at the Kaiserhof Hotel or the Adlon. Here he met the men with whom he did business; some eminent, successful men; some shady characters who only dealt in cash and operated under aliases. He thought that some of these, at least, were Jews, whose last and only lifeline was their business. He saw these men in his suite where large sums of money changed hands, promises made and deals done. The prominent Berlin businessmen, with impeccable Aryan pedigrees, he entertained lavishly. Sometimes they were Party officials who were also after a steady supply of arms from European sources. There was just no end to the opportunities presented by the arms race. Not only was the legitimate German army after arms, there was a proliferation of smaller groups, some opposed to Hitler, who smuggled themselves into the hotels via the back entrance to try and win favours from this powerful English businessman and pay him over the odds.

And after business there was pleasure, lots of it. Berlin was the capital of decadent fun, something that Hitler had not yet been able to clean up. Most of his supporters were enthusiastic patrons of the casinos, strip joints, bars and beer cellars which proliferated on the Kurfurstendamm and Friedrichstrasse, the Jagerstrasse and Behrenstrasse, the Unter den Linden and the Munzstrasse. After hours of tough business discussions there usually followed a visit to an expensive restaurant, a few hours in a casino or strip joint and a visit to a brothel, though sometimes the high-class whores came to Bart at the hotel. The dissipation reminded him of his heady days in Rio and Buenos Aires. It was a great contrast to the luxuriousness, the dullness and decorum of his life in Wenham, and the infidelity of a worthless, scheming wife who had none of the accomplishments of the prostitutes in Berlin, Frankfurt or Munich.

However this visit, as far as Bart was concerned, was not straightforward. He was able to offer his clients a much better service now that more transport was on offer, but there was information to be extracted too. It was a case of bargaining one thing for another.

Herr Anton Lippe was a mysterious man who always came into the hotel by the back door. He was short and insignificant-looking, a rather shabby dresser, badly shaved, with a head of sparse, thin, greying hair. He was the sort of person you would never notice in a crowd, but he had a serious manner and a first-class business brain. There was never any small talk with him, or the suggestion of a visit to a bar or strip joint after the business discussions, which were intense.

Bart had found him a mine of information on almost everything to do with Nazi Germany. He had no idea whose side he was on. Herr Lippe did not look Jewish, nor had he a Jewish name, but that meant nothing. Bart was pretty sure he was Jewish, although he sometimes felt that he was acting for the Nazis and sometimes for the opposition. His name was surely not his own and from his accent Bart, whose own German was progressing, suspected he might be Austrian, or even Czech. However, whoever he was and wherever he came from Lippe, though he drove a close bargain, seemed possessed of unlimited funds. Merchandise was paid for promptly in Swiss francs by a draft on a Zurich bank. In the past year he had supplied enough small arms to Herr Lippe to equip an army. Now he wanted Herr Lippe to do him a favour.

Herr Lippe sat opposite him in his suite at the Kaiserhof. On the table between them were several bottles of beer, two glasses and an overflowing ashtray. It was late at night and both men, now in shirt sleeves, were sweating, but a deal at last was in sight.

"You drive a hard bargain, Herr Sadler," Herr Lippe said, sitting back and lighting one of his endless supply of cigarettes which had stained his heavy moustache yellow. "But I think we can conclude the matter satisfactorily."

"There is just one other thing." Bart leaned over towards him and, taking an unnecessary precaution, lowered his voice to a whisper. "On behalf of a friend I need some information. I must emphasise I have nothing to do with the person concerned. In fact I have never met him. His name is Schwartz, a well-known Berlin art dealer, and he has disappeared, probably into a concentration camp. Now if you can help me trace him and, if possible, effect an early release, I am able to offer you even better terms than the ones we have under consideration. Say an extra two and a half per cent ... and immediate delivery to any destination you name. How does that sound?"

January 1938

The days were very long for Deborah. Even in her nice new house within sight of Wenham, with her mother and sister nearby and James to care for, time hung heavily on her hands. She kept a small staff: a cook and a maid who lived in, a daily who came to clean, a nursemaid for James – Jemima had come with him – and a man who lived in the town and came at intervals to do the garden and odd jobs around the house.

Deborah had never been a good house-keeper, nor was she an instinctive mother. Babies and small children bored her. It was only after Bart had ejected her from Upper Park that she had missed her children. It was a long time since she had given so much as a thought to the son, who had never known his mother, growing up in Bristol.

But now, as a divorced woman with an adequate income and not enough to do she felt in a position to look around, to play, as it were, the field – not to be tied down by the past. She had lost her reputation, so there was nothing left to lose and men of all kinds were attracted to her: rich farmers, local businessmen, professional men, store-keepers, but none of them got very far. As the ex-Mrs Bart Sadler she felt she had standards to maintain, bigger fish to land. So she was lonely, isolated and yet a subject of some fascination and much gossip in the local community. When she was a little more sure of herself and her new-found freedom she thought she might go to London and stay with her cousin Martha, familiarise herself with the ways and perhaps the temp-tations, of the big city.

Then, one day, Solomon turned up, unannounced, probably in the expectation that she might not receive him. Well, he might have been right. She couldn't say what she might or might not have done, because Betty the maid merely flung open the door of the drawing room, where Deborah was idling over a novel and some magazines, and announced him.

"Mr Palmer, madam."

And in had come Solomon. He stood there gazing at her diffidently. He looked pale, dishevelled, ill at ease. She didn't get up but stared at him.

"Solomon," she said.

"Debbie."

"Well I never did." She knew she'd flushed, with irritation rather than embarrassment. Betty would certainly get a talking to after this visit was over.

"I hope you don't mind me coming. I was passing and thought ... well ... I thought I'd like to see how you were. And..." he hesitated "...and little James."

"Not so little now," she said, pointing imperiously to a chair. "You'd better sit down now you're here."

"I can understand how you feel, Debbie."

"Oh can you?" She knew her voice sounded shrill. "I think not."

"Oh yes, I can understand. It was an awful time ... for both of us. I can't tell you how grateful I was ... well you sacrificed everything for me."

"Not for *you*, Solomon." She corrected him sharply. "I thought that if you hanged I would have it on my conscience. I may not a very good woman, very religious or God fearing, but—"

"But for you it would have been an open and shut case." His expression was humble. He seemed to have shrunk, grown thinner. Looking at him Deborah couldn't imagine why or how she'd ever found him attractive. She thought she must have been very bored indeed to risk losing all she had for a man who had not one tenth of Bart's sexual allure, and none of his power or wealth.

Now she despised Solomon. She liked a

man with a bit of character, even if he had too much, like Bart. And, although she didn't think Solomon could have murdered Sarah-Jane, sometimes she wondered. Despite the evidence of the time factor you always had that little niggling doubt that somehow he might just have done it, the law might have got it wrong.

Her eyes narrowed. "Funny they never found the man they thought killed Sarah-Jane. It must weigh heavily on you, Solomon."

"Oh yes, it does." He gazed disconsolately at the ground. "Sometimes I think people still believe it was me. It wasn't."

"Oh, I know it wasn't."

"He went to ground. Colonel George. Obviously a false name."

"Obviously."

The conversation petered out. Deborah stifled a spasm of guilt at the suspicion she'd harboured a moment or two before. She knew that Solomon was incapable of the emotion, let alone the hatred that you would need to put a piece of piano wire round a woman's throat and tug at it until she was dead. Bart could, but he would probably do it with his bare hands or shoot you. Bart was capable of a great deal of violence, but poor Solomon wasn't.

"What are you doing now, Solomon? You

said you were passing. I heard you'd left the district."

"I work for a building supplies firm as a commercial traveller. It's not much of a job, but it is a job. I don't usually come to the West Country but I've business in Yeovil and then on to Exeter. I'm based in London."

"I see." Deborah began to feel fidgety. He would be someone she would be sure not to look up if ever she went to stay with Martha.

"Solomon, it is good of you to call, but I don't feel we've anything in common any more."

"I really just wondered how James was," Solomon said looking up. "He *is* our son, isn't he Debbie?"

She thought his pale dejected face showed a little hope. Well it would be easy to squash that. He had, after all, cost her her marriage and she had no intention of taking him back. She had paid a heavy price for that particular bit of fun.

"I wouldn't be too sure about that, Solomon."

"But I thought Bart—"

"Bart didn't know. He just thought, one of those funny spur-of-the-moment notions, and he always thinks he's right. No one knows. Not even I, his mother, know for sure. You see the funny thing is that, despite his many differences to Bart, in some ways the older James gets the more he resembles him. He has a little mole, a birthmark, on the side of his face; Bart has one just like it below his left ear. Frankly, I think he has Bart's nose. As I say the older he gets—"

"But Bart has adopted Sam!" Solomon sounded outraged.

"Oh, well, he can have Sam." Debbie gave a false, unattractive laugh. "Good riddance. Even though Sam is my half-brother, I can't stand him. Never could. My mother didn't like him either. Now Sam *is* very like Bart. No doubt whose son *he* is, but James..." she looked slyly up at Solomon, "I'm not sure."

"Could I ... may I see him?"

"I'm afraid not." Deborah rose and glanced briskly at her watch. "I'm sorry to end this visit, but I'm expecting guests. Oh, and look, please do remember that we have nothing in common, not even a child, and next time you 'happen to be passing', be sure you go straight on."

Deborah kept her finger firmly on the bell by the side of her chair until the door opened and Betty, looking rather startled, popped her head round.

"Yes, madam?"

"See this gentleman out please."

Deborah went over to the window and, as Solomon crept out, she didn't even turn her head to watch him go.

378

Alexander came into the restaurant and paused on the threshold. He gazed across at the woman sitting at a corner table, her face in profile to him, smoking a cigarette. She looked sophisticated, elegant, poised – the product of a cosmopolitan, cultured European Jewish family. She didn't look bored or irritated that he was late, but quite happy, self-assured, composed, a woman at ease with herself.

She wore a short black velvet evening frock, with a gold lamé jacket. She had a single row of pearls round her throat. A little pill-box hat, also of black velvet, perched slightly towards the front of her head, her black curls carefully arranged round it. A fine-mesh half-veil that ended just below her eyes added to her mystery, her undoubted allure. From under the tablecloth he caught a sight of her black silk stockings and high-heeled shoes, one ankle crossed over the other.

As usual she was heavily made up. The slash of scarlet lipstick, the heavy use of rouge and mascara making her seem at once exciting, exotic and slightly dangerous.

Hastening over to her he apologised for being late.

"Oh that's all right." Irene looked up, and smiled her lazy, relaxed, reassuring smile.

She would never put a man down or make him feel uneasy. You felt that she had experience beyond her years gained, undoubtedly, during the Bohemian life she had led in Berlin.

He sat down opposite her and produced his cigarette case.

"Did you at least order a drink?"

"I only just arrived. Really."

Alexander looked around the Savoy Grillroom and beckoned to the waiter.

"Shall we have champagne? Or would you prefer something else? A cocktail, perhaps?"

"Champagne sounds marvellous."

"A bottle of your best Krug, please," Alexander instructed the waiter. "Pre-war if you have it."

"Yes, Mr Martyn."

"You know about champagne?" Irene cocked her head on one side, her eyes behind the gossamer-fine veil shining tantalisingly, a little teasing perhaps.

"A bit. Many negociants of course didn't get going again for a long time after the war. Prosper had a very good cellar, a lot of pre-war vintages, and I've been studying wine – in what spare time I have," he added as an afterthought.

"How's Kate?"

"Kate is simply beautiful. She's in the country at the moment with Lally. Lally wants to meet you again, oh and your mother of course. She asked me to bring you both down."

"Sounds lovely." Irene nodded with an approving smile.

The waiter arrived with a bottle in an ice bucket and two glasses. While he removed the cork Alexander offered Irene a fresh cigarette. Surreptitiously observing her face, as he lit it, he wondered at the source of his growing interest in her, and if it was reciprocated.

They had met half a dozen times since her unexpected visit to him, ostensibly for him to report progress on Bart's complicated and top-secret negotiations in Germany. There had been dinner at the Café Royal, dancing at Ciros and a visit to the Criterion to see the new Rattigan play *French Without Tears*. She was a stimulating, knowledgeable companion, but she also liked a good time. She was fun. She was not at all like Mary, not in the least, but there was an indefinable attraction about her, a sexuality and maturity that his dear little wife had completely lacked, and which he found intoxicating. This was a woman you felt you wanted, yet who you would never completely know. So far there had been no intimacy, but only because he held back. He felt that, in being fascinated by another woman, he was being disloyal to Mary. But, after all, she had been dead for three and a half years. Was it wrong for a man to try and find happiness again after a suitable period of mourning?

Alexander thought that if he waited too long he might lose a chance of happiness with a woman who, surely, must have many admirers, real or potential.

The waiter finished pouring the wine and after handing them their glasses left them.

"Are we celebrating something?" Irene looked at him eagerly and carefully drew back the veil – as though it had formed a slight barrier between them – and tucked it nonchalantly under the brim of her hat.

He had already hinted on the telephone that the news might be good.

"We have found your father." Alexander leaned so far towards her across the table so that their heads were nearly touching. "He is in Sachenhausen concentration camp."

As one of Irene's hands flew to her mouth Alexander quickly reached for the other, pressed it reassuringly. "We are getting him out with the help of contacts Bart Sadler knows. With any luck your father will be here within weeks, if not days. I am afraid that he will never recover his property or money, but that, I think, is a small price to pay, perhaps for his life."

Her fine eyes brimming with tears, Irene

took hold of both Alexander's hands and held them tight.

"I don't know how to thank you."

"I'll think of something," he said, and brought her fingers to his lips.

Her skin was white, soft and perfumed, her scarlet nails glistening wickedly in the candlelight. He wanted to draw her to him and kiss her, but he knew that would come later. Without any doubt he was on the brink of falling in love.

And Irene? As he looked at her her rapturous expression suggested that she felt the same. Their gaze spoke volumes. He pressed her hands again and kissed them, aware of an answering response.

Because the future was uncertain the present was so very precious. The moment had to be seized, held on to, savoured. Momentarily the dark clouds surrounding them seemed to have parted, and let in the sun.